The Decadents

M.C. SCHMIDT

Published by:
Library Tales Publishing
www.LibraryTalesPublishing.com
www.Facebook.com/LibraryTalesPublishing

Copyright © 2022 by M.C. Schmidt
All Rights Reserved
Published in New York, New York.

For general information on our other products and services, please contact our Customer Care Department at 1-800-754-5016, or fax 917-463-0892. For technical support, please visit www.LibraryTalesPublishing.com

Library Tales Publishing also publishes its books in a variety of electronic formats. Every content that appears in print is available in electronic books.

9 7 8 - 1 - 9 5 6 7 6 9 - 0 4 - 3
9 7 8 - 1 - 9 5 6 7 6 9 - 0 5 - 0

PRINTED IN THE UNITED STATES OF AMERICA

The
Decadents

M.C. SCHMIDT

PART ONE

Chapter 01

It had been the best year of Phil's long business career, but still he was losing. The frontrunner was a new edition to the Chamber of Commerce, a startup that made instant millions from the fabrication and online sale of testicular implants for neutered domestic pets. Vanity dog balls, as Phil thought of them, those unexpected silicone eggs that had rolled into his path to trip-up his victory lap.

The Outstanding Entrepreneur wouldn't be announced for weeks, but Phil had gotten wind of the Chamber's leanings from a reluctant source on the deciding board, a member he'd cracked that morning after days of nagging and cajoling. With the wound from this news still freshly bleeding, he turned into the parking lot of his Columbia Fry Buddy distracted by thoughts of injustice and the visitation of vague calamities on his professional rivals. He pulled into the space nearest the fast-food restaurant's doors, trapping beneath his tires the stenciled words, *Reserved: Phil Ochs.*

For most of his six decades he'd shared this name with a famous liberal folksinger, a coincidence that provoked enough teasing to leave him leery of handshake introductions and transactions that required his photo ID. These days, with the folky long dead from suicide, such teasing had become rare. But the famous Phil Ochs persisted in his mind like a trauma: a shape given to the feared inadequacy that shadowed his outward bluster, to his suspicions that he was mocked where he most desired respect, to his belief that he was seen as less each time his name triggered recollections of that more successful man. The folksinger was often on Phil's mind, and to Phil's mind the folksinger meant all of this.

He was crossing the parking lot now, his Lexus locking behind him with a confirming bleat. From the restaurant's glass vestibule and lobby to its service counter and kitchen, he moved swiftly, greeting his employees' gazes with a boarded-up face as unwelcoming as abandoned property, until he made it to the office and shut himself in.

Without taking a seat, Phil hunched over the office PC and opened an Internet browser. He needed to understand how he was losing to a business like this, how the Chamber could respect ornamental pet genitals more than they respected him. Surely, these hustlers weren't the first to think up a thing like this, not in a world full of pandering dog owners. Was it something to do with innovation? Had they found a way to make their product itch or throb when kicked?

Or maybe it was a size thing, the way smartphones used to get smaller with each advancing model, this company stealing Phil's award for their pioneering restoration of little creatures' manhood—hamsters and guinea pigs and those sugar gliders the flea markets sold.

Into the search field, he entered the company's name: *FauxGnads*. As he waited out the lagging white screen that was a hallmark of the restaurant's service provider, his phone began to vibrate in the muffler pocket of his tracksuit. David Samuel, of course.

"Keep it short," Phil said into the phone, "I'm tied up here."

An audible gust of wind crackled in the speaker before the caller said, "Dad?"

"What is it, David Samuel?"

This query too was met with interference, and then a stoic voice said, "Dad? Dad, I'm calling to let you know something: I'm on the roof. I'm on the roof, and I wanted to let you know while I still can that I don't blame you, not for anything."

"Creeping Jesus, David Samuel," Phil moaned, "where are you?"

"I'm—I'm on the roof. Don't ask me to come down because I've made up my mind. There's nothing you can say to stop me. Mom isn't here because I didn't want her to see this. I don't know how long she'll be gone, though. Can you come home right away so you can take care of things before she gets here?"

Phil rubbed at a pain in his temple. "Will you be in the front or back?" he said.

"What?"

"The front or the back? Which way are you jumping? If I can make a request, do you think you'd be able to hit those gaudy lawn ornaments in the Shepherd's yard? I don't have the perspective you do, but it seems to me that you could clear the fence with a good solid leap."

"Oh, my God!" David Samuel said in his alarming, near-feminine lilt. "You're a monster!"

"Maybe," Phil conceded. "But I'm also at work. Do you have any idea how busy I am? Do you think I need this kind of aggravation?"

"Your needs? What about what I need? Have you ever thought of that for one miserly second?"

"And what is it that you need this time? Is it taxidermy school? I swear to God, boy, if this is about taxidermy school…"

"I need to go to a good school!" David Samuel pleaded.

"You're a moron, kid," Phil said.

"Maybe. Maybe that's true. So, I may as well jump."

"David Samuel, if you jump off that roof because I won't pay for you to go to taxidermy school, I swear to God that I'll find the valedictorian of the best taxidermy school in the state of South Carolina, and I'll pay him to stuff your ass for display in one of my stores. Now, how's that sound to you?"

As he awaited his son's reaction, Phil's Internet search results loaded. He clicked on the company's official link. Another round of the hallmark lag.

Finally, David Samuel said, "Well, if you won't send me to school, then I want a leave of absence to recompose. A few weeks of Me Time."

Phil groaned in anticlimactic disappointment, as if saddened that the resolve of his only child would lead him to deal rather than to jump. "Really, boy?" he asked. "'Me Time?' You'll get one week after you've accrued it. June or July, maybe."

"I can't wait for June or July!"

"Well," Phil said, "you better jump then, because that's the deal." There was silence on the line. "David Samuel," Phil called, "jump, goddamn it, or I'm going to drive home and turn on the hose and wash you off that roof."

"You wouldn't! You wouldn't do that to Mom!"

"Oh, now you think of your mother," Phil said. He missed his son's response as a smiling German shepherd bounded onto his computer screen. "David Samuel, I have to go." By way of parting, he added, "Mind the shingles."

The dog sat centered on the lawn of a regal American home that rose in the background, its white porch railing seeming to embrace the family that posed beyond it in a chaste and wholesome hug. It occurred to Phil that a better promotion might have been an action shot of the canine, an image whose subtext was 'full recovery.' The product being sold wasn't visible in the image. They made you go deeper for that. Instead, the salesmanship was in the dog's satisfied eyes. Eyes that stared into Phil's own with the clear communication: *I finally have my confidence back.*

For twenty minutes, Phil poked around the site, learning more than he cared to about veterinary psychology and the symptoms of K9-PTSD. Of technical surgical details and the disturbing requirements of post-surgery cleansing. He studied the crushing photos of the company's owners posed on charity golf courses with powerful businesspeople and smiling candidly backstage with celebrities famous enough that even Phil recognized some of them. Local boys gone good. He took particular notice of a page titled *Our Story*, where he learned of the company's origins: a father and son—one a vet, the other a polymer scientist—sharing a vision and starting a company and changing the world, even if only the exclusively privileged world of animal-loving crazies with disposable income to burn.

Soon enough, he'd read all he could stand. He was bested. These were the better men. Phil was a successful regional fast-food franchisee, but these characters had a photo with Rachel Ray. He closed the browser, defeated. Phil rose to his full five feet, six inches, the ache in his back from crouching signaling a second defeat.

It had been foolish to think he'd be chosen as the year's Outstanding Entrepreneur. He'd been a member of the Chamber for three decades, after all, and they'd always kept a public distance from fast food, believing his industry to be cheap and indulgent, shrinking from its association with obesity and heart disease and toxic predation on the lower class.

But still. This year.

He'd opened his seventeenth franchise; added sixty employees to his payroll; achieved, finally, the status of on-paper millionaire. After all this time, was he wrong to expect the admiration of his business peers, a long overdue pat on his old and aching back?

Phil allowed himself only a moment's self-pity. Then he crossed the office floor and opened the door to the distant resonance of a living restaurant. He continued toward those sounds as if their hiss and sizzle and chime and clatter were coded tones arranged in a message that beckoned him, come. When he rounded the partition wall that separated the back from the kitchen, that message became a clear entreaty for perspective. His kitchen demonstrated the clockwork efficiency of mass-production. In the front of the house, tidy queues of demand and delivery repeated and repeated and repeated. If the Chamber of Commerce disagreed that his operation was a thing of beauty, it was they who were wrong, not Phil.

Would he prefer the sort of success that attracted talk show interviews and rounds of golf with powerful business leaders? Of course, he would. There'd be no greater joy than being a father/son team, identifying a hole in the market, collaborating on a mission statement, then building the bones and watching the profits come. But Phil's son wasn't a vet or a polymer scientist. He was a truculent boob, prone to flights of fancy. Phil had fought for a lifetime to achieve what he had. He, the first successful Ochs in a pedigree of losers. His own belt-wielding father had never come to him with a mind to change the world, so he wouldn't be made to feel inferior. Not by the prejudice of some regional deciding committee. And he wouldn't let go of this award without a fight.

As this thought hurtled past the bounds of affirmation toward something resembling monomania, Phil's eyes fell onto Register Three, trapping what he saw there into the issue like misfortunate creatures into amber.

The register was manned by Ruzanna Singh, a part-time high school Junior whom Phil had hired suspecting she was pretty enough to bring the boys in. Having only ever possessed a sputtering lust, such an evaluation by Phil was a leap of pure theory. But Columbia sales had gone up since her hire, so he felt his judgment had been sound. It wasn't Ruzanna he was focused on, though. It was the boy she was ringing up, a recognizable young man Phil knew to be her boyfriend.

His name was Collin Radaszewski, a mid-level star of the Mt. Early Senior High School basketball and football teams, teams Phil cosponsored. From the bleachers, he'd admired Collin at play: his graceful, easy athleticism; his charming good looks. Phil, himself, had been too small to be an athlete, but he believed he had the athletic stamina, the champion's drive to succeed.

The phone in his pocket vibrated. He knew without looking it was David Samuel. David Samuel who, at twenty-three, had yet to put a point on the board, who had, in fact, fouled so frequently that a dozen points would do little to lessen the deficit.

It was at this intersection of feelings—envy of the dog balls, desire to edge them out for recognition, admiration for Collin Radaszewski, and this refreshed frustration with his son—that a lightbulb flashed in Phil's brain. To become the Outstanding Entrepreneur would be a matter of winning the Chamber's respect. If expanding his regional footprint hadn't done it, perhaps building his legacy would. If he could present David Samuel as a star of the next generation of regional business leaders—the sort of man young Collin promised to be—then they would have to acknowledge Phil, wouldn't they? They may even be so moved as to reimagine him as the likely patriarch of a future powerful family. A South Carolina kingmaker.

He only had a few weeks, and it wouldn't be easy. But he saw a way that it might work. The problem, of course, was that rebuilding David Samuel into a respectable heir would first require breaking him. Phil would need help with that. But, in Collin Radaszewski, he believed he was staring at just the man for the job.

Chapter 02

Across town, in their big house on Ellery Lane, Lillian Ochs sat erect on the edge of a sofa cushion. Her phone was pressed to her ear. On her right hand, she wore a recently ordered device that she'd found delivered to her porch upon returning home from an afternoon meeting of the Daughters of American Patriots. The device was called the Microfiber Miracle Mitt. Its chamois palm rested flatly against her thigh. The hundreds of dust-grabbing fiber noodles that covered its upper surface slumped and wilted and haphazardly leaned into and away from one another. While she waited, she shook the hand a little and watched the noodles tousle and reshuffle. Tanya Tucker's "Delta Dawn" played in her ear.

Before the second chorus, a lyrical male voice broke into the line and said, "Thank you for calling Miracle Products. My name is Raj. Who am I speaking with today please?" Lillian delighted in the long O's and retroflex consonants in his pronunciation. She found the friendly purr of it so common to these calls that she'd come to think of this as the accent of customer support.

"Hi, Raj," she said with seductive friendliness. "You're speaking with Lillian Ochs."

"Hello, Lillian Ochs. Are you calling to place an order today?"

"No, I already placed an order. For the Miracle Mitt. I'm wearing it now."

"Are you unsatisfied with your order?"

"Well, it's only just come today. So, we'll see."

"I see."

"It's very soft," Lillian said.

"Very soft," Raj agreed.

"How is that?"

"The Microfiber Miracle Mitt uses five types of cloth to give you superior dust attraction. The leading competitor uses only three."

"Types of cloth?"

"Yes."

"That's marvelous. Listen, Raj," Lillian said in a tone that suggested they get down to it, "you're probably wondering why I called."

"Was there something I could help you with today?"

"What I wanted to ask you is: is it safe to use on an animal?"

"On an animal?"

"Yes."

"No, we would not recommend this product for use on an animal."

"Right, well, let me be clear: the animal is dead."

"A dead animal?"

"Yes. He's stuffed."

"Stuffed to mean like the grizzly bear?"

"A beloved pet, actually."

"My condolences."

"Bless you, Raj. So?"

"The beloved pet is dead," Raj said, considering. "And does the dead pet suffer the day-to-day burdens of household dust?"

"Dust is an issue, yes," Lillian confirmed gravely. "Also, food spills."

"On the dead pet?"

"Yes. Is it safe to dampen the mitt to remove spills?"

Raj paused and then walked cautiously through his reply: "If it's safe for the dead pet to be wet," he began, "then you could rub the damp mitt on the pet. But this would not be recommended."

"But—I still could?"

"Yes, you still could. But it would not be recommended. Not by Miracle Products."

"Hmmm," Lillian said.

"Was there anything else I could help you with today?"

"Raj, let me tell you what we'll do," Lillian offered. "Let's give it a week. I'll dust him with the mitt when it's dry. And I'll dampen the mitt to clean off the food spills. Then, when the week is up, I'll call back to let you know how it works."

"The dead pet gets many food spills in a week?"

"You'd be surprised," she said. "But if it all works out, then you could recommend it. To other callers, I mean. And if it doesn't—well, then we know."

"I could not recommend it."

"Not *yet*," Lillian corrected.

"No."

"I'll call back in a week, then."

"Please feel free to call back any time. But please also know that this call has been recorded and that Miracle Products cannot be held responsible for any damage or desecration to your beloved stuffed dead pet, may he rest in peace."

"Raj, you're a pip. It's been a pleasure talking with you this evening."

"You were satisfied with your call today?"

"Oh, goodness, yes. And, Raj?"

"Yes?"

"I'm excited to see what happens. Are you excited to see what happens?"

There was a pause before Raj said, "Yes, thank you and have a good day."

Lillian set her phone on the coffee table. She was half-risen from the sofa when a crash arose from behind her. "David Samuel?" she called over her shoulder. There was no answer. Slowly, she rose and navigated around the living room furniture toward the first-floor hallway. The hall was dark, but Phil's office door was open. "Phil?" she called, unclear why he'd be home at such an hour. There came another crash, as if in response. Cautiously, Lillian craned her neck to peek past the door, and as she did, David Samuel burst through the doorway toward her. Lillian gasped and leapt out of his path. David Samuel regarded his mother with widened eyes. "David Samuel, what are you doing in your father's office?"

"Your husband," David Samuel said, "is an ass." He tossed his long hair and moved past her down the hall. Dead leaves clung to his sweater and to the seat of his pants.

Lillian stepped into Phil's office to find that several of her husband's trophies had been knocked from the shelves: his three heavy crystal yams won for outstanding regional sales; his autographed headshot of Wendy's founder, Dave Thomas; the framed nutritional facts flyer from his pilot Fry Buddy store; the phone camera snapshot Lillian had taken of Phil smiling over his father's casket at his funeral. She pulled the Miracle Mitt from her hand and slung it over her shoulder, petting it momentarily as she worried over these men and their fighting. Then she set about righting the room.

Once done, she found David Samuel standing at the kitchen sink with his back to her. "David Samuel," Lillian said, "what's the matter?"

David Samuel snorted. Without turning to her, he said, "Nothing of any consequence, Mother. The only matter is my self-regard and personal sense of respect.

No concern to anyone in this house."

Lillian moved past the kitchen's long granite island and joined at his side. He turned away, intent on the work of finishing a sandwich. On the counter sat Bernie, his head and back sprinkled with crumbs of white bread.

Received as a birthday gift when David Samuel turned sixteen, Bernie had lived six respectable rabbit years in a cage in the boy's room before permanently hopping from his mortal coil the previous spring. The trauma of the animal's passing had been so significant to David Samuel that—rather than burying him or, as Phil had suggested, flinging him into the dumpster by his goddamned ears—Lillian had surprised her son by having the rabbit stuffed and mounted. This had led to a heightened level of posthumous affection from David Samuel, who took to carrying the lacquered beast under his arm and absently stroking it in his lap while writing in his journal or when lost in a television program. As a creature no longer prone to shitting and chewing the furniture, Bernie had gone from being a boarder whom the senior Ochses sometimes smelled but rarely saw, to being emancipated to the full freedom of their home. "I must have mislaid him while fetching preserves," David Samuel had said when Lillian found Bernie in the pantry. "There's no need to be shy. He doesn't know what you're doing," Phil was told after retiring to the bathroom with a newspaper and finding the rabbit sitting voyeuristically atop the laundry hamper.

"Oh, I wish you two could get along," Lillian said. "Do you know it breaks my heart that you two can't ever seem to get along?" She touched her son on his thick arm.

David Samuel shook her hand away. "That man is stifling."

"He's under so much pressure, hon."

"Pressure?" A small wad of wet white bread accompanied the word from his mouth. "And what am I under? Besides your husband's boot, I mean. I have aspirations, Mother. Would it be too much to have him provide even a word of support? For him to stop stepping on my dreams to make himself feel taller?"

"Oh, he doesn't do that, David Samuel. It's just that your interests are so far reaching that sometimes it feels like you move between things without really committing to them." The reflexive glance that they each made toward Bernie at this suggestion was met with neutrality by the rabbit's glass eyes.

"He's an autocrat who's determined to see me fail," David Samuel said, moving to shield the beast from his mother's view.

Lillian puckered her lips in a pout. "He's the hardest working man I know," she said. "Look at all his hard work has given us."

David Samuel made a show of eyeing the Miracle Mitt that was draped over her shoulder like a sash.

Lillian clutched self-consciously at her fiber noodles. "What I mean, David Samuel, is that everything we have is because of your father's dedication to his work. And that doesn't leave much of him for us. I know that better than anyone." She reached and took her son's broad face in her hands. "You have a beautiful soul. The privilege your father has given us makes it possible for you to explore your gifts. And you have so many gifts. Not everyone gets to have the freedoms you do. That's all because of your father. Even if he can be grouchy sometimes. You should be expressing yourself through your art, not by destroying your father's office. Do you see what I mean, hon?"

David Samuel was silent for a moment, then he set down the last of his sandwich on Bernie's driftwood base. His expression conveyed that something in her words had touched him, while simultaneously communicating shock that anything his mother might say had the power to do so.

"Maybe I see what you mean, after all," he said. "It's cheap, isn't it, acting out this way?"

Lillian tipped her face to him in loving affirmation.

"I mean—anyone can break Phil Ochs' knickknacks. But only a real talent could destroy him through art." Before Lillian could object, David Samuel grasped his mother's shoulder and squeezed. "Thank you, Mother. This has been an unexpectedly enlightening talk. But, if you'll excuse me, I have poems to attend to." He lifted Bernie from the counter, tilted him until the remainder of the sandwich fell off his base and into the sink, and then disappeared through the kitchen door. The quickness of his stride caused two leaves to detach from his sweater and drift serenely down to the kitchen tile.

Chapter 03

A day after his epiphany, Phil sat on the Mt. Early Senior High School bleachers considering how the coach's taunts sounded neutered. His boys were all dingleberries and numb nuts and chuckleheads. Phil remembered when high school coaches would get at boys by calling them girls. Or, more seriously, parts of girls, girl genitals specifically. Or, most seriously of all, specific parts of girl genitals, which the boys of Phil's day had little practical knowledge about other than the knowledge that a young man should endeavor to perform in a way that wouldn't lead to his being compared to these mysterious organs. But, times, he supposed, had changed.

The chuckleheads' Nikes squealed and pattered and reverberated in the chamber of the high school gymnasium. Phil waited for ninety minutes, from the pre-game warmups to the post-game stretches, always with an eye on Collin Radaszewski. When they were through, he watched the players sprint or amble off the court, keyed up by physical activity or worn out from it, horsing around or huffing for air. "So, what do you think?" a voice asked him, Coach Blevins having quietly climbed the bleachers while Phil's attentions were elsewhere.

"Oh, well, your boys look good," Phil said, playing his role.

"They need to look better if they're going to square off against Sedgewick next Friday. Can you believe they put that meet so early in the season?"

"It's early," Phil agreed, unclear on the implied importance of the referenced opposition. He kept an eye on the last of the boys as they filed out of his view into the locker room.

"Don't worry, though," the coach said, "I think we'll be ready. We'll give you your money's worth."

"Radaszewski looks pretty good," Phil said, steering the conversation to his topic of interest.

"Radish? Oh, he could be fine if his head was in it."

"His head's not in it?" Phil said. He stood, having begun to feel emasculated by the coach towering over him.

"Well, we'll see," Blevins said, making a show of shaking his head and rolling his eyes. "He got himself a steady girlfriend this season, and that always spells trouble to me. It's still early, but you can see the difference in his game, or I can anyways. Why do they got to get involved in all that drama? That's what I want to know. I mean, you're a high school athlete. Never mind the scholarship opportunities a kid like Radish could have if he knuckled down, it just seems to me a high school athlete ought to have the social capital to fuck and run. Between you and me. But kids that think they're in love... Well, they never put in the effort to really do something out on the court."

"Fuck and run," Phil said, parroting more than agreeing.

"But," Coach Blevins sighed, "you can't come right out and say nothing to them about it. Most wouldn't listen even if you did." He stared into the distance as if mourning the fate of contact sports in a world where love was king.

Boys soon began to trickle from the locker room's gaping mouth. Phil presented the coach's arm with a supportive rap of his knuckles then moved with the first of these boys toward the interior gymnasium doors.

He stood in the school hallway for some minutes with a phone to his ear, occasionally shaking his head and saying important-sounding things to create the illusion of someone listening on the other end of the line. He kept his eye on the gymnasium doors, on the fitful knots of athletes as they appeared through them. Eventually, Collin emerged, laughing together with a well-built Black boy.

Into the phone, Phil said loudly, "Because what I say goes. And if you don't like it, you can find yourself new employment. Get me, Buster Brown?" The athletes glanced at him. Phil shoved the phone into the pocket of his tracksuit jacket and followed at a distance behind them. They parted at the end of the hall, the Black boy continuing through a pair of doors into the school parking lot while Collin turned into the boy's lavatory. Phil paused momentarily outside the lavatory door, then pushed through it.

Collin stood in a broad-legged stance at a urinal. Phil sidled to the next urinal and undid his Velcro fly. He stared at the wall ahead of him in observation of a universal urinal etiquette. "Jesus, kid," he said, "congratulations on that flow."

"Huh?"

"You got a robust stream there. You get to be my age, you lament the days when you could take a good, satisfying piss." His own urine sputtered and splashed in the porcelain trough, decorating the front of his pants in tiny freckles of reflected fluid. "You boys looked good out there today."

"Yeah," Collin said.

Unable to move his eyes in the boy's direction while he was genitally exposed, Phil couldn't judge the temper of Collin's reaction. He continued: "I got a kid—older than you, grown now—wasn't ever any kind of athlete. A real disgrace, that one."

Collin voiced a single pulse of laughter.

"I'd have given anything for that kid to play ball. It would have given him some spine. Which, in this kid, is much-needed. But, instead, now he's just a mooch. Just an over-sensitive, disgraceful goddamn mooch."

"That sucks."

At the sound of Collin's zipper, Phil's eyes un-locked, and he turned his head toward the boy. "What he needs, if you ask me, is a good ass-whipping. Do you know guys like that?"

"I guess," Collin said. He moved to the bank of sinks behind the urinals.

Phil secured himself inside his pants and joined at the boy's side. "And do you ever give them that whipping?" He smiled in assumed complicity, staring at the mirror reflection of Collin's face.

"I mean, maybe. I don't know what you mean, I guess."

"I don't mean anything. I don't mean anything at all. All I mean is, sad as it is, sometimes it's the only thing you can do for a guy. A well-deserved ass-whipping. But it's for their own good, so it's got to be done, right?"

Collin said nothing.

"Yeah," Phil tried again, retracing his main point to underscore it in Collin's mind, "I think the best thing for that boy of mine would be for someone like you—an athlete, I mean, a champion—to give him one good, solid whipping. That would set him right."

Collin cocked his head then and said, "Aren't you my girlfriend's boss?" He'd finished washing his hands and now stood at the sink, drying them on his t-shirt.

"Maybe," Phil said, "I'm a lot of people's boss." He

pulled a brown paper towel from the dispenser.

"Yeah, I think you are," Collin nodded, studying Phil's face.

Phil opened his palms and shrugged as if to accept the inevitability of his role as a job creator. "Like I said, that may be. I'm a community leader." Collin's body language suggested he was preparing to exit the lavatory. "Say," Phil continued, as if the thought had only just occurred to him, "that thing we were talking about. Is that something you'd have any interest in?"

"What thing?"

"Ah, you know. Helping a guy to…get back on the right path."

Collin's face was blank.

"Teaching him how a man should behave, I mean. Like a lesson. Teaching a guy a lesson to show him the…error of his ways." With a growing sensation of drowning, Phil continued, "And, of course, for helping me out—by helping *him* out—you'd naturally require a little something for your trouble. That much is obvious without being said." He recognized he was stammering. The words he needed were forbidden and speaking around them was imperiling the quality of his sell.

Phil raised his eyes to the boy then and found that Collin was staring down at him with what he recognized as judgment. He'd dived into this thing with such certainty—so sure of his belief, not only that this was a job that needed doing, but that Collin Radaszewski was the man to do it—that he could scarcely make sense of this reaction. Then it dawned on him: perhaps today's young jocks really were just chuckleheads after all, a generation neutered by sensitivity training. Or, perhaps Phil had simply misjudged Radaszewski's character. Perhaps he wasn't a man in Phil's own image after all.

"Eh," Phil said after a pause, "just forget it I guess." He threw the wadded towel into the bin with a forceful snap of his wrist.

"Five hundred," Collin said.

"How's that?"

"I mean, you're trying to pay me to beat-up your kid, right? Five hundred."

Phil squinted at Collin with cold eyes. The boy met his gaze and held it. Ultimately, it was Phil who blinked. "Son of a bitch," he said, reproaching himself. Collin hadn't been judging him after all. He'd been sizing him up as a mark, determining how badly Phil wanted this done and translating that value into dollars and cents, a rate of extortion. It was a trait he couldn't help but admire. With a proud, near-paternal delight, he countered the offer: "Two hundred. He's a pancake. There's no risk in it for you."

"I could get arrested. I could get expelled. Kicked off the team." Collin laid out each of these possibilities on an outstretched finger. "I need five hundred."

"You won't get arrested," Phil protested. "You'll push him around, maybe sock him in the gut two, three times, and be on your way. I'll do two-fifty. Max."

"No, there's too much risk."

"No risk," Phil said. "No risk."

"That's easy for you to say. You're not taking the risk. Five hundred."

Phil pulled back: "All right," he said as if outdone, smiling up at the boy. "You win. Only because I like your style, I'll do three hundred. Three hundred and we'll call that that."

"Look," Collin sighed, "I've got to get home to babysit my kid sister. Five hundred or I don't do it."

"Fine," Phil said, sensing a bluff, "forget the whole thing then."

"No problem," Collin said. "But give me the three hundred anyway."

"For what?"

"For keeping my mouth shut," Collin responded with affected innocence. "For not going to Coach and telling him that an old man—a community leader—

just solicited me in the bathroom."

Phil responded with a one-syllable sound, raised at its end to denote a question, but not, strictly speaking, agreed-upon vocabulary.

Collin feigned shock. "That's an accurate description of what just happened here, right?"

"You little piss ant."

Collin smiled and shrugged and extended an open palm. "Come on, I'm going to miss my sister at the bus stop. And when she gets mad, boy, she's a shin-kicker. You've seen our team's shorts. My legs are my livelihood." His fingers waggled in a 'gimme' gesture.

Phil blushed uncharacteristically, blinking away his disbelief. But, finding himself with no choice, he pulled out his wallet and removed three bills.

Collin accepted them graciously. As he folded the money and stuffed it into his front pocket, he said, "Hey man, this was a real pleasure. So, you know what I'm going to do? I'm going to give you a bundle rate. Since you gave me three hundred to keep your secret, I'm going to take care of your son for your original price. I'm in for two hundred."

"That's five hundred dollars," Phil shouted.

"No," Collin said. "It's three. And two."

Phil shook his head.

"Do you really want him to go the rest of his life as a—what did you call him? A pancake? Come on, it's for his own good. Don't you love your son? Two hundred dollars."

As upset as Phil was at the turn this negotiation had taken, he was aware he had no alternative solution, no other fixer he could lean on. His thoughts turned to the Chamber of Commerce, to the Outstanding Entrepreneur.

Phil retrieved the money and held it just out of Collin's reach. "How do I know you won't just take this and welch?"

"Well," Collin said, "I guess you don't have any

way of knowing that for sure. But don't worry about it. You can trust me. I'll come by your restaurant tomorrow after school and you can give me the details. The one where Ruzanna works, the one in Columbia. I need to go now, though." He reached out and snatched the money. At the bathroom door, he turned back to Phil and said, "Listen, I really appreciate you trusting me with this thing. I have a good feeling about it." He smiled then and disappeared through the door.

Phil stood. Ego bruised. Wallet lightened. In that moment, he had only the comfort of knowing that his original judgement of the boy had been correct, after all: Phil Ochs and Collin Radaszewski were every bit the same kind of man.

Chapter 04

After his shift at the Irmo Fry Buddy, David Samuel retrieved his oversized leather-bound journal and checkered duffel coat from his employee locker. Owing to the simplicity of his job in the front of the house, he ended a typical shift with a pocketful of sketches and budding verses scratched onto folded paper napkins, the best of which he would transfer into his journal for reworking in pursuit of what he thought of as 'high art.' On that afternoon, however, his pocket contained only one single napkin on which he'd scribbled five modest words: *damn the father with love*. It was a confounding phrase, but one which made him flush with excitement when he considered its elegant simplicity.

From experience, he knew that the sterility of the Ochs house would stamp the life from an idea this unformed. The home was like a creative gas chamber that only the most robust and tenacious of his prompts could endure. Were it to survive that artistic Gulag, he would need to first blow flames into its smoking embers, to strengthen and steady the fitful beat of its heart. So, at the bus stop outside the Irmo Fry Buddy, he boarded a Greyhound for Lake Murray.

He saw a seat free beside an older Black woman. David Samuel declared his intentions with his eyes then folded his body into the available space. The woman frowned and leaned away from him. She was that toothless sort of older person with collapsed lips and a jutting chin, and when David Samuel smiled at her after settling in, it was unclear to him if her continued frown was intentional or inevitable.

It was a fifteen-minute bus ride from Irmo to Lake Murray, and David Samuel filled those minutes by flipping through his journal. Peripherally, he saw that the woman had noticed the book, so he laid it out across his thighs—a discrete repositioning that would allow her to see what was written and drawn on its manila pages. His movement through the journal became a service to his audience: when he noticed her eyes squinting down onto a page, he lingered; when her head turned back toward the window, he loudly and showily flipped ahead. He fantasized that her eavesdropping might lead to questions: *"Are you some kind of writer, son?" "Where did you learn to sketch that way?" "Do you mind if I take down that poem, so I can have your beautiful words in my life?"* But no questions came. The deeper he got into the journal, the faster her eyes left the pages, coming to study his face with a look that, when he finally turned to meet her gaze, appeared to him to be less awed than troubled, the eyes of a concerned citizen on the brink of crying out for the authorities. David Samuel promptly slapped the book shut and secreted it inside his unbuttoned coat, turning his body away from her for the remainder of the ride.

Murray was a manmade lake, allowing its beach the unlikely features of black tupelo and flowering dogwoods that rose high out of the sands like shipwrecked travelers from a southern wood. It was to such an out-of-place tree that David Samuel came after exiting the bus, kicking sand onto the toes of his black work shoes as he trudged forward. The November breeze was cool off the water, but the beach was unusually crowded. Snatches of conversation as he passed fully-clothed families on blankets and in beach chairs told him that this was due to a watching party for the evening's new moon.

The shade beneath the dogwood would be prized on a hot summer's day, but in these conditions, David Samuel's only company in the dusk of the tree's canopy was a middle-aged man with a cash box and a balsa wood sign that read, *Two-Headed Root Doctor.* David Samuel eyed the man warily, then situated himself on the opposite side of the trunk, turning his back to him. Despite an attempted delicacy in his landing, he fell hard against the sand and he emitted an involuntary, "Oomph." He opened his journal to a clean page. From his jacket pocket he pulled a heavily-chewed and under-sharpened number two pencil and the folded Fry Buddy napkin. He read the napkin's phrase then leaned his head back against the tree trunk, closing his eyes to the lower branches. *Damn the father with love.* In his mind he saw his parent's roof, the tall casement window that had bitten into his arms when he'd crawled through it onto the shingles. He could feel a connection coming between these images and the words on his napkin prompt.

"Nice evening for a new moon, isn't it?" a quiet voice asked into his ear. Startled out of his meditation, David Samuel's body was skittering away from the sound even before his eyes opened. The man with the lockbox and sign had joined his side of the tree. "Hey, I didn't mean to scare you, buddy." Even in the shade of the dogwood, the man's right molar was visibly gray when he smiled.

"Couldn't you see that I was in the middle of something?" David Samuel said in a voice that was faint and put upon. "What do you want?"

"Only to be friendly. And to see what was in your

book. Are you some kind of a writer, son?"

"Yes," David Samuel said, attempting to express a look of bother while still cocking his head to invite deeper questions on this line.

"What kind of a writer are you?" the man asked, scooting closer in the sand.

"Every kind. Any kind I need to be. It was a poem that you interrupted. And now it's probably gone forever."

"Like catching moths in your hand," the man sighed.

"I beg your pardon?"

"A creative friend of mine said that to me once. That finding ideas was like catching a moth in his hand. Not hard to do necessarily, but more will get away than you can ever grab, so to say."

"Well," David Samuel said, "yes, that's a way of putting it. But I fear this moth almost had my fingers closed over it until you scared it away."

"I'm real sorry about that, buddy. I thought maybe you was a blogger or something, come to write about the new moon."

"I am not a blogger, and I do not care about the new moon." The lock box caught David Samuel's eye and he said, "Are you soliciting donations for this tree?"

The man appeared confused. "This tree?" he said, laying his fingertips on the dogwood's bark.

"Yes. Is that why you interrupted me? Is this tree sick?"

"This here tree?" the man said again. "Buddy, this tree is fit as a fiddle. This tree is having the time of its life. What makes you think this tree would need me to give it money?"

"Your sign," David Samuel said, nodding at the message, *Two-Headed Root Doctor.*

The man read the words of his sign as if they were unknown to him, then he abruptly laughed, causing a reappearance of the gray molar. "Oh, I see. You saw

'Root Doctor' and you thought, 'arborist.' Is that it?"

David Samuel responded with a single, self-conscious nod of his head.

"So, you took my sign to have literal meaning—to mean literally that I'm a doctor of tree roots—and your most pressing question is about this old dogwood? If you took my sign that way, I'd have thought the bigger question would be, 'Where's your second head?'" For a moment his face was challenging, his eyes staring into David Samuel's, but then he broke into a second fit of laughter that caused him to fall backward onto the sandy beach.

"I didn't come here to amuse you," David Samuel said. "I came to be alone and to find inspiration. So, if you don't mind." He shooed at the man with the back of his hand.

"Oh, hey now, buddy. I'm not here to get at you." He tucked his thumb into the collar of his shirt and wiped it at the corner of his eye. "Look it, I'll explain it to you." He sidled closer and moved an index finger across each of the words on the sign. "Two-headed root doctor," he said. "Two-headed, that's hoodoo-speak for one what's got psychic gifts. And root, that's like a mojo-hand. You know, like a talisman. Get it?"

"So," David Samuel said, "you're a witch?"

"Eh," the man said with a more-or-less shrug of his shoulders.

"And why are you here?"

"I came for you, buddy."

David Samuel scoffed. Then, in a skeptical test of this answer, asked, "What's my name then?"

"I got no idea."

"How did you know I would be here?"

"How could I have?"

"Then what do you mean you came here for me?" David Samuel said.

The man scanned the horizon, moving his eyes over the beach-goers. "I came for all of you. But you especially." He grasped David Samuel lightly on the shoulder, allowing his hand to linger before releasing him.

"Why me especially?"

The man laid back on his elbows and crossed his ankles. "You're the one who sat under my tree."

To David Samuel, the logic of this was sound. "So, you want to give me a reading, I presume?"

"If that's what you need."

"And the lock box is for me to pay you."

"If you paid me, that's where I'd put it." A moment passed during which the two men stared silently at one another. Finally, the root doctor said, "Let me show you something, buddy." From his relaxed position, he stretched an arm around the far side of the dogwood's trunk. When it returned to David Samuel's view, the hand was cradling a bird's nest with a cracked blue egg inside it.

"What's that?" David Samuel said with a sickened scrunch of his nose.

"A bird's nest with a cracked blue egg inside it," the man said. "A starling, I'd guess. But do you know what might interest you about this old nest? When I showed up at this very tree not one hour ago, there was two fox squirrels grab-assing through the branches there," he said, pointing upward. "They scared away at the sight of me, but as they run off, this nest fell out of the branches."

"Is that what cracked the egg?"

"No," the man said with a smile. "This guy's brothers and sisters would of flew off months ago. But do you know where this nest fell to? It fell right to the very spot where you're sitting now." He enunciated these final words slowly and clearly, punctuating them with wide, astonished eyes.

"What does that mean?" David Samuel said, eager for any sign the universe had to offer that might announce him as being charmed.

"I have no idea," the man said.

David Samuel scowled. "What kind of a psychic are you?" he said.

"My abilities concern the roots of things. This here is a sign." He waggled the nest. "I don't know what it means, but I know it means something to you."

"It means nothing to me."

"My abilities tell me it does," the man said with a confidence that caused David Samuel to reconsider his knowledge to the contrary.

"Well...then what might it mean?"

"Now, of course, signs are personal. Only you could know that."

"But I don't. I don't know."

"Just think about your life," the man said, casually offering the nest to David Samuel. "And the short, aborted life of this poor baby bird. Then ask yourself, 'What do these things have in common?'"

David Samuel pondered the nest in his hands: the ugly, brown bowl of grass; the lovely symmetrical curve of what remained of the brittle ovate; the dried goop that had seeped from the crack and now glued the shell to the grass. That goop, he realized, was the very stuff of life, as much a bird as any of those that patrolled the waters of Lake Murray even at that moment, only shapeless and carelessly spilt. Nature had given this baby bird armor and a soft bed intending that these protections would one day allow it to take flight, to literally rise above its humble beginnings. But something had gone wrong, and now the bird would not only never fly, it would remain fixed in that filthy nest by the vengeful clutch of lost potential. Slowly, his head rose from the nest and his eyes found those of the root doctor. Despite the chilled air, sweat had beaded at David Samuel's hairline. "It's me," he said with wonder in his voice. "I'm the aborted baby bird. Is that right?"

"Sure," the root doctor said with a shrug. "I mean, it ain't up to me, but sure."

There was a pause then, David Samuel taking time to get comfortable with the closeness the fates had allowed him to their quiet magic. The root doctor whistled tunelessly through his teeth. "Your abilities," David Samuel eventually said, "are deceptive. But astonishing."

The root doctor grinned. "See? I got a second head on me after all. But look, buddy, now that your mind has been verily blown, how's about a donation to the cause?" He gave his lockbox an economical shake.

David Samuel nodded understanding. "Of course," he said. "This experience, I have to say, has been truly eye-opening." He pitched forward onto his hands and knees and rose to his feet, a necessary readjustment to allow him access to the back pocket of his work pants. In the process, three of his fingers punctured the bird's nest, and when he got to his feet, the nest adorned his hand like a set of brass knuckles. He withdrew his fingers then extended the nest to the root doctor.

"I'm good," the man said, wrinkling his nose as if he hadn't been holding the nest moments before. "Why don't you keep that as a receipt of our transaction?"

David Samuel worked the tips of two fingers into the tight slit of his pocket and tweezed out a folded five-dollar bill. He handed the money to the root doctor, who accepted it with a gracious bow of his shoulders. "I hope you won't think me rude," David Samuel said, stooping to collect his journal, "but I'm going now." The last of these words came as a croak as the waistband of his pants cut into his diaphragm. When his hand reached the leather binding of the journal, he felt a crackle of excited energy pulse from it like a mild electrical shock. He erected himself and pushed out a showy, restorative breath. "But you, Mr. Two-Headed-Doctor, have inspired me. Rest assured that this experience will be memorialized in my very next piece."

"Cool, buddy, cool," the root doctor said as he un-folded the bill and placed it into his lock box. Looking down into it, David Samuel saw that his was the only money it contained. Its other contents appeared to be a half-eaten pack of bologna, a paring knife, an un-used candle, and what might have been a black and shriveled human finger. David Samuel held the journal in crossed arms against his chest and waited to share a meaningful exchange with this man whom he now felt he'd been destined to meet. But the root doctor seemed to deliberately avoid such a moment, keeping his focus on rearranging the contents of his box. So, in time, David Samuel lumbered off through the sand, his mind abuzz with artistic possibility.

Chapter 05

The Number Three combo was comprised of two cheeseburgers with onion and pickles—known as 'regular buddies' in the parlance—a medium beverage, and a medium fry. Phil, who always made a point to pay for meals in his restaurants, ponied the additional forty-nine cents for sweet potato fries. The markup for sweet potatoes was low, given the extra time and cooking oil needed to prepare them, but they were a legacy item that dated to the original Fry Buddy restaurant and remained a powerful symbol of the brand.

Collin didn't eat. "See?" he said upon arriving. "Here I am. And you thought you couldn't trust me."

Phil had played over and over his rhetorical loss to the boy a day earlier in the high school's lavatory, so now scrupulously said nothing. He merely gestured for Collin to join him at his booth.

"I can't stay," Collin said, sliding into it. "Ruzanna's got a shift here in an hour, and this isn't the kind of thing she'd be down with, if you know what I mean. My boy, A.J., drove me, and he's got to go."

"I don't need you for long," Phil said in a reproachful tone meant to suggest that he was equally inconvenienced by this meeting.

With an air of mislaid pride, Collin continued, "A.J.'s got a girlfriend whose parents are gone overnight to a funeral in Augusta. So he's got the meter running on me. Every minute I keep him out there in the parking lot is a minute she's home alone. I've probably already cost him a handjob, and that's not the kind of debt I want to have to repay."

"Let's get down to it then," Phil said.

"Cool. What's that?" He nodded toward a small pile of papers to the right of Phil's tray.

Phil placed a reverent hand on the pile. "Fry Buddy's application for employment and employee handbook." He continued quietly, "In case anyone notices us talking, they won't be suspicious." His eyes moved to a pock-marked team member who was crisscrossing the floor, wiping down empty tables with a sodden rag.

"They won't be suspicious that you're eating during my job interview? Don't I deserve some respect? It's that kind of thoughtlessness that'll force me to take my talents elsewhere."

Phil responded to the boy's grin with what he hoped was an equivalent display of displeasure.

Collin held his gaze for a moment, then seemed to lose interest and said, "So, do you have a picture of this guy or something?"

"No," Phil said. He hadn't thought to bring a photograph of David Samuel, but it occurred to him now that he wouldn't have known where to find one even if he had.

"Not even on your phone that you can show me?"

Phil gave the slightest shake of his head. The team member was wiping his rag on a table two booths down from them.

"WTF, man? How am I supposed to know who I'm looking for?"

"You'll know him when you see him. Don't worry about that."

"Whatever. Where will I find him?"

"He works at my Irmo store," Phil said, then thought better of this: "but don't do it there. He spends a lot of time in Oswald Park. That'll be better."

Collin's eyes rolled upward as if to study a map on the ceiling. He nodded. "All right," he said, "I know where that is. When will he be there?"

"I don't know."

"Seriously, dude? This," Collin said, splaying his fingers on his chest to indicate his own body, "isn't a detective agency."

Phil returned his gaze to the team member and acted to hush Collin with a lowering of his hand. "He goes a lot on the weekends," he said. "Try the weekends."

A car horn sounded in the parking lot.

Collin's exhalation seemed purposefully showy and brimmed with melodrama. "Fine," he said. "So, how will I know it's him?"

The team member nodded at Phil as he put a knee in the booth seat directly behind Collin to wipe crumbs from the windowsill. Phil cleared his throat and said firmly, "So, what hours can you work? Are you available on the weekend?"

Collin peered over his shoulder and, recognizing the game, said, "No, man, weekends are out for me. Oh, and I want to tell you up front: I'm going to need a company car. That's on my list of must haves. It's off the table. Late model four door. You pick the brand. Nothing domestic, though, God!"

The team member moved on and Phil signaled with his eyes that the coast was clear.

Collin leaned in and annunciated slowly, "How will I know it's him, boss?"

Phil closed his eyes and shook his head, troubled by the image he conjured. "He carries around this book, like a big scrap-book-type deal. And he's got this hair. Long and oily, like, I don't know, like a girl that gave up on ever being loved, maybe. And he's got one of those faces that, something about it, just makes you uneasy. And he's big. Husky, I mean. But soft too, like there's no bones in him, nothing so solid as that." Following this description, Phil was quiet for a moment, eyes tightly shut, his face lowered toward the table. Eventually, and as quietly as if he were speaking only to himself, he muttered, "Circumference, not angularity."

"Shit," Collin said, startling Phil's attention back to the table. The boy was staring at him in a way that left Phil unsure whether this outburst had been in response to his alarming description of David Samuel, or if it was meant as commentary on Phil, himself.

Before he could get a better read on him, Collin slid out of the booth to the accompaniment of more horn sounds from the parking lot. He reached and swiped one of Phil's sweet potato fries then continued while chewing it: "We have a game Saturday night, but I'll hang out at the park a little bit on Sunday. If he's not there though, it's not on me. This isn't something I'm devoting my life to."

"He'll be there," Phil said, blustery.

"Like I said, it's not my fault if he isn't." Collin punctuated this declaration by smacking the back of the booth seat, then he hurried away before Phil could answer.

Phil watched as the boy pushed through the outer restaurant door and crossed the parking lot, then curled into the passenger seat of a dented Corolla. The driver appeared to chide him, but Collin responded with a mischievous smile and greatly exaggerated masturbatory strokes of the air between the driver and the steering wheel. The driver pushed Collin and punched him on the arm and then the Corolla backed out and drove away, and Phil was left alone with the thought that all he wanted was a son like that.

Later that evening, Phil returned a file of month-over-month sales figures to a cabinet drawer in the Columbia Fry Buddy's office, then walked to the back of the kitchen and took a position he favored between the store's two rolling garbage cans. From here, he could see the entirety of his operation at work: the economy of the two-sided grill press; full baking sheets of buns being toasted or steamed, depending on their purpose; the simple efficiency of the timer lights on the deep fryer indicating when to put down baskets of fries and when to bring them up; the predictable movement of clockwise assembly from cooking to dressing to wrapping to delivery. He stood with his hands clasped behind him, like an admiral on the deck of a destroyer. From the garbage cans, there rose the sweet fragrance of food waste just beginning the rot, and he found this sensory experience complementary to the pride he felt here, a pride like that of a God watching over a universe he'd spun to life. Beyond the kitchen, in the front of the house, cashiers moved customers quickly through the register lines, into the dining area with plastic trays or out the door with paper sacks and cardboard drink carriers. He could see the back of Ruzanna Singh's head at register three, her black hair redacting her lovely face from his sight. She turned abruptly, her eyes passing over Phil like he was just another piece of sterile kitchen equipment, searching until they found Tony, the floor manager. She beckoned him, and Tony came to her, looking particularly tall and gangly from Phil's vantage, with the stooped posture of a post-autumn scarecrow. They shared a brief exchange, and then Tony took Ruzanna's place at the register. Phil used this as a cue to end his surveillance, and he moved forward through the kitchen to the front of the house. The scene he saw at Ruzanna's register momentarily stopped him until his brain coded it as an emergency and he charged forward, his face a furnace of anger.

Across the counter from Tony stood Jim Trebek, smiling, one hand resting on the countertop, the other in a fist on his hip. As he approached, Phil intoned a loud and startling growl that brought Tony to attention. The manager was upright and nearly convulsive by the time Phil arrived at his side. "Phil, I—" he began.

"Phil," Trebek said with bright music in his voice.

"You!" Phil said with a sneer. "What are you doing in my restaurant?"

"Woah," Trebek laughed, "that's a heck-of-a how are you."

Jim Trebek had come to South Carolina from Greater Sudbury, Canada. He'd worked for eighteen months as the sales manager for J.T.P. Parts, the restaurant parts distributorship that was owned by Phil's closest friend and career-long supplier, Jerry Tatum. He'd then stolen Jerry's business model, along with half of his salesforce, and opened a rival distributorship in the same Gadsden commercial district as J.T.P. Save for Phil, all the major South Carolina franchisees had migrated from Jerry's shop to Trebek's.

Phil turned his attention from Trebek to Tony, glaring at him with silent accusations of betrayal. Too meek to return Phil's stare, Tony froze, possum-like. Phil noted the dampness of the manager's uniform shirt, the way his badge angled down as if wilted from the heat of the kitchen, or from disappointment at its association with so pathetic a namesake. A thought of the folksinger—Phil's own sad eponym—flashed in his mind, and he was angered further.

"Phil," Tony explained, "Ruzanna was in need of *the lady's room.*" He leaned in and whispered this object of Ruzanna's need. "I was just minding her register."

To Trebek, Phil repeated, "What do you want here, Jim?"

"Well, gosh, Phil, there's not anything I want in particular," Trebek said, feigning hurt. "I was just on my way home from the shop, and I thought I'd stop in for a bite." His pleasant tone turned to one of inquiry, "Hey, Phil, I couldn't help but notice: you're missing some signage, aren't you? When I walked in, I didn't see anything about the Bacon Buddy promo. Started Monday, yeah?"

"There's a sign above your head, Jim," Phil corrected.

Trebek leaned far back and appraised a two-sided cardboard sign suspended an inch below the ceiling. "Oh, yeah," he said. "Wow, you really got it up there, don't you? If only I were seven feet tall, eh?"

"You want food? Order it and get out. I know your game, you Canadian bastard." The bastard's game, as Phil understood it, was to grow his sales staff by casing Phil's restaurants and stealing his most talented managers. He'd lost two in just the last fiscal quarter.

"Geez, Phil, I had a long day, is all. So, I came to a friend's restaurant for something to eat. That's all this is. But, of course, if I'm not welcome…"

"I'm not your friend. And you're welcome to take your food and get out."

Trebek nodded. "Then that's what I'll do. Once my sweet potatoes are up, I'll be on my way." In the brief silence that followed, Trebek worked his thumbnail over a crust of dried ketchup on the counter, a performance of apathy that ratcheted the moment's tension with each repetitive scrape. After what seemed to Phil a carefully-timed pause, he added. "Oh, by the way, Margaret says 'hi.'"

Phil flushed. Margaret had once been the manager of his Eastfield store and was the most recent of his betrayers. Trebek's reference to her stabbed Phil in a still-soft and undefended region of his ego. He squinted his reply.

"Yeah," Trebek continued, "Margaret's been a real delight, a real giver. She already feels like the heart of the shop. Says she's never been happier." His eyes moved to Tony but stopped short of winking.

Tony blushed.

"Maybe you should come by and see her, Phil. You've never seen the shop, have you? You too, Tony. Come on by sometime, the pair of you."

Phil took a sideways step that forced Tony back and that inserted himself between them. "We've never seen your outfit and we never will," he assured Trebek. Then, to Tony, he said, "I think I just heard the fries ding, bub."

Tony's body jolted, but froze when Trebek said, "Hang on there, Tony. Don't bark at the man, Phil."

"Go," Phil instructed.

"Wait," Trebek said.

Tony's eyes fixed on the counter, as if by diverting his gaze he could render himself invisible.

"Phil, you know, I have to say: it's not right to treat your people like this," Trebek said. "I never talk to my folks that way. Where I'm from that's just not polite."

This statement riled in Phil a jingoistic pride that was vaguely defined but trained to easy upset. "Tony," he said, pressing an index finger into the tall man's chest, "I want you to get this Canuck's order together now before I grab that stinking mop and shove its handle straight up his crooked ass. And when I'm through with him, you'll be next, get me?"

"Hey, now. That's enough," Trebek said. "Tony, tell this man to treat you with respect."

Tony appeared as if he might explode into a nimbus of nervous sweat.

"Has he beaten you down so badly?" Trebek said of Tony's non-response. "That breaks my heart, big man." He paused to glare at Phil. "No! You know what? I can't stand for that. I won't!" He continued with what Phil regarded as amateurish theatricality: "Call me a bleeding heart. Say what you will, but I want you to come with me, Tony. I'll always have room for a man of your talents. We can get you on the payroll by Monday."

"You rat," Phil growled.

Tony was silent. His white shirt heaved noticeably. His face had gone red, and a thin mustache of sweat glimmered in the restaurant's fluorescent lighting.

Trebek continued to coax him: "Don't worry, I know the wages he pays. You won't do any worse with me."

With a bull snort, Phil said to Tony, "Don't you dare."

Tony staid put, his lips working in silent puckers as if emitting a series of invisible smoke rings.

"No?" Trebek inquired with a tone of finality. "Well, suit yourself. Forget the fries. I've lost my appetite." He shot a final, reproachful look at Phil then took a step away from the counter. "I wish you luck, big man," he called to Tony.

In the seconds that followed, Tony's eyes rose to meet Phil's. A bead of sweat traveled down his cheek from the receded hair above his temple. An intensity came into his stare, and the corners of his mouth began a downward curl. When Trebek was nearly at the inner door of the glass vestibule, Tony emitted the slobbering exhalation: "Wait, Jim! I'm coming too!" He shouldered past Phil, knocking heavily into him. Reeling, Phil could only turn and watch as Tony withdrew through the lobby, an ebbing shape of treachery.

Chapter 06

When Phil arrived home, he found Lillian on her aluminum step stool rubbing the Microfiber Miracle Mitt's cloth noodles across a platoon of jade elephants that lined their fireplace mantel.

"You home, hon?" she called over her shoulder. She took a downward step on the stool and stood with one foot on the floor, the other propped on the stool, the fisted mitt pressed against her stomach in a posture that recalled that of Washington crossing the Delaware.

"Well, he did it again!" Phil called. "He poached Tony. While I was standing right there to see it."

"The Canadian bastard?" Lillian said with a disconnected usage that robbed the words of their intended offense. "Oh, Phil, I'm sorry."

"Tony was a dim bulb anyway, and I got someone I can fast-track through the management program. But still. It's the principle of the thing."

Lillian's response suggested he'd buried the lead: "Oh? Who are you fast-tracking? You haven't said a word."

Phil cleared his throat. It seemed unlucky some-how to bring her into his plan for David Samuel on the near side of the assault. He was sorry he'd let this much slip. "It's too early to talk about it," he said. "A need-to-know sort of thing. But, this shake-up means I've got to jump on this quick. I've got planning to do, so don't wait up." He made for his office with hurried steps.

"Phil?"

He stopped and turned, his shoulders sunken to communicate the significant burdens they bore. *Just one more thing,* those shoulders signaled, *that's all it will take to break this man.*

"What is it?" Phil asked.

"It's David Samuel."

A small munition of panic lit and blew, and Phil was briefly fuddled under a rain of displaced frag-ments of thought. *If she'd guessed he meant David Sam-uel, had she worked out the darker parts of the plan too?* Eyes cycling, he searched the debris for a fast answer, then blinked his wife into focus again and demanded, "What did you mean by that?"

Lillian cocked her head. "You asked, 'What is it?'" she said with a curious note in her voice. "And I said, 'It's David Samuel.' Because it is. David Samuel is what I wanted to talk to you about. He wrote me a poem." She produced it from the mantle and extended it as evidence. "Are you feeling okay, hon?"

"Oh," Phil said, "a poem. Well, then...how about that." He turned again in the direction of his office.

"Don't you want to hear it?"

Phil shook his head. He wasn't sure which mad-ness was greater: his son's for inflicting this sort of thing on them or his wife's for adoring him for it. "Ev-erything's just kind of a lot right now," he said.

"But it's beautiful," Lillian protested.

Facing away from her, Phil hung his head and

nodded to the carpet. "Read it."

"Okay," she said, invigorated, "it's called 'To a Mother.'" Tittering, she added, "By D.S. Ochs." She proceeded to read:

Once, a happy zygote, I,
pushed into the world's cold fingers.
Boo, Mother! To pull that little caper.

You laid with an ice cold man
and let his frost bite me
Boo times two for you!

In your house it was warm
But he is the wild,
icicled outdoors where you evacuated me, Harpy,
and on whose tundra my bitten skin aches in
memory of you.
Achoo!
Achoo, Mother!
Mother, adieu.

When she was through, she remained silent, presumably to allow Phil time to meditate on the poem's deeper meanings. "Isn't that something?" she said, finally. "And, look, he illustrated it." She moved to her husband and offered the page for him to see.

Phil reluctantly appraised the charcoal images that bordered the text. "Is that a tit?" he asked.

"I think it's supposed to be." Lillian frowned and brought the page closer to her face. "But, from this rendering, I'm forced to wonder if he's ever actually seen one. A mother's sustaining breast? That's how I took it."

Phil scratched at his temple and stared at his wife. A narrow bird of a woman. Batty as all this was, he couldn't help but feel a twinge of appreciation in that moment for her loyalty. Loyalty to Phil and, God knew, to the boy too. In a world where you bring people in, encourage their potential, train them to be effective leaders—only to have them double-cross you, take all that investment and push their chips into the pot of some no-good Canuck—there was something reassuring about someone having your back. Even when their taste in allegiances was questionable, as was the case with Lillian, who may have just wiped at a tear from something she'd read in that bullshit poem.

With his office door locked, Phil did thirty minutes on his elliptical, willfully forcing out the day's anxieties with each suspended step. Once done, he dismounted the device and wiped his damp face and arms with his discarded tracksuit jacket. He stepped out of his shoes, pulled down his moistened pants and used them to rub dry his white and balding inner thighs. In only a t-shirt and underwear, he fell into his desk chair with a force that rolled the chair backward until its casters struck the baseboard of the wall behind him.

He opened the Lenovo on his office desk and entered the complicated password he'd chosen to protect it. His screen brightened to a wallpaper image of Wendy's founder, Dave Thomas's *Dave Says Well Done*, the fast food bible and a piece of writing that Phil suspected to be amongst the most important of the twentieth century. He navigated to a multi-tab, color-coated spreadsheet that broke down the staff at each of his franchise locations. On the Columbia tab, he took great delight in highlighting Tony's name and mashing his finger into the Delete button. "Back-stabber," he muttered to the now-empty cell. Then he moved back and forth amongst the other tabs. Cells tinted yellow indicated managers, blue were assistant managers. There were desperately few of both in the wake of Jim Trebek's pillaging. Orange cells were the up-and-comers: hourly employees whom Phil had witnessed performing exceptionally, or who comported themselves with confidence or with a neat, well-groomed appearance that at one time or other he had recognized as suggestive of potential. He moved to the Irmo store and stared woefully at his son's name highlighted in punitive red. It made him shudder to think of the work it would take to turn this boy's cell yellow. As he was puzzling over this, he heard faint movement in the hall beyond the door, the quietest creak of floorboards shifting under carpet. "Do not knock on that door," he instructed, then waited a moment before returning his eyes to the spreadsheet.

A faint scratching began at the door.

"Lillian, it's really not a great time."

Scratch. Scratch. Scratch. Scratch. Scratch.

"Please go," he called, then squeezed his temples with the fingers and thumb of one hand and repeated this wish to himself in the muttered mantra, "Go, go, go, go, go..."

Scratch. Scratch. Scratch.

"I'm not feeling my sanest just now."

Scratch. Scratch.

"Go away!" he finally erupted, punctuating the command with an involuntary side-fist strike of his computer keyboard.

The sounds in the hall abruptly ceased. Phil listened, his eyes fixed on the elliptical beside the door. A full minute passed in silence. His anger began to subside. His heart rate slowed.

Finally, Phil returned his gaze to his computer. From the blow he'd struck it, a line of pixels, whiter than the whiteness of the blank screen, now traveled rapidly down and to the right, down and to the right, until it reached the bottom of the display, only to reappear in its upper-left corner where it began its descent again, his spreadsheet lost somewhere behind that pale curtain.

Scratch.

"Creeping Jesus!" Phil exploded. He bounded to his feet and the chair fell back with a clamber against the wall. He slid on his shoes and stomped half-nude through his office, the office rug muting each step, neutering his intended bluster. He reached for the doorknob, took it in his hand and pulled the door open to find a hall that was dark and empty. There was no light from the living room. It appeared Lillian had gone to bed. He looked left and then right. Phil took a step forward and his foot hit something light and small on the hall carpet. He looked to see Bernie on his driftwood base, teetering from the blow. The stuffed rabbit fell backward, revealing a sheet of notebook paper folded into thirds. Phil's miniaturized reflection peered back at him in the rabbit's glass eye.

Phil stooped and snatched the folded paper. Once fully risen again, he delivered a swift and powerful kick to the rabbit and it ricocheted off the opposite wall, then landed with its backside pointed momentarily up at him before finally settling on its side.

Floral handwriting on the back of the paper read, "To Phil Ochs." Phil unfolded the paper to reveal what he correctly suspected to be his own poem. With a preparatory intake of breath, he read:

The Baby Bird
By D.S. Ochs

The baby bird is beautiful. The baby bird is blue.

With his broken body mangled 'neath your orthopedic shoe.

Some nights, he sits on peaking rooves, his wings too bald to fly, just hoping to be noticed by a kinder father's eye.

And 'cross those shingles (shining with the moon's unblinking glow), his shadow runs beyond the eaves to skies he'll never know.

And in that shade, he's swallowed; in that shadow, he's eclipsed, until he's without certainty that shadow's even his.

Could it be another's silhouette the bird cannot escape?

That baby bird whose twisted bones are darned with glue and tape?

Could that shadow be a specter? A black ghoul of creosote, who's wrapped his demon hands around the baby's feathered throat?

And is that shadow even there? Or a trick of naïve eye?

A truth taught to the baby on foundation of a lie?

Fore, it may be the father's shape, that swindler of Oz, who swore the shadow as a truth, so the babe believed it was.

The father! Damn the father! That's right: damn his blasted pride!

His arrogance, and wastrel-making, showy, hollow pride!

God blast him as his consequence! God blast his spiteful soul!

God free the baby bird and everything in his control!

Free the breeze the baby needs to lift him through the air!

Free the wings the father plucked and left so bald and bare!

And if you will not free him, with your grace from up above, then teach the father how to live with love! With love! *With love!*

When Phil finished reading, he forgot himself and spat onto the hall carpet. The poem left him momentarily lightheaded. At its border were illustrations of a sideways bird's nest with a cartoonish cracked egg inside it and what appeared to be a two-headed man. As he reflected on the page, however, he realized that it was the title he found most offensive, so twee and inappropriate to have come from a grown man's brain. How was it possible for the boy to find so many ways to disappoint when Phil's expectations for him were already so low?

It didn't matter now, Phil reminded himself as he crumpled the poem and tossed it into his office wastebasket. There was a reckoning coming and this kind of foolishness would soon end. He closed his office door with a smile at the thought that what would come next had been planned with love, with love, with love.

Chapter 07

On Sunday morning, Collin brought some boys along. A.J. drove, of course. And Tom bitched until Collin let him tag along. Tom was fourteen and not above ratting the whole thing out to their parents if he didn't get his way. So...

Before the park, Collin said to A.J., run by Fry Buddy, and he did. Collin made Tom pay to make up for being a blackmailing little nark. Ruzanna was on the register, and she asked what trouble they were planning and Collin assured her none at all, babe.

He didn't tell the boys he'd be kicking no asses that day. They'd sit for a minute at the park, and Collin would talk tough, but there was no way they'd even see the guy. He made it sound like a sure thing, but really Ruzanna's boss had left it up to chance, and there was no chance it would happen. Then, Collin would say fuck it and they'd go play Xbox at A.J.'s or to the mall. And Collin would have all that money for absolute free.

They ate in the car at the park. The joke was to be like everyone they saw was their guy, even when it was a woman or a little kid. Tom had a few good ones, but then he belched and made the whole car smell like pickles and ass, and they had to roll down the windows or else die.

But, the thing that happened then was, they saw him.

He came up the hill right in front of them, just like he was in on the plan. It was like that thing with the old televisions? The horizontal lines? The guy rose up from behind the hill into more and more of the lines. Incrementally like that, until he was framed right in the center of the windshield.

This guy, he looked like if you'd never seen a human in real life, but you'd heard them described, and you made your best guess. Arms longer than the legs. And the hair. God, the hair! And clothes that were, like, lady's clothes? Vests and shit? Silk, maybe, like pictures of Collin's dad from the nineties.

Big, just like her boss said. He was all covered in his lady clothes, but he was still visible in, like, an anatomical way. Not balls and joints, but like when Tom covered the dogs in a blanket and watched them worm their way out of it. The way those blankets looked before the escape. His body was a thousand dogs in silky blankets all moving in different directions.

And his eyes were round. Like, legitimately. Buttons sewed onto a beanbag. And his feet pointed way out to the side, like they wanted to go two different directions but had to settle on straight ahead.

And he had the notebook under his arm. It was big and square like those old photo albums with the sticky cardboard and the plastic window. When Collin was a kid, he liked the crackle of lifting that plastic at his grandmother's house, playing in her closet. The notebook looked like that, like his grandma's photo albums.

And the guy was looking all around him. At, like, the trees and the birds and shit. Like he saw something there that Collin couldn't. Fairies or pixies or whatever.

Or, like he was the lady on the hill from that musical, the one with the Nazis, and he was playing it up for the cameras.

When Collin saw him, his cheeks went hot, and his ball sack walnut-shelled. He started to say something like maybe they should go. Something dumb like that, as if the boys hadn't seen him too and something that lame would work. But then Tom was out of the car. Fucking Tom. And he slammed his door hard like the sound of it would remind Collin to man up.

Collin looked to A.J., who looked scared but happy too. He had his phone and was getting it to his camera. He said something that sounded like a heart beating in Collin's ears, and he had this crazy grin. Then he was out of the car too. Collin just sat there. A.J. pushed his head back inside and asked was he ready to do this, killer. He was pointing the phone at Collin.

Collin glanced at their guy on the hill then back to the camera. And then he fake-smiled and said, "Yeah, man, let's roll."

Chapter 08

When Lillian attended state functions of the Daughters of American Patriots, it was as Mrs. Phil Ochs. The *Mr. Man* formality of DAP name badges always seemed to her quaint and proper, and she delighted in these occasional opportunities to become that version of herself. Who wouldn't delight in being Mrs. Phil Ochs, wife of the successful restauranteur? Certainly, she thought, Mrs. Ernest Fishback or Mrs. Bob Packer or Mrs. Jeffrey Combs—women whose names she could read from across her luncheon table, and whose husbands were surely not so accomplished nor well off—would leap at the chance to swap badges with Lillian. Sooner or later at one of these events, she expected someone would read her name and ask if she were the wife of the Fry Buddy franchisee, and Lillian would nod and bat away the question and say yes, she was, but she really only thought of him as *her Phil*.

The luncheon was being hosted by Lillian's Columbia chapter and was something of a loser's banquet, an event for South Carolina Daughters who were unable to attend the high-profile American Heritage luncheon which, by lottery, had been held this year in

Beaufort. Over the next two days in that out of the way southern city, Daughters would be treated to pageantry, choreographed presentations, speeches by various state regents, a national congresswoman and even the state lieutenant governor. Columbia, by contrast, had a six-hour reservation at the Holiday Inn Express where Daughters served themselves buffet-style lasagna and salad from tinfoil trays at thirty-two dollars a plate. All because these Daughters' poor health or advanced age or fear of a changed routine had kept them from traveling to the real show. Ironic disqualifiers, as these tended to be the very traits that led women to pursue membership in the first place.

The lasagna went quickly, the Daughters apparently resolute to get all they were due from their admission fees—their future heartburn and stomach cramps acceptable souvenirs of a day they'd wrested from mediocrity to make memorable. *Today, I ate half a tray of room temperature pasta in white gloves and a pioneer skirt.* It seemed to Lillian, however, that the day's primary menu item was sour grapes.

Stoic, though the Daughters professed to be, a collective malaise hung over the Holiday Inn Express like smoke in a bar hall, a stagnant smog of green-eyed awareness that, by attending this event rather than the state's premier function, they had each outed themselves within their group as an *other*—when the very point of membership was to demonstrate an exclusive pedigree, to single out your line of descent from all those *others* who couldn't make the roster. So, the jealous ladies stayed their tongues beneath huge mouthfuls of catered cuisine. Glances were made at the bareness of the room's decoration. Heads were shaken. In acts of temper, some daughters removed the sorority ribbons and pins from their blazers and cast them heretically onto their plastic tablecloths. "Flaccid," said Mrs. Dale Cole when her plastic fork extracted salad from her Styrofoam bowl. Clucks of solidarity arose from the

Daughters of Lillian's table. Mrs. Cole shoved the fork into her mouth, and then, in as un-ladylike a manner as was possible from a woman dressed as a colonial-era aristocrat, opened her mouth and let the unpalatable bite fall from her tongue back into her bowl. Each of the banquet hall's two dozen tables, it seemed to Lillian, felt like the back-corner table at a wedding: overflow depositories for illegitimate and unwanted guests.

The event's entertainment had been billed as a 'historic presentation of DAP fashion by decade,' but now proved to be the Camden regent standing at a lectern and modeling a succession of costume hats. "Eighteen ninety," the regent said, tying on a duck-billed Leghorn bonnet. She nodded four times in a left-to-right sweep of the room that allowed every table a direct look at it. "Nineteen hundred," she said before donning a floppy feathered Edwardian.

Unlike most of the women in the banquet hall, Lillian could have gone to Beaufort, but she'd opted not to. She had the time and the money and, save for the quiet fear that without her mitigating presence one of the men in her house might kill the other, no real obstacles had prevented her. She simply wasn't one of those Daughters who wore membership as a badge of honor, one whose personal identity was molded out of the history or mission statement of the organization. "I am the modern DAP," was a proclamation she'd heard dozens of times by such Daughters through the years—retired teachers who were drawn by the group's works in education, or the widowed homemakers whose loneliness had led them to commune with their ancestral dead, or the middle-aged women who tended to be the youngest of the Daughters and were driven by their ultra-conservative worldview. Lillian had joined for the simple reason that no woman should presume herself an island. And, as comfortable as she was to barricade herself in her big Prosperity house, an island dweller who never ventured to the mainland might well be judged a castaway, a dispersion which would undermine Lillian's happy island life. So, after proving herself a descendant of American Revolutionary War patriot, August Emerald Byrd—who killed lobster-backs and Waxhaw Indians with equal relish—she'd long ago settled on the DAP as the ship to which she occasionally fastened her dingy.

"Nineteen twenty," the regent said, pulling on a three-cornered musketeer.

A Daughter at their table spoke and Lillian turned just as Mrs. Gilbert Bonk asked, "Did you say something, dear?" Mrs. Bonk's eyes were fixed on the Daughter seated to her left, a forty-something with a dark, teased hairstyle that framed her face like a hood. From Lillian's perspective, the richness of the forty-something's tanned skin and dark hair against the backdrop of table upon table of aged white-haired women had the effect of a bruise on a banana, making the room, by her single point of contrast, look more rightly like the Grandmothers of American Patriots.

When the forty-something spoke, it was with a tone of polite derision: "I said that this is riveting." As she spoke, the regent nodded toward them in a nineteen thirties' linen cloche and met Lillian's eyes, and an association was made in Lillian's brain that this look may well have been a personal rebuke for not keeping order at her table.

Mrs. Gilbert Bonk looked down to the forty-something's name badge in what was, at first, a manner of quiet casualness, but Lillian recognized her alarm in what she saw there. Lillian looked too and saw that the forty-something's badge was one of the few she'd ever seen at these events with a feminine construction: Ms. Lydia Parker.

"I'm...not married," Ms. Parker said at the behest of their table's eyes.

With a lack of subtly, the Daughters now studied Ms. Parker's enviably youthful face to determine what about it might forbid a man's attraction. It was a curiosity Lillian shared.

Perhaps aware of their judgment, Ms. Parker clarified, "I used to be married. But, when I suggested my name badge read, 'Ex-Mrs. Gordon Secretary-Fucker,' my regent got a little longwinded on the bylaws."

"Language!" said Mrs. Gilbert Bonk.

"Filthy…Gracious sakes…In all my life…" said the table.

"Nineteen fifty," said the regent, her head crowned by a slight, polka-dotted silk cap.

Loudly, Lillian said in the direction of the regent, "Oh, Ginger Rogers had one like that," drawing the attention of Mrs. Gilbert Bonk and Ms. Lydia Parker and several others at her table. "I read somewhere she was a Daughter." And, one by one, they each turned to the hatted regent and seemed to remember themselves and the supposed formality of their congregation.

Non-confrontational by nature, Lillian had spent two decades caught in the battle between Phil and David Samuel, an experience that had heightened her instincts as a peacemaker. She had no hope of defanging either of them, not meek Lillian Ochs, not against wills as strong as her husband's and son's. So, over the years, her desire for peace had been trained in the techniques of distraction, a tactic which suggested that if one was not actively engaging a problem, then that problem ceased to be.

"The swinging sixties," the regent said with a jaunty shake of her shoulders before slipping on a fur and netting pillbox.

Lillian glanced around the table and felt pleased that her peace was holding. And, in the quiet of that peace, she shifted her gaze to study Ms. Lydia Parker. Here, before her eyes, at her very table, sat a victim of infidelity. It wasn't a rare status, she knew. But having a victim so near her, Lillian felt the kind of guilt-laced pity that occasionally led her to sponsor a balloon-bellied African child or to throw a handful of change out the window of her Audi when driving by dented cars with open hoods broken down on the side of the road: her own life was charmed, while others' were not. She'd been Mrs. Phil Ochs for half of Ms. Parker's life and yet Ms. Parker's marriage sat burned out in a ditch of time that was well in Lillian's rearview. This wasn't due to chance, of course. It was because Lillian had the good sense not to build a marriage on such caustic a foundation as lust or physical attraction. Phil was a born provider. And Lillian, in the most honorable sense, was a homemaker, charged with interpreting and demonstrating Phil's success through the things she chose to surround them with. If Phil was a light then Lillian was a prism, one perfectly cut to reveal his many attributes. For Lillian, the practicality or beauty or convenience of her well-bought things reflected those same traits onto the man who provided them. It was a simple point of compatibility on which to base a marriage, but it was the undramatic secret of their longevity. Phil didn't drink, and he wasn't violent. For all his bluster, she'd never feared for hers or David Samuel's safety. But while it may have been true that the Mr. and Mrs. Lydia Parkers of the world brought on their hardships by their own caustic passions, Lillian couldn't help but feel sorry for them.

"The solid gold nineteen seventies," said the regent who was now in a sequined beret of that decade's stated color.

The phone in Lillian's purse began to chime. She removed it and looked at the screen to see, as if he knew she'd been thinking of their collective good fortune, that the caller was David Samuel. She rose from the luncheon table and brought the phone to her ear and quietly said, "Hey, hon."

"Mrs. Ochs?" a strange, male voice said, "This is Deputy Sheriff Slattery."

"Deputy?" Lillian began, looking around her as if

seeking clarification from the indifferent eyes of the Daughters, then increasing her pace toward the exit. As she pushed through the glass, she asked, "I'm sorry, what is it that's happening?"

The deputy cleared his throat. "Ma'am," he said, "first off, I want to assure you there's nothing to be concerned about. Your son is fine. However, I'm calling to inform you that David has had an altercation."

"David *Samuel*," her son's voice corrected from a distance.

"An altercation?" Lillian said, supporting her body against the hotel's brick exterior. "I don't understand. David Samuel had an altercation?"

"Yes, ma'am, with a gang of roughnecks. Three, by his count. They was dispersed by the time we got the call. He ain't hurt too bad, just banged up is all. Still, to be safe, we're transporting him off to Lexington Medical for a look over."

"My God, he has to go to the hospital?"

"Yes, ma'am. But don't misunderstand me: it's just a precaution. In case he has any internal bleeding or broken bones or hemorrhaging or whatnot. We let him go with something like that, that we're not aware of? He could turn around and sue us—or the family could if the injured party died—and we got budget trouble enough as it is. It's a bad deal. The budget, I mean. And your son too, of course. There's no good here, ma'am."

Lillian began to wail.

"Ma'am, I need you to understand: your son is fine. He ain't going to die. We're just taking him to get checked out to make sure I'm not wrong about that."

"I want to talk to him!" she demanded. "I want to talk to my son!"

"Mm, that's probably not the best idea right at the moment. He's pretty worked up right now."

"Woebegone," she heard David Samuel yell. "I'm woebegone."

"Ma'am," Slattery said, "he's claiming to be woe-begone."

"Where?" Lillian said. "Where did it happen?"

"Here at Oswald Park. A hiker found him curled up on the floor of that concrete bathroom they got here. Upsetting to think of the contagions a person could get exposed to on a floor like that. Mighty upsetting, if you ask me."

"I'm coming there," Lillian said, pushing herself off the wall and into the parking lot.

"Ma'am, no. By the time you got here, we'd be gone. Just as soon as he stops slapping at the EMTs, they're going to have him on this gurney and on his way to Lexington. Better you go there too. And ma'am? You might could bring him a change of pants."

In the background, she heard muted protestations from her son. "What's that?" Lillian said. "What's he saying?"

"Who knows," Slattery said with a weary thread in his voice. "He's been screaming about a journal they stole off him. Ma'am, can I ask you: your son claims he didn't have any money on him. Is there a chance he was in possession of medication that might have made him a target? Anxiety pills? Antipsychotics?"

"No."

"Lithium? Something like that?"

"No."

"Zyprexa, maybe? Mood stabilizers?"

"David Samuel doesn't take medication."

"Huh," Slattery said. "I'll be danged. Never mind then. It was just a hunch. Tell you what let's do: just grab him some clean shorts and meet us at Lexington Medical, okay ma'am? I'll see you soon." With that, Deputy Sheriff Slattery disengaged the line.

More than a minute passed. Lillian stood on the parking lot blacktop, the forceful beat of her heart was enough to sway her body forward and back, forward and back, ever so slightly, her phone gripped precariously in loose fingers. On the phone with the deputy sheriff, she'd felt called to action, but his abrupt termination of the call had stranded her. Apart from the call. From the situation. From any idea of what to do next. And it was from this stupor that she became aware of having lifted her phone to her ear, of its speaker ringing. Then Phil said, "Yeah?"

* * *

When the call came, Phil was in the Columbia office crafting the language of an incident report about Tony for corporate. Jagged red and solid blue lines blossomed on his screen as he typed, scolding rebukes of his poor spelling and careless punctuation. He sighed at the interruption of his lighted phone screen, the vibrating dance it did across the countertop. He snatched the device and accepted the call: "Yeah?"

"Phil?" Lillian said in a voice that sounded hoarse and unsteady. A car horn honked in the distance.

"Yeah?"

"Phil—David Samuel's in the hospital." She spat these words as if a force had built up behind them, one that might push them away from her and place their burden on him.

Phil's pulse rose in his throat. It had occurred to him that the boy might play this for drama, expecting a full body cast for a slug in the gut. "The hospital?" he said, pulling off his cheaters and squeezing the bridge of his nose. "Why would he end up at the hospital?"

"He was jumped. They say he had an altercation."

"Wait. Who says?"

"The police. The sheriff's office."

"Sheriff?" Phil said, rising from the desk chair. This was a wrinkle that he hadn't previously considered. Thinking it through now though, his eyes moving left to right as if speed-reading all the potential outcomes of such a turn, he found no immediate cause

for panic. In a worst case—Radaszewski being appre-
hended and taken into custody—it would be Phil's
word against that of the delinquent who'd beaten up
his son. "Did they catch the guy?"

"No."

"Oh, good—uh, good God, that's terrible." Phil
directed a relieved wink at the dead-eyed poster of Fry
Buddy's founder that hung above the office desk. His
body felt light when he leaned on the back of the chair.

"The deputy says there were three of them." Her
voice sounded stronger now.

"Three?" Phil said with a skeptical rise in his voice.
It would undoubtedly be good bang for his buck—the
services of a mob for the cost of a hitman—but it
wasn't the plan. A one-on-one brawl, that's what was
needed to straighten the boy out. A good, honest scare.
But victimize him too much and you might push him
further in the wrong direction, sissify him into becoming a shut-in, jumping for cover when the mailman
comes and growing his fingernails into curled defen-
sive talons. "How is he? Did he hit back?"

"I don't know," Lillian said. "I haven't seen him
yet."

"How's he acting?"

"I don't know, Phil, I haven't seen him. I guess I
will, though. I guess I'll go now. They said," she paused
here as if to honor the gravity of the message, "that he
soiled himself."

"What?"

"I think they said he soiled himself, Phil."

"Creeping Jesus." He closed his eyes to a stab of
pain in his temples. What Phil found most upsetting
about this was how characteristic it seemed. He'd never known David Samuel to shit his pants, but thinking
of it now—God, he seemed like the type. "How bad
did they beat him up?" He asked this question expecting the answer to be that he was scared but fine, so he
was unprepared for Lillian's response.

"They said he might die." Her voice was choked and quiet.

"They did not."

"I'm sure they said something about him dying."

"Not a chance. What did they say exactly?" When he touched his palm to his cheek, Phil's face felt cold and bloodless.

"I don't know now. My head, it's all muddled," Lillian said. "But I know he said the word 'die.'" She'd started into those pinched sobs whose pitch always triggered Phil's instinct of fight or flight. He inched the speaker away from his ear.

"Lillian, don't do that," he scolded. But he was on his feet now and heading toward the glass vestibule. "A person doesn't die from getting beat up."

"But...what if they...really hurt him? What if they...broke our boy?"

Phil emerged into the sunlight of a bright autumn Sunday.

In his ear, Lillian's tears turned to anger, to panic: "They're monsters. They're monsters for laying their dirty hands on my boy. Oh, my God, Phil, I need to go. I need to go see him. I—"

Phil disengaged the call. He tossed his phone onto the passenger seat of the Lexus, then climbed in and slammed the door. Lillian was wrong. The boy wouldn't die. He wouldn't die because that wouldn't serve anyone. Still, he needed to get to the hospital and to the bottom of it, to take charge of the chaos—like when a disgruntled manager quits mid-shift and he gets the call that the ship was sinking. And he needed to get a first look at his investment, the value he'd gotten for his money. And, perhaps also, he needed to abate a quiet worry that he may have caused something honestly bad to happen here, and to prove to himself that it wasn't so.

Chapter 09

Lillian and Phil arrived at the hospital together—she coaxing her Audi into a space in the parking garage a mere moment before his Lexus squealed to a halt across two spaces to her right—only to find that David Samuel had been released.

No stitches. No slings or casts or doctor's somber decrees. No pants, other than the pair folded into the hazard bag that he held in the lap of his paper dress.

All the way home, Lillian begged descriptions of the assault and of her son's mental state, encouraging him to cry out for her, but David Samuel said nothing. Upon arriving in Prosperity, he defied her further by immediately retiring to his room and locking himself in for the night. Briefly, Lillian took to sobbing outside his door, knocking and slapping at the obstacle of it, unsuccessfully plying her son with promises of homemade treats or the application of ointments, decorating her offers with choruses of, "my boy, my boy." Eventually, though, her motherly grief was bested by a self-respect that prevented her from a second hour of prostrate begging on the hall carpet, so she collected herself and advised her son's door to call her should it need anything, and then she joined Phil downstairs.

"The sheriff told you he was going to die, huh?" Phil said, flattening his lips. The cable news show he'd settled into was on a commercial break.

"Don't, Phil."

"What did he say when you were up there?"

Lillian's throat felt constricted like she'd spent this last hour escaping from a burning building and smoke inhalation had damaged her breathing. When she spoke, her words were all sighing defeat: "He didn't say anything at all to me."

"Well, maybe he's just taking it in stride. A situation like this, it has a way of toughening up a guy, making a man of him. Sure, he shat himself, but maybe that was just a symbolic evacuation to make room for a little personal growth."

Lillian ignored this. On the television, a failed former presidential candidate espoused the security of investing in gold bullion. "He wouldn't even open his door to me," she said.

Phil said nothing. His demeanor was calm, but Lillian noticed how his eyes shifted around the room as if each place he focused them stung and made them flinch away. Evidence, she reasoned, of the pain he was privately suffering on behalf of their son. *Oh, the frustrating beauty of her two prideful men.*

"I think we should talk about this," Lillian said after settling on the sofa, but her declaration was met with silence. "Do you think they'll catch the punks that did it?"

A disgraced Alabama governor advocated for reverse mortgages. Phil's eyes flitted to and then away from him, but never toward Lillian.

"I just don't understand how this could happen. How could someone do something so vile?"

Phil cleared his throat.

Sensing that Phil didn't want to talk, Lillian said quietly to her knees, "I never thought I'd see this in my own backyard."

Unexpectedly, Phil erupted: "Okay, Lillian! I get it, you're upset. But, would you give it a rest?" He slammed his flat palms onto the arms of his recliner, causing air to push through a tear in its plastic cover with a high-pitched toot. "He's a grown man for God sakes. You act like he's made of glass. It does no good to coddle him. It does him no good at all."

"Phil, don't."

"No, listen," Phil said, rising to his feet. He turned toward her, but, as he spoke, continued to avert his eyes: "I kept hands-off in how you raised that boy. Lord knows I had my reservations about it, and I've been struggling to deal with the consequences for twenty years. What's that they say about reaping what you sow? It's like that. Like you used bad seeds or the wrong fertilizer or that, and what grew out of it was a weird, sad version of the picture on the seed packet. And instead of looking at it and admitting it wasn't right, you doubled-down and planted your feet and treated it like the most perfect version, threw both arms around it and encouraged every freakish thing wrong with it. Meanwhile, everybody else is looking at what you grew and saying, 'are those supposed to get that big? What's with the lumps on it? I think it might be rotten.' He walks around like a weird little spook, Lillian, because you made him feel like that was okay. What happened today was basic assimilation: if you don't teach him to be part of the larger group, then the larger group is going to rise up and do it for you. This was your work these kids did today, the work you—and when I say 'you,' yes, I do mean 'we'—didn't do." Phil wiped his sleeve across his forehead, which had become noticeably damp.

"You…blame me for this?" Lillian said quietly, sitting forward on the sofa.

Phil coughed. "Blame?" he said. "Sure, maybe to a point I do. But, I mean, no, it's not like that exactly."

He stuttered to a stop, then narrowed his eyes at her. "Why do you want to bring blame into it?"

"You just said..."

"I said what I said. Maybe it's your fault. Maybe it isn't anybody's fault. These things, they happen. Why look for culpability? Whatever the cause, you can't change it now. Just, maybe you should try to be grateful is all. For these kids picking up the slack, I mean."

"Grateful." Lillian said, not as a question, but as a concept that had been laid before her for consideration.

Phil moved back to his recliner. He looked tired and small. The cushion wheezed as it accepted his weight. "Grateful," he said, "sure."

"Well, I hope they catch them then, so I have an opportunity to thank them."

Phil shook his head and stared at the television. "They aren't going to catch anybody. That's what's so smart about doing this sort of thing to a stranger: no connection to trace back to them."

"Smart," she said, adding this to her concepts for review.

There was a thump from upstairs which drove Lillian to her feet.

"Leave him be," Phil said.

Lillian took a step toward her husband. "Phil, I'm going to go see if my son—who was just battered by thuggish monsters, remember—needs his mother."

"Yeah? While you're up there, check to see it there's any more of his development you can arrest."

"I'm going, Phil. But when I get back, we can talk about why he was even in that park today. He goes there to think up his poems. Poems he uses to get the attention of his father. So, I don't know—maybe one of us here is to blame after all."

"Me?" Phil leapt to his feet. Lillian had to step backward to avoid a collision. "So, it's my fault?" he said. "That's rich." He was suddenly moving toward the living room's open doorway. "You want someone to coddle him? Well then, why don't I go?" He continued from the stairs: "Maybe it'll be a nice change of pace for him if we switch for a while: I'll indulge his non-sense, and you can get real for a change."

Lillian stood, her eyes on the ceiling. She heard Phil's knuckles on David Samuel's door. "You all right, bub?" he called. She listened, but no answer came. Soon there were sounds of Phil opening their bedroom door and proceeding with getting ready for bed.

Lillian took a seat on the edge of the sofa. It was past her bedtime, but it would be a long time before she could sleep. She turned and peeked through her curtains at a darkness that seemed complicit in hiding the bad people who lived within it. Frustrated by that dark and by the silence of her house at a time when the emotion raging inside her demanded confronta-tion, she sat forward, picked up her phone from the coffee table, and dialed.

"Thank you for calling Miracle Products. My name is Raj. Who am I speaking with today?"

"Raj, this is Lillian Ochs."

"Hello, Lillian Ochs. Would you like to place an order today?"

"Raj, this is Lillian Ochs," Lillian repeated, by way of clarification.

"Who please?"

"Lillian Ochs."

Raj was silent. Then, meekly, he said, "The beloved pet?"

"Of course," she said in a perturbed exhalation.

"How are you today, please?"

"Well, I have to tell you, Raj, I'm not doing partic-ularly well this evening."

"The stuffed pet is not doing good?"

"The stuffed pet has a sneaker scuff that your mitt will not rub out."

"Sneaker scuff?"

"Yes. Where someone kicked him. Phil, I would guess, but either of them are capable."

"Of kicking a dead pet?" Raj said.

"I tried to wet the Miracle Mitt, like we talked about. But, I rubbed and rubbed, and nothing happened. And I know this isn't the mitt's intended function, but wouldn't you expect that a quality cleaning fabric would be able to handle a simple sneaker scuff? Does that seem to you to be too much to ask, Raj? It doesn't me." She allowed him time to respond, but no response came, so she continued: "And, now, in the spot where I wet the mitt and rubbed it on the scuff mark, the fabric is balding. When I was through, it looked like the sneaker scuff had irritated his skin or something and given him blue dander. It was upsetting, I'll tell you."

"The Microfiber Miracle Mitt is not recommended to be wetted and rubbed on your beloved deceased."

"I should hope not. Recommending it for a thing like that would be irresponsible, considering."

"That is the view of Miracle Products."

"Good. I'm angry, Raj."

"Me too."

"And now I need a new Miracle Mitt."

"Okay," Raj said. "With your warranty violation, I can have a new mitt delivered in three to five business days for the original low price of nineteen ninety-five. This is no problem."

His agreeability caused Lillian to drop her head and sigh. "Raj," she said after a moment, "It may be that I owe you an apology. Can I tell you? My ruined Miracle Mitt is not the only upsetting thing in my life right now. There's more by a long stretch."

She interpreted the sound he voiced as a groan of curiosity.

"My son was jumped. Raj, he got mugged."

Raj said nothing.

"Exactly. What does one say? It was the simple

work of hooligans. An awful, awful thing. And in a public park in broad daylight too. This used to be such a nice neighborhood. Do you live around the Prosperity area, Raj?"

"Prosperity?" Raj said. "No."

"Well, you might want to think twice before considering it. I tell you, in the car, on the way to the hospital, that Elvis Presley song played on the radio, and it was like he was singing about right here in my own hometown."

"The...*All Shook Up*?"

"*In the Ghetto*, Raj, naturally. But can I tell you something? I'm all 'shook up.' Over David Samuel." She waited for his response.

"*Teddy Bear*," he offered.

"Oh, he is, Raj, such a teddy bear, and that's the real tragedy," Lillian agreed. "What do people do in situations like this? Pray? Aren't there Bible passages about tragedy being a blessing in disguise, something like that? What do you think about that? Do you think there's a God that challenges us to make us grow?"

Raj swallowed audibly.

"I mean, it's crazy, but my first thought is that I want a Bible passage like that or some kind of motivational quote. Something I can say to him to lift his spirits, you know? Aid his recovery? 'Scar tissue is stronger than the skin it heals,' something like that. Do you know that expression, Raj?"

"I am not familiar, no."

Lillian thought about this. "I thought I'd heard that one, but maybe I made it up myself. See? I'm not equipped for this," she said. "But it's apt, isn't it? Because he's literally healing from an attack. Do you see what I mean? And adversity can make us stronger in spirit?"

"You have the soul of a poet, Lillian Ochs."

"Oh, Raj, stop that. Now's not the time."

"Stop like hang up?"

"Mercy," Lillian said with a sudden self-awareness. "I'm keeping you, aren't I? Do they listen in on these calls? I've heard that they do. Well, if they are, Raj is doing a great job. In fact, he just upsold me. Sell me something else, Raj."

"Sell you?"

"Anything at all. You deserve a commission for the kindness you've shown me tonight. Sell me a gift for my son. Something that says, 'get well soon.' How about the Grab It Ratchet Reacher?" A commercial for the item had played as she was dressing for the DAP.

At this, the tone of Raj's voice shifted: "The Grab It Ratchet Reacher means no more bending, straining or stooping. Its miracle reaching ratchet can comfortably hold up to five pounds due to its ergonomic handle, slip-resistant claw and reinforced aluminum stalk."

"Yes, that sounds like the perfect gift. What do you think, Raj?"

"Your son has issues bending, straining, and stooping since his jump?"

"He's convalescing, so that seems reasonable. And he wasn't exactly an athletic specimen to start. Raj, if someone surprised you with a Ratcheting Reacher, would you be thrilled?"

"It would be the thought that counted," Raj said.

"It is very thoughtful, isn't it? Oh, well that's just it then. You've convinced me." Lillian managed a measured smile. "I'm so glad I called to yell at you, Raj. Now look where we are."

"The Lord works in his ways," Raj said.

"Amen," Lillian said.

"Yes, okay," Raj said, "amen."

Chapter 10

When Phil awoke in the night, he wasn't sure what he'd been dreaming about, but it had been sufficiently spiny and poisoned to send him upright and panting.

In her Sleep Number bed, which was mated to his own, Lillian had stirred at the sounds of his panic. She seemed briefly to have awakened, but then her bed whirred some readjustment and she turned on her side and was quieted.

Phil rose and paced a few short laps in the darkened bedroom to calm himself. Once his breathing steadied, he perched on the stool Lillian used at her vanity and adopted a thinker's position to try to recall what his nightmares had been telling him.

After a moment's concentration, he recovered a premonition of the next morning: he and Lillian waking to find David Samuel's door still locked; busting into it to find the pale, Sleeping Beauty form of their son laid out peacefully on his bed, hemorrhaged or succumbed to an invisible rupture in the soft vault of his body; the wrecking ball smashing a hole in the outer wall of his room to give access to the crane that would be needed to lower him down to the ambulance; the muddy treads that would linger in their lawn long after their son was buried; the light-colored nubile grass that would announce those former treads for years after. Then into this mournful scene appeared the unlikely addition of Collin Radaszewski, deranged in that way of dreams, into some manner of smirking devil. In the nightmare, he'd chased after a running and terrified Phil. The devil had been calling out as he pursued him in a voice of graveled menace.

But what was it he was saying?

Phil considered this, his elbow pushing a red circle onto his bare thigh. "A boy needs opportunity," that was it. Phil snapped his fingers in triumph, but then his face fell at the recollection of what had happened next: as soon as Collin's message had reached his ears, Phil became aware that his own clothes were suddenly changed to those his son had with him when he and Lillian recovered him from the hospital, the same stained pants and ripped shirt. Collin had called out again, "When you hurt him, you hurt yourself," and Phil's body had begun to swell to several times its girth. Recollection was coming easier now, and Phil's face contorted in horror as its images played behind his eyes. "The boy needs roots," Collin called, and dream-Phil's vision had become impaired by greasy locks of his son's hair. He'd pulled the hair out of his eyes to find himself outside the Columbia Fry Buddy, staring into its big front window, David Samuel's broad silhouette reflected back at him. Here, Collin had caught him, had taken him by the shoulder and turned him. Collin had stared threateningly at Phil and growled, "Your boy is your future." At this, Phil became aware that his David Samuel body was now clad in a Fry Buddy manager's uniform, a realization that caused that body to shrink, quickly and startlingly, back to Phil's regular proportions. He'd turned then to see his own familiar reflection in the glass. With one wry smile, Collin's devil face morphed into one of mocking sweetness and he said, in perfect high-pitched mimicry of Lillian's voice, "Show him his value, okay? Okay. Love you, hon," and then he disappeared into an explosion of light that had likely been the event that woke him.

On the vanity's stool, Phil opened his eyes and considered the meaning of this scene. It was a nightmare, sure. But, perhaps, also a vindication, a reaffirmation that his plan was sound. "David Samuel is going to be a great manager," he said out loud as if to silence any of the room's invisible skeptics.

He rose, heart rate elevated with residual dread, and scooted in bare feet to the attached bathroom. At the sink, he cupped his hand and drank from the faucet, then washed the damp hand over his face. His reflection in the darkened mirror calmed him, his stern eyes a reminder that this was his goddamned pony show, whether or not the assault had gotten out of hand. "He'll be a great store manager," he said again, smiling at himself, droplets of water pin-balling through the bumpers of his midnight beard. Wise old fox, his eyes teased.

Phil shuffled back to bed then, thinking about the Outstanding Entrepreneur, the joy of winning. He pictured where in his office he'd display the physical prize that signaled his conquest. If any more dreams were to come that night, he wanted to offer these happy thoughts as their subject.

Chapter 11

David Samuel had promised Lillian a tour of his pain. After three days of recovery, he accompanied her to Oswald Park, or as he referred to it, "the scene of the crime." For the reenactment, he'd dressed in the clothes he'd worn on the day of his attack—the ripped top and vest, the laundered pants he'd soiled, everything but the notebook that had been stolen by his attackers. On the car ride to the park, he'd lamented the notebook, supposing it to be the sole representation of beauty in whatever viper's nest or drug den it now occupied.

Lillian wore a broad hat and the HD Vision Wraparounds sunglasses that the television had promised would block harmful UV rays, those agents of cancer and crepe paper skin that she'd only then learned were conspiring against her. The wraparounds fitted over her regular eyeglasses, protruding far off her face, dwarfing her fine nose. She was being led up a hill by David Samuel, who breathlessly narrated. He'd adopted that dramatic flourish of his, the one that Lillian always favorably compared to a Tennessee Williams heroine:

"I was coming up this way from the pond. 'Sauntering' would put an adequate image in your mind. And I remember thinking, perhaps fancifully, 'why will these little turtles let geese—which to them must appear as veritable giants—walk right up to them while they're sunning on a log, but when I, gently and quietly, come within fifty feet of the bank they frighten into the water?' I scratched a quick poem about that in my notebook—the last I ever wrote," he added gravely. He turned his head and let his eyes play over the pond behind them. The brightness of the sun against his pale skin lent his facial bruises and scrapes a new significance. "Of course," he continued after a moment, throwing one leg in front of the other to climb the steep hill, "now I wonder if they had recognized me as a marked man, if they sensed in that way animals can that I was someone the fates had turned a cold eye to, if they felt the chill of trouble blown into my path."

At the top of the hill, David Samuel stopped and struggled for breath. Lillian skittered and crested behind him then stood at his side. "Shoo," she said, removing a tissue from her sleeve to blot her forehead and wipe the back of her skinny neck. While her son reconstituted, she looked one way then the other in open-mouthed wonder at the landscape surrounding them. "These glasses, I swear," she said. "It's like walking through a movie."

David Samuel grimaced at his mother's oversized, reflective amber eyes as if staring into the face of a housefly. Ignoring her, he continued, "They were right there." He pointed down into the parking lot. "That parking space. Right. There." He kept the arm outstretched, following the finger like a compass as he trudged clumsily down the hill toward the paved lot. At the bottom, he stepped over the concrete barrier into the dramatic emptiness of the space he'd indicated. David Samuel raised his arms with upturned palms and turned to face Lillian, who remained at the hill crest. "I can feel it," he yelled, "all of their rage. Their hatred as they watched me. I was right where you are now, Mother, innocently—maybe even naïvely—trying to peer below the scarred surface of this world, hoping to glimpse some beauty underneath." He frowned up at his mother, his eyes narrow and angry. Then abruptly, he turned away. "Mother," he called, "Mother, you had better come down here with me. Standing here, I feel all their hatred, and it's all directed at you, just the way they directed it at me. Come down now before I'm overcome by their rage. Come quickly, Mother, for the good of us both."

Lillian trotted down the hill like a prancing dressage horse, the wraparounds slapping up and down on her nose. David Samuel swayed and sat, landing heavily on the blacktop between the painted lines of the parking space. By the time she came to the concrete barrier, he was lying flat on his back on the asphalt, his limbs outstretched.

"David Samuel," she scolded, looking from her prostrate son to the immediate area surrounding them, "get up, hon. People can see you."

"No, Mother. You committed to hearing my story, and this," he said, tapping the pavement, "is an integral part of it. I feel them. I feel them all." He caressed the concrete in a manner that could be mistaken for sensual. From Lillian's angle, south of her son's outstretched legs, it was a spectacle that was nudging toward the edges of obscenity. She averted her eyes. "Him! He's the one!" David Samuel continued in a put-on voice. "His grace intimidates me! Me too! Even a thug like me can feel the elegance of his spirit! The devil has presented us a martyr for our adolescent rage, our wild, brutish passion!"

"David Samuel," Lillian scolded again.

Abruptly, he sat up, then rolled onto his hands and knees and awkwardly stood. "Don't run from it, Mother. This is the unflinching truth of my assault.

I came down that hill, just as you did, an unwitting deer in the crosshairs. As I approached, I saw them get out of their car. I even began to say hello to them but thought better of it when I saw their denim pants and short sleeved shirts. I swiftly turned and began walking away from them, toward a vile-smelling bathroom." He grabbed Lillian's forearm and hurriedly led her toward the concrete structure. "Were they following me? I wasn't sure. But I was taking no chances. I clutched my notebook close to me. As I look back on it, I was more concerned with protecting my art than my safety. If you take away anything, it should be that."

"Slow down, David Samuel," Lillian protested, "you're going to rip off my arm."

"But then I saw two of them flanking me on either side. They were fit and fast. I threw my notebook at one, not in defense of myself, but as if the art had the power to save one and all of us from what they were planning."

Lillian was breathless from a combination of physical exertion and the excitement of David Samuel's storytelling. "What happened?"

"One called me an ass ranger. Another, a rear admiral."

"Oh," Lillian winced.

"That's nothing compared to what happened next," he cautioned. "They grabbed me, put hands on me physically."

They arrived at the restrooms. David Samuel released his mother and pressed his back against the concrete bricks to the left of an open doorway labeled, 'Men.' He continued: "And two of them, they beat me. Savagely."

Lillian echoed his posture on the right side of the doorway. A foul odor escaped the bathroom's labyrinth of concrete walls. Lillian's stomach turned at the thought of her son lying on the floor of these facilities. She hoped that he wouldn't drag her inside to reenact that portion of the story. "What about the third punk?" she asked.

"I can only see him in flashes now. But he had an outstretched phone. Mother, I believe he was recording a video with that device, documenting my indignity. No doubt they've had a barrel of laughs watching and re-watching my pitiful tragedy."

"Oh, I hope they catch those thugs," Lillian said, smacking a weak fist into the palm of her hand.

David Samuel raised his face toward the sky with a dramatic toss of his hair. "Naturally, you would hope that, Mother. And, that's sweet of you, I suppose." He smiled absently and closed his eyes to the sun. "Of course," he said, as if pausing for the moment of maximum impact, "it's only right that I tell you that I've decided to call off the investigation."

"You stop that!" Lillian shouted at her son just as a senior citizen exited the bathroom, intently palming-off a nickel spot of dampness from the crotch of his pants. He glanced at them with guilty eyes, then hurriedly shuffled away, holding his hands in a manner to conceal his shame.

"Oh, David Samuel, you can't say things like that," Lillian pleaded. "They have to pay for what they did."

"It will do you no good, Mother. I've already informed Deputy Slattery that I have no intention of pressing charges." He turned to regard her as if peering into the carnage of a bomb he'd thrown.

Lillian's eyes affected a disappointed pucker, an effort that she realized was lost behind two layers of eyewear. "But why?" she whimpered.

"I don't know that you could understand it, honestly. All I can say is that when those punkers attacked me, they left me with a little piece of them. I feel stronger now, wiser. Tougher, if I can be blunt. And I can't help but think they experienced a similar awakening, that maybe I left a little of myself with them. So pursuing them would be, in a sense, pursuing myself."

"That doesn't make any sense to me, not any sense at all."

"Maybe not to you. But those of us who have known true hardship see with different eyes. We see with clarity."

Lillian self-consciously fingered her HD glasses.

"You know," David Samuel continued, "the most savage of those boys was very tall—in my altruistic moments, when I can scrub my memory of his animalistic violence, even handsome. I'm overcome with the thought that he's the one in possession of my notebook, that he looks it over at night when the peer pressure of his youth gang has lifted, and he gets to be his true private self. I think of him reading it. And my hope for him is that he fills its empty pages with his own gritty sensibilities. Sensibilities that I, perhaps, had a hand in waking. My only regret is that I'll never get to read those nascent, streetwise longings."

"David Samuel, you're sounding crazy."

"Please, Mother! I need you to accept that I'm the authority here. What may seem crazy to you is simply a matter of—the ignorance of the beholder."

"Well, I may be ignorant," Lillian said with a gentle defensiveness, "but I think this is something you should bring up to your father. Invite him on your pain tour. Talk to him about your newfound grit."

David Samuel stepped away from the lavatory. A fly buzzed determinedly around his sweaty hairline. "Yes, I'm sure he'd be bursting with rejoinders on that subject. Perhaps I'll save myself that humiliation for his birthday."

"I don't know," Lillian sang in an interrogative melody that suggested she knew something he didn't. "It may be he's seen it himself already. He's taken a recent interest in you."

David Samuel snapped his head toward her, one eyebrow cocked. "An interest of what kind?"

When Lillian continued, it was with the burst-ing-dam aspect of a teenaged gossip defeated by the force of her secret: "He wants to make you a manager in Columbia! And you know how he loves that store. I mean—after all these years of loggerheads—he wants you to skip the kitchen and Key Holder and AM and make you the head of his flagship store! I overheard him going all through it with himself on the night of your gang-bang. And I've kept an eye on how he's been watching you since then. Never saying anything, just quietly watching." Here, she stopped and bit her fist in anticipation of her son's response.

His response, in a word, delivered through a mask of unconcealed disappointment, was "Gross."

"Hon?"

"I have standards of dignity, Mother, and your husband's nocturnal epiphany that his son has value is well beneath them. Besides, what makes him think I'd want to be a restaurant manager?"

"Well, the prestige for one thing. The accomplish-ment of it."

"It's the same boot I'd be under, just advanced from the heel to the toe."

Lillian walked through the grass to join at David Samuel's side, her thin arm weaving around his like a vine. She removed her HD glasses to encourage a con-nection of eyes. "Do you honestly feel that he's treated you so badly?"

David Samuel snorted. "I'd defer to the Trojans for advice on what accepting a gift of Phil Ochs sort would portend."

Lillian tilted her head and allowed a look of con-fusion to play over her face. "You see this as your father giving you a gift?"

"What else? You'd have me believe that he re-spects me, suddenly?"

"David Samuel, I know that you and your father haven't always seen eye to eye. But you're thinking of this the wrong way. It's you who'd be giving the favor, not him. Do you know how many managers your father's lost to that Canadian character? He lost another one just this week. I know he's too proud to ever put it to you this way himself, but Phil needs you, hon. I think you're wrong that he doesn't respect you deep down, but if that's how you really feel then this is your chance to be the bigger man. Show him he's wrong to feel that way." Here, Lillian paused. She could see in her son's face that she'd said enough, and that what she'd said had hit the mark.

David Samuel was staring into the middle distance, the impish glint of scheming in his eye. It was a look he'd inherited from his father—one that in the senior man signaled to Lillian that he was planning some real estate acquisition for a new franchise location, and in the junior meant the beginning of some new art project or similar creative scheme. "Yes," he said finally, "that Canadian headhunter does get under Dad's skin when he walks off with one of his managers, doesn't he? Okay, Mother, you've sold me. Sign me up to be a hamburger manager."

Lillian squealed.

"I won't even make him beg me. But I'll only do it on the condition that he stays out of my way. He has a nasty habit of trying to impede my particular verve. It won't work out for either of us if we're elbow to elbow in this thing. I think we should go now, Mother. It's time for lunch, and you've given me a lot to think through. Strategy's going to be key to my working this out."

Lillian smiled her agreement. Side by side, she and David Samuel started down the hill, each of them sated by the belief that they'd outwitted the other through their subtle deployment of cunning.

Chapter 12

Collin was on the edge of Ruzanna's bed, feet on the floor, hands where you could see them, proper as a gentleman. Ruzanna sat sixteen inches to his left—sixteen inches, he knew, because they each sat on one of the pony heads printed on her comforter, and the pony heads were exactly sixteen inches apart. She'd measured it. It's what her parents had called a 'respectful distance' to keep when they studied, the space between two pony heads. Ruzanna was leaning forward like she was praying over her history book.

It was hard for Collin to concentrate, all things considered, and he realized she'd asked him a couple of times now what document the Constitution replaced. "Mm, the Mayflower—no, the, what's it? Particles of Confederation," he said.

"Articles," she corrected, then made this adorable little you-are-correct dinging sound as if he hadn't actually bombed it. But then she went stiff again, like she remembered all of a sudden that this was no time for adorability.

Collin looked out through her open doorway into her parent's room. Mr. Singh sat across the hall from him with a mattress corner poking out from between his legs like a saddled-up cowboy. Collin did a smile-wave reflex, but her dad just shook his rolling pin like, "I'm watching you, buddy."

So, Collin read, "Which of the following Constitutional amendments have been repealed?" getting the message.

Ruzanna answered, "the eighteenth," before he could even give her the choices.

Brains and beauty, Collin thought. Instead of what he should have thought, which was: *Don't yell out across the hall like you're about to.* "You have a really bright daughter. Very smart. You should be," he called, but then his nerve got all limp-dicked and he finished with a wimpy, "proud."

Mr. Singh smacked his own thigh with the rolling pin, and that was a sound that wasn't going to do Collin any good right at that moment, given his state of affairs. So he leaned over and told Ruzanna he'd rather fail this test, babe, than tempt murder by psycho-daddy.

"Radish," she pouted.

To which Collin bluffed: "I'm actually being serious right now. I'd, legit, kiss my top five schools goodbye. I'd go to a public to get him to stop cleaning and dressing me with his eyes."

Ruzanna laughed, but in a way that didn't use her voice or face.

"So, I'm going to bolt, okay?"

"Seriously?"

"Yeah."

"Seriously-seriously?"

Collin nodded and gave her a sincere look that was all: believe it, babe. She looked back at him disappointed and maybe kind of judgy. Collin lifted up off his pony head and turned his back to Mr. Singh for a private moment, but when Ruzanna stood up he stepped back to save himself a thump from that fucking rolling pin for suspected groping of her illegal parts and pieces. He knew that he was coming off a little squirrely himself right then, so he took some effort to lay on a little game before he grabbed a hat: "Hey," he said, "this band, El Escarabajo, is coming to the Metro Credit Union Amphitheater. You want to go if I got tickets?"

"How would you get tickets?"

"I'd pick them up tomorrow after practice."

"But I mean, what would you buy them with? Do you need me to give you the money?"

Ruzanna knew Collin's parents didn't let him work during sports seasons, so this wasn't an insult in actuality. But still.

When he told her that no, he had the money, his whisper got louder, like his honor didn't give a shit about the angry man with his kitchen club. And then it was rapid fire, like: "I just mean do you want to go with me."

Then, "Where?"

"To the Metro Credit Union Amphitheater."

"No, I mean, where did you get the money?"

"What difference does that make? I just have it. Do you want to go with me?"

Then there was another smack from across the hall that made a legit little-frightened-kitten sound come out of Collin's mouth. Mr. Singh was hanging out his bedroom door, waving around the rolling pin, that little nubby handle threatening them in unpredictable, violent-looking arcs. "This does not sound like study!" he screeched. "This does not sound like study!"

Ruzanna went all red in the face and looked at Collin like, 'sorry, babe,' which meant she probably wasn't coming with him to the concert.

He bought the tickets anyway. If Ruzanna couldn't go, he'd take AJ or, God help him, even punk-ass Tom.

Collin went to school and to practice and then to the Kroger with the Ticketmaster because buying tickets online meant you needed a credit card, and he only had cash. In other words: he went on like nothing at all was wrong. He came home, took a shower and banked his jersey and shorts into the bedroom hamper. He jumped into bed, stretched and scratched the happy trail under his belly button. He reached into his boxers to peel sack skin off leg skin, woke up some places that needed a scratch, and he scratched. He checked out new texts on his phone. He closed his eyes for a nap, but that camera in his head was still spitting pictures of Oswald Park.

He stared at the ceiling instead. When the pictures started projecting on the ceiling too, he rolled over and grabbed the concert tickets from the drawer in his bedside table. He read everything on them: date, seat numbers, venue, corporate sponsors, taxes and disclaimers. That distracted him for all of a minute. When he leaned over to put them back, he saw the rest of the cash in the drawer, wadded and folded. He stared at it for a long time with this sort of out-of-body feeling, then he brushed the cash away and pulled the notebook out of the drawer.

Collin didn't know shit about art or poetry, but he'd been in sports since pee-wee t-ball, so he understood weakness. And this notebook reeked of it.

No one would believe him if he told them this probably, but he didn't mean to take that book. His body was just off-script, blackout manic. A let's-get-our-shit-and-go kind of impulse was the best he could understand it. But now he had it. Proof of purchase. He hated to admit it, but when he first flipped through it, what was his selfish thought? That this thing could be useful for creative writing assignments. What a dick, right?

But that didn't even matter because he started reading and saw it was far too lame to put his own name on any of it. But that was beside the point. The point was he didn't want to have it in the first place.

Or he didn't want to be the person that created the opportunity to take it. If that made sense.

For maybe the fiftieth time, Collin opened the book and started thumbing through it. It was touching the bare skin of his chest which made him feel skeevy, so he lifted it up so no contact was made.

It was mainly poems and, like, mini-manifestos? But a lot of drawings too. He stopped at one sketch toward the middle. It was skinny, straight up and down, like if you traced the outline of a pencil, but with a pretty clear ball sack at its base. He'd seen his share of dicks drawn on locker room walls, but the thing about this one was that where the head should be it split into three heads, each with an animal face: a bunny on the left, a cat in the center, and a duck on the right. The cat made sense to him in a figurative sort of way. But why the rabbit and the duck? The thought of sharp buckteeth and hard clamping bills made him close the book and lay it protectively over his crotch.

His phone buzzed and he swiped away a text. Then, without even thinking about it, he pulled up the video A.J. had sent him from the park. A.J. and Tom both thought it was hilarious. They told him so, like, every time he was alone with them now. He doubted this was true, but thought that maybe if he watched it one more time he'd get the joke too.

Chapter 13

"There comes a time in every man's life," Phil was saying, "when he starts to experience changes." He was staring through the windshield of his Lexus, David Samuel squeezed into the passenger seat beside him. He'd insisted on driving David Samuel to his first day of management training. "He's not a boy anymore, is what I mean."

"It's nothing to be nervous about, hon," Lillian chirped from the backseat. When she'd learned of Phil's ceremonial delivery of her son to his rites of passage into professional adulthood—a three-week training at the Irmo Fry Buddy—she'd tweaked the plans to include herself.

"I'm not nervous, Mother," David Samuel said distractedly. In the side mirror, he was studying a lesion on his forehead. It hurt when he touched it, so he touched it often and with mindless impudence.

"Of course, you're not nervous," Phil said, continuing what David Samuel presumed to be a motivational speech, "when a boy becomes a man, he's got no time for such emotions."

Of David Samuel's lesion, his three bruised ribs, and his busted nose, it had been his nose that initially caused him the most pain, but it was also the nose that had mended most quickly—to a point that now, even when he smashed and waggled it with his fingers, he couldn't reproduce that original violent throbbing.

"Time comes for him to set his fears aside," his father was saying.

The tenderness of his ribs had become similarly unpredictable. He could occasionally aggravate them to the point of taking his breath by rocking his flank into the back of a wooden chair or thrusting himself into the frame of a doorway, but not consistently, not anymore.

"You look so handsome all dressed up," came a call from the back. "You look just like pictures I've seen of your father when he was starting in management."

Both of her men hit Lillian with scornful, disbelieving glares.

"In his general aura, I mean," she clarified. "Responsible. In charge. A man in uniform."

"Anyway," Phil said. "Business is a game. Business is a game for sure, with rules and objectives and all that."

David Samuel knew he needed to be careful with the lesion. His skin was so pure and white—not a facial freckle or mole or pockmark—that it would be a crime to encourage a scar with his picking and pinching.

"There are winners in business. And that means there's also got to be losers."

David Samuel pushed himself closer to the mirror. The lesion seemed smaller today, little more than a thin red line above his eyebrow. With one finger, he covered the eyebrow to solicit the illusion that the lesion was his actual brow and so positioned as to leave him in a state of perpetual angry surprise. He smiled at this, then reexamined the texture of the abrasion, pulling the skin taut with a thumb and finger to better observe its rippled surface.

"I think this is so great," Lillian said, laying a hand on her husband's shoulder.

"An overdue acknowledgment," David Samuel said absently, "if somewhat suspicious."

"It isn't," Phil said with a snappish defensiveness. "It's strategic and perfectly timed."

"Oh, sure, it is." Lillian laid a complimentary hand on her son's shoulder and said to him, "And you can still do your art on the side. I'm sure a lot of artists have other careers with responsibilities and everything. Who knows, maybe someday your staff will all say, 'I knew him when. He was my manager back before he stole the show at the'—what? Not the Emmy's, that's TV. Not the Grammys. What would it be? What's the thing for what you do?"

"Lillian!"

"You're embarrassing yourself, Mother."

"No," Lillian protested, "I can see it. I can see it."

There was a pause before Phil picked up his thought: "So, what I was talking about was winners and losers. What side of that line do I fall on? I've got a pair of luxury vehicles, a nice house in a good neighborhood, and money in the bank. But none of that came easy, boy. It was hard work that got me where I am. A good head. A killer's instinct."

David Samuel interrogated the response of the lesion to being gently squeezed and separated, then lightly scratched across its surface. Moving closer still, he was able to illicit a sharp, satisfying jolt by knocking himself in the place of the scar with the cool glass of the passenger window.

"So, what does all that mean to you? You took a hit, bub. That was your old life saying, 'sayonara.' Now it's time to toughen up. Move forward. Switch gears. I think pretty soon you'll think back on this scrape and come to see that it was the best thing that ever happened to you."

"Oh!" came an explosion from the backseat, "the Pulitzers!" Lillian blurted with the air of having cracked it. Then, doubtfully, she added, "Wait, are those even on TV?"

"Mother, please."

"Fine," Lillian said, briefly lifting her hands from her men's shoulders as if in surrender. "I just think it's great, is all. And, who knows? Maybe you'll get to like management so much that it turns out *that's* your thing. Making speeches, giving orders. Maybe it'll turn out that you and your father aren't so different after all. Maybe you'll own your own stores and I'll be filling the mantel with crystal yams that say, 'David Samuel Ochs: Outstanding Regional Sales.' What do you think, hon?"

"We're here," Phil said. He turned into the backstreet behind the Irmo Fry Buddy and stopped alongside the topless shed that housed the metal repositories for grease trap renderings. Once the Lexus was stopped, he turned his head toward David Samuel, keeping his eyes low, addressing his son's feet, "So to sum up what I was getting at…"

"Yes, I know," David Samuel said, "Eye of the tiger, killer instinct, aphorisms on the unchanging view of any but the lead dog. Lesson noted." He opened the passenger door and pulled himself to his feet, then turned and slammed his door, catching and unclipping his tie from the collar of his shirt. The tie dangled where the car door held it, its faux knot fallen and half-submerged in a puddle whose surface glinted in the sun with an oily sheen. When he recovered the tie and clipped it on, the knot smelled loudly of days' old deep-fried starch.

David Samuel offered his parents a pestered wave, then clomped around the side of the building and entered through its heavy glass door. The store manager—a middle-aged woman whom David Samuel had always found too frumpy and dower for the casual, spunky energy suggested by Jen, the nickname she insisted on—was placing fresh tills in the cash registers. "Hey," she said upon seeing him, "look what the cat dragged in." There was an uncommon lightness in her voice that suggested to David Samuel that she may be as relieved to see him go as he was to be going.

"Jennifer," he said to her. "I see you've managed without me."

Jen snorted and slid a cash register drawer closed, its chime like the rim shot that follows a bad joke. She raised her eyes then wrinkled her nose and said, "What's that stain on your shirt?"

David Samuel appraised himself to see that, beneath his chin, his damp tie knot had bled into the fabric of his shirt and made a gray oil stain the size of a tennis ball below his collar. "Mm," he hummed distractedly, wiping at the spot, then rubbing his thumb across slick fingers. "I had a misfortune behind the building a moment ago," he explained, snatching a succession of napkins from the condiment island then vainly polishing his shirt with them, managing only to spread and lift the pungency of the frying oil. "Maybe it's best I don't do customer-facing work today," he said. "It's my suspicion this won't come out without a washing. Mother likely has a miracle elixir that can save the shirt," he added as if to allay his manager's fear for the garment's future.

Jen allowed a register till to drop onto the counter with a solid, singing smack that worked as a kind of throat clearing to focus his attention. "That's not how this works, David Samuel," she said. With a top note of frustration in her voice, she now sounded like herself again. "It's a three-week training program, and you can't just hide from the customers. It begins with floor management. There's a program. A process to follow."

"Two weeks," David Samuel corrected, coming to join her on the employee side of the counter, the oily napkins balled in his fist. "I did the first week at my new store last week. Dad wanted to expedite my training." Jen's put-upon, holier-than-thou attitude often goaded David Samuel into these lies.

"That isn't true," Jen asserted. "Your father didn't tell me that. He said to do the full training."

"Well then, perhaps my father," David Samuel said calmly, "is compromised with senility."

"Oh, he is not. I saw him yesterday."

"Believe what you will," David Samuel said then yawned as if above arguing with her. "Call and ask him if you want to break his heart. Or we could get down to training. It's all the same to me."

Jen's eyes called bullshit. But something—be it professional etiquette, fear of redressing her employer's only son, or a simple weariness with him—restrained her from doing more than stare at him through her glasses with their thick metal frames and large lenses of a multi-sided, trapezoidal shape whose name he was unsure of, but which affected in him thoughts of an old-world orphanage donation more so than the free choice of a modern consumer. He'd come close to her now, and she caught her first whiff of him. "Shoo," she said, wiping a hand in front of her nose, "your clothes stink."

David Samuel lowered his face to his chest. "It isn't the most pleasant of odors," he allowed.

"Go clock in and clean yourself up. I don't have time for this foolishness, David Samuel."

"Perhaps a change in your tone would be helpful," he said, walking in the direction of the time clock. "I'm your equal in this organization now, Jennifer. You can't strong-arm me anymore."

"You're three weeks from being my equal."

"Two weeks," he reminded her, then turned to see her dramatic inhalation, one that suggested preparation for an explosive response.

But the anticipated explosion was a dud: "Fine,

whatever," was all she said. "Just do what you can to clean yourself up."

There was nothing David Samuel could do, however. His attempt to wash out the spot at the bathroom sink only resulted in a spreading of the odor and a weakening of the stained fabric, leaving it pilled and tufted and making it necessary for him to spend his day with one large hand covering the spot as if he were pledging allegiance to every employee and customer with whom he interacted.

At shift change, Jen finally allowed him to leave the restaurant floor. She led him through a narrow hall, past the dual drive thru windows, to the store office. They carried two first shift register tills apiece, Jen's neatly stacked in two hands, David Samuel with one laid on each of his forearms, his fingers gripping various bill compartments, in a configuration that repeatedly caused the edges of the tills to bang against the tiled walls, spilling dimes and pennies out of their troughs and onto the floor.

Once seated in the office, David Samuel became aware of an ejected nickel that had come to rest on the protuberance of his stomach. He sucked in and then forcefully out to project it onto the office's countertop. Jen watched the nickel humorlessly, as if its spinning were the very mechanism that perpetuated her hatred of him. She waited for the coin to slow and settle, heads up, on the counter before casting a sidelong gaze at him. "We'll get into this more next week, but we count the tills and put them in these bags," she said in a monotone, holding up a small zippered pouch. "These forms are for writing down the totals."

"Of course, they are," David Samuel said, "I know that." He'd become distracted by the knot of his tie, which had now dried with an encasement of flaky, translucent crust like the glaze of a day-old doughnut. He pressed a light fingertip to it and a flake floated downward, twisting like confetti and landing on the back of Jen's hand.

"You've been trained to prepare bank deposits?"

"Yes, I told you. Last week."

"That can't be, David Samuel," Jen said, manually creasing her forehead with a pinch of her thumb and fingers. "It's a three-week program and it's taught in a specific order." Here, she retrieved a three-ring binder and opened it to him so that he could study the grid of tasks and check boxes that comprised the three-week training, as if such visual evidence would prompt him out of his lie. "Even if you did do a week in Columbia, which I'm sure you didn't, you wouldn't have gotten to this. Right here, see?" She indicated with the ball point of her pen.

David Samuel made a show of looking at the form. "At a cursory glance," he finally said, his eyes still on the form, "I don't see a thing here that I haven't already been trained on."

"Last week, you mean?" Jen said. "In Columbia."

"I mean last week in Columbia," he said, raising his eyes to her with a terse nod.

"You got through everything on here? You're trained on all of this?"

"Well, I mean, at first blush. You know, you really are a very suspicious person, Jennifer."

Jen slapped a flattened palm on the countertop, causing various troughs of coins to tinkle. "It's Jen!" she said. She brought her face close to David Samuel's, the pen in her fist positioned such that its point could stab a hole in his jugular vein with a mere upward jerk of her arm. "You know—I shouldn't even be here. I have a degree," she hissed. "I have a BA in Theatre Arts. From the Harvard of the onlines. Jerry Mathers, himself, called it that at our tele-graduation." The pen rose toward his throat, but at the sight of David Samuel's widened eyes, Jen seemed to regain a measure of self-control. Her torso pulled back. With deep inhalation, she settled against the back of her chair, eyes addressing the ceiling. "Don't do this Jen," she said to herself between calming breaths and slow, meticulous rolls of her head, "it isn't worth it. It's only temporary. All life's trials are only temporary. Remember what Jesus would do. What would Jesus do, Jen? He wouldn't stab the little nut; he'd be cool. Jesus would be cool." She inhaled deeply through her nose and released the breath with a melodic whimper of a sort that might be inspired by particularly appealing food or sex. "Back on the horse, you'll get back on the horse one of these days. And, if not, you still have a decent apartment and a son who loves you, probably. It's all good, Jen. It's all only ever good. You are not the architect of your life's disaster. But you can be the renovator of its façade. You are a dynamite lady, Jen Beaver. A dragon-blooded miracle." Then she stopped speaking, eyes closed, head dropped limply over her chest.

"Wow," David Samuel said.

"I'll tell you what let's do," she said, snapping to attention, "you mark it all down, you just mark down the training you say you've had. And I'll sign off on it."

"You'll…sign off?" David Samuel repeated skeptically.

"On every single thing you say you know. You're my boss's son, right? Who am I to question you? You're the prince of this place. So, go on. Fill it out, Your Highness, and I'll sign it." She curtsied as best she could while seated.

David Samuel hesitated, weighing Jen's offer.

"Go on, My Lord," she encouraged with a deferential roll of her fingers.

He pulled the binder toward him and began to tick its boxes, feeling obliged to mark them all, given the boldness of his claims.

"Mm," Jen intoned to the occasional tick of his pen, imbuing certain of the boxes with implied significance. "You really did learn a lot," she said. "In Columbia. In a week."

"Well," David Samuel said conciliatorily, "They're rather efficient in Columbia. It's Dad's flagship store."

"Isn't it ever?" she agreed. "Oh, coupons?" she said, indicating a mark he'd made on the form. "You learned that too, huh?"

"Of course, I did," David Samuel said. "In—"

"Columbia," Jen said. "Last week."

"Right." When he ran out of boxes, David Samuel clicked his pen shut. Jen pulled the binder toward her, and began to sign enthusiastic initials beside each of his pen marks.

"Well," she finally said. "It looks like you're all clear. You've done it." She ripped out the training form and presented it, unceremoniously, to him. "Time's up," she said, "and you pass. Dun-da-da-dun," she mock-trumpeted. "You're an inspiration to us all."

"Thank you," David Samuel said. And, when the clock struck five, David Samuel Ochs became the only trainee in Fry Buddy's storied history to complete its three-week management program with two weeks and four days to spare. Nevertheless, he supposed he'd continue getting up each day and dressing in his white shirt, then spend a clandestine few weeks collecting his training pay while lounging at Lake Murray or visiting shops downtown before handing over his completed training form to his father and announcing himself as fit to serve.

*   *   *

Across town, at the very moment David Samuel was muttering to Jen a terse and final goodbye, South Carolina State Legislator, Senator Ernie Holcomb, arrived at a Swansea motor lodge. He'd not been feeling well that day, and when the occupant of the room opened the door to him, he informed her of this. Her name wasn't Dawn, but she'd allowed him to address her as such for one and a half senatorial terms. "Dawn," the senator said, "I'm not feeling well today." She suggested he lay on the bed, and he did. She loosened his tie and called him, "baby." She rubbed away the sweat from his forehead and cooed like a mother. The senator said, "Probably not tonight."

Not-Dawn said, "We can just lay here." So, they did.

In time, though, he was overcome by her silk garment with its tiny straps and everything.

She said she could do a thing that wouldn't be strenuous for him.

He said for her to go on.

Not-Dawn did as she was told. On and on.

The senator smiled and sweated.

At the time his smile grew biggest, the senator's heart abruptly stopped, and he simultaneously came and went.

No longer technically in his company, abruptly technically alone, Dawn became Brenda. From Sioux Falls. With parents and a brother and the rest. She checked the senator's pulse for confirmation.

Brenda fought to extract the wallet from the former senator's pocket and removed her fee plus payment for the evening's emotional damages. And for his near two-term commitment to her, Brenda repaid him with an anonymous courtesy call to one of his aides: Motel 6. Room 17A.

Chapter 14

Two weeks later, Phil led his son into his home office and presented him with a name badge whose laminate tape read: *David Samuel Ochs, Store Manager.* There was a tremble in his hand in that exchange, a low-grade electrical crackle.

As this day had drawn closer, a stirring had begun in Phil's gut, its intensity having increased with the shortening of time, so that on the day's arrival he found himself quietly burping gas from the gale of acids churning in his stomach. He tried to explain away this feeling as the effects of excitement—his body acclimating to the altered gravity of his new world, one of respect and awards and a son he could count on—rather than as the distress of self-doubt. Nevertheless, he'd felt a funereal aspect in closing the Columbia store the previous evening. He'd hung around for hours after his employees had gone, taking a memory tour of his flagship restaurant as it currently stood, as if the next time he saw it would be through the barricade of police tape or via his insurance adjuster's photographic evidence of what remained after the explosion.

David Samuel accepted the name badge with no fanfare, with no indication that he was similarly moved. He insisted on taking the Greyhound to Columbia, a longtime preference of the boy which Phil had once presumed to be a desire to sit shoulder to shoulder with the community's other weirdos, but that now he tried to see as a kind of self-reliant bootstrap pulling.

Accepting that the leaping in his gut would prevent him from accomplishing meaningful work that morning, Phil opted instead to drive to Gadsden for a visit with Jerry Tatum, his closest friend and the supplier of his restaurant parts. He was sitting in the J.T.P. parking lot when the crew arrived to unlock the doors at seven o'clock.

Jerry was saying something to Phil now, something that—with his out-of-state southern accent and interdental lisp—Phil didn't make out. Whether a lifelong speech impediment or the consequence of Jerry having lost two of his four front teeth, Phil respected his parts supplier for never shying away from the difficult words. And, should verbalization prove too difficult, Jerry was always quick to get his point across with a stiff middle finger.

"How's that, Jer?" Phil said, narrowing his eyes to concentrate on what followed.

"I thay he'th a goddam bathtard!" Jerry squawked. The topic of conversation was Jerry's rival, the Canadian, Jim Trebek. Phil had just gotten through relaying Trebek's recent visit to Columbia, his pilfering of Tony, and Phil's resultant promotion of his son. "I told you, didn't I? I told you that Canuck got hith eye on Tony, the tall, ignorant thumbitch. I told you, 'you best watch yourthelf, elth you going to be out one more manager to that clown.'"

Phil nodded. "Truer words."

They were standing in a packing room framed by a half dozen tall metal shelves that were stocked with toilet seats and salad spinners and ten-foot-long sheets of polypropylene that would be cut to custom sizes and sold as cutting boards, and by unfolded bundles of banded shipping containers, and stacks of loose cardboard. On one side of the packing area, a thin drywall partition separated the backroom from customer service specialists who sat at cubicles and took phone orders with telephone headsets and occasionally served the stray restauranteur who arrived in person to procure emergency solenoid valves or three-sided gaskets. It was for such sales roles that Phil's managers had been headhunted.

He stood with his back to a suite of bay doors. Jerry leaned on the shipping table, facing him. A bustling shipping crew worked around the men, depositing orders on the table in plastic baskets, then packing and processing those orders for shipment.

Phil and Jerry had fallen into a silent commiseration on the hardships of the job creator, when a voice from Phil's right said, "You all's talking about Jim Trebek?" Together, he and Jerry turned their attention to the speaker, then stared with profound judgement at having been disturbed in such a moment by the whim of a wage-earner, a sucker of the tit. He was wiry and tall with deep creases in his cheeks. Over forty, but a recent addition to the crew. Likely a drunk, Phil intuited. "That's who you was talking about wasn't it?" he asked again.

Jerry's expression was that of a parent whose child has overstepped their bounds in front of his preacher or an old high school rival. The others on the crew worked silently, deaf and blind and wiser than the new man. Undeterred, he continued, "Did you hear about his sister? Or, whatever she is: sister-*in-law*. She's that gal that run for Senate a few years back."

"Yeah?" Jerry said impatiently.

"Well, they say she's going to win it this time around. This special-election-deal. On account of that old boy 'dying in the arms of his wife.' Which, the fact that they say it like that—don't that sound like a load of bull-crap?" He had stopped working and now rested a hand on his hip. He placed an unlit cigarette between his lips and left it to dangle.

"What election?" Phil said.

"This one coming up, the special one. That's the rules in South Carolina if a seat comes empty. 97.1 was saying there's more than a year left in the term, so they can't just appoint someone. They got to let people vote. And the thing of it is she damn-near beat him last time, which means they're putting her as the favorite this time. Also, you got to remember that the gal would be running as a Democrat."

The word landed in Phil's stomach with the same hollow weight as in a patient's whose doctor has just somberly uttered, "Cancer."

The thin man palmed a lighter from his shirt pocket and picked up a stack of three labeled boxes. He passed Phil and hit a button on the wall that caused a bay door to rise, slow and loud. Sunlight poured over them as the door rose and curled above their heads. The cigarette waggled up and down between his lips when he spoke. "Represented by a Democrat. Can you believe that crap?"

"Eh," Phil said, looking straight at Jerry to reclaim the privacy of their conversation, "somebody will run. Somebody will beat her."

"Ain't no Republican even declared. Not as of this morning, anyhow," the thin man called from behind him. He was pushing the labeled boxes onto a detached UPS trailer.

"Jethuth Critht," Jerry muttered. "The goddamn Democrat'th. Jethuth Critht"

"Say," the thin man bellowed from the trailer to Jerry, with a grin that Phil read as decidedly shit-eating, "you're a Republican, ain't you, boss? You ought to run. You're a respected business man. I might even do it myself if I had a pot to piss in. And if it wasn't for my erroneous sex offender status."

"Trebek's sister-in-law," Phil said. Just as the situation's gravity was beginning to dawn on him, the phone buzzed in his tracksuit pocket. Its screen displayed the number of the Columbia Fry Buddy. His hand trembled. "Yeah?" he said, bringing the phone to his ear.

"Yeah," a female voice said, "who's this?"

"The owner of this store," Phil barked. "Who's this?"

"This Phil?"

"Who is this?" Phil demanded.

"Yeah," the voice confirmed, "that's you. Phil, this is Wanda Perkins. Out at the Columbia restaurant? I called the emergency number in the office."

"What emergency?" Phil said, nearly breathless. A wave of acid lapped at the back of his throat. "What's the emergency?"

"I don't know, man," Wanda said with a sarcastic lilt in her voice. "But you might want to come down here. Your son done left us."

"What do you mean left?"

"I seen him go out the front door, and I ain't seen him since."

"Creeping Jesus," Phil muttered. "Yeah, I'll be there." He ended the call with the swipe of his finger. The phone blackened, and the time floated onto the screen. It was eight-fifteen am. The boy had only lasted fifteen minutes.

Chapter 15

"I don't want you to think of me as your leader," David Samuel was saying to a collected group of AM restaurant staff. It was ten minutes before the Columbia Fry Buddy opened for breakfast. "I *am* your leader, and I want you to know that. But, I want you to push it to the back of your mind so when you look at me, the first thing you see isn't a boss. Instead, I want you to think of me as a mentor. And when you see me, I want you to realize that someday this could be you. Hold yourself to that standard, and if you feel yourself wavering, just lift your head and let your eyes find me to remind you that your life is full of possibilities. Are there any questions?"

An older woman raised her hand.

"Yes?" David Samuel smiled.

"But, what if my daddy don't own a restaurant?" There were snickers from the group.

David Samuel glared at her nametag. "Well, Wanda," he said, "then, he probably didn't listen when his superiors tried to inspire him. Maybe you might learn from his mistake, yes? Are there any *real* questions?" This time, he made a show of considering every face except for Wanda's. The employees fidgeted or stared down at their phones or rolled their eyes. "Okay, then," David Samuel said with muted excitement. "Let's make this a great day."

The group broke up, sluggishly moving to various work stations, spreading in all directions like a slow-motion replay of shrapnel spray from a detonated munition. David Samuel, the fuel for that explosion, stood in his dress shirt and tie, mentally recording the scene of his first crew positioning themselves for the Monday breakfast rush.

He checked his watch, then hurried through the front of the house, positioning himself in the store's glass vestibule. It was two minutes to eight. Consulting the watch again, he rested a finger and thumb on the outer door's lock, then waited. On the other side of the door, a dirty-looking man stood waiting to come in. David Samuel glanced at him, and the man waved. A look of mild disgust passed over David Samuel's face. He averted his eyes.

"Is it time?" the man called. David Samuel twisted his arm in response, so the man could see the watch face. The man nodded and adopted a casual, resting posture, supporting himself with a flat, callused palm on the door glass.

David Samuel tapped the glass with his fingernails, then scolded the man with a tisk-tisk waggle of his finger.

"Sorry, buddy," the man said, removing his hand then buffing the glass with the worn elbow of his shirt sleeve. He briefly returned to his posture of repose, this time propping himself with a hand on the brick of the building, but then appeared to rethink whether this would be similarly offensive and erected himself with crossed arms.

After a moment, David Samuel heard the handle of the door being tried. He scowled at the man, who shrugged innocently then scratched his nose with the back of his hand.

The man stared up at the sky and then began a series of stretches, his arms bent behind his head, pulling an elbow to the point of resistance with the opposing hand, then switching sides and repeating. The action looked, to David Samuel, like that of an athlete preparing for competition, and it flashed in his mind that this dirty creature might well back up and attempt to sprint through the glass panel and into the restaurant. He looked discretely around him as if for a panic button. But, when the man again locked eyes with David Samuel, he lowered his arms and stood smiling, then puckered his lips and blew David Samuel a kiss.

The watch's alarm announced eight o'clock. David Samuel's fingers turned the lock reflexively. The man burst into the restaurant. The force of his entry and the sudden suck of air from the vestibule through the open door left David Samuel momentarily disoriented. He wedged himself against the window to allow the man to pass. "Thanks, Beautiful," the man said, helping himself to a handful of David Samuel's ample belly and giving it a gentle, pulsing squeeze. David Samuel recoiled, tripping one shoe on the other, then lost his balance and landed hard in a seated position on the tile. The man disappeared into the restaurant.

David Samuel clambered to his feet and pulled open the inner vestibule door, crying loudly into the dining room, "Stop! Do not serve that man."

The man turned to face him, along with a male employee behind the counter and a succession of visible faces from the kitchen. Wanda peeked her head in from the drive thru window. "What in heaven's name," she muttered into her headset microphone.

"You, sir!" David Samuel shouted to the man, his finger outstretched and accusing, "I want you out of my restaurant." To the male employee at the register, he clarified, "this man is a fiend."

"It's just Al," the employee said, as if the identity of the man should not only be obvious, but that the character associated with that identity were a definitive rebuke of David Samuel's accusation. Al smiled at the invocation of his name.

"I don't care who he is. He physically assaulted me in the vestibule. Throw him out."

"I don't really do that," the employee said.

From a measured distance, David Samuel said, "Did you ever hear of PTSD, Al? I'm a dangerous person to mess with. An uncaged animal. I'm the very recent victim of a mugging, and there's no telling what I might do when provoked. I suggest you leave before we find out."

"Wait," Al said, "who would mug an uncaged animal?"

"Call the authorities," David Samuel called to his crew.

"Hey holdup, Beautiful," Al began.

"He just wants a cup of coffee," the employee said.

"A cup of coffee," Al confirmed.

"He's a regular."

"Here every morning."

"This is the boss's son," the employee explained to Al.

"Oh, shit," Al said with a smile. "I'd have never thought it, a big boy like you. My condolences. I would never have got friendly with you like that if I knew you had them kind of genealogical burdens." He stuck out his hand. "Friends?"

David Samuel leered at him.

"Oh," Al said then, as if with understanding. He dropped the hand. "I think I get it: do you have feelings against the homeless, Beautiful?"

"What?" David Samuel said. "No."

"I think Beautiful, here, has feelings against the homeless."

David Samuel intoned a sound of incredulity. "That's baseless misdirection. I love the homeless."

"Do you? And what is it you love about us?"

"Well, not you, obviously, but…"

"The other homeless?"

"Yes."

"Which ones exactly?"

"Well, I mean," David Samuel began. "There's a man I know, a two-headed root doctor. He's a dear friend of mine."

"Root doctor?"

"Yes, a practitioner of the spiritual arts."

"And where does this spiritual practitioner live?"

David Samuel paused to examine the trick of this question. "I mean—he's homeless," he finally said. "He doesn't live anywhere."

Al stared with skeptical eyes.

"Under a tree, I guess. At Lake Murray. A fine, um, fine old dogwood."

"And you love this doctor?"

"Yes, I said I did, didn't I? I saw him not, well, I don't know, it's been a few weeks back, but I gave him money. I gave him money!"

A broad smile bloomed on Al's face. His eyes looked wet and friendly. "You know what, Beautiful? I think I was wrong about you. You might be a bona fide guy, the Lord's own right hand. Do you want to call this off now and let me have my coffee?"

David Samuel appraised his assembled staff and the smattering of customers who'd come into the restaurant, all of them staring in anticipation of his response. "Fine," he said with a put-upon air, like a monarch sparing a head. "Have your coffee."

"That's just beautiful," Al said, then, "Nick, one black coffee." He reached into his pocket and withdrew a fistful of pennies and nickels and slapped them with a polytonic jangle onto the counter.

David Samuel smiled at the other customers then headed for the opening at the end of the service counter.

"Oh," Al called, "Beautiful?"

David Samuel stopped and turned.

Al opened his arms. "We need to hug this out, brother." He started forward quickly, his arms waggling with faux menace, laughing and goading as he came.

David Samuel shrieked and ran, Al close behind him, doing a full lap around the lobby, nearly kneeing a toddler in the face for which he turned back to apologize, but became nearly caught, so left the little girl behind, finally conceiving a way out through the glass vestibule door, taking the exit and escaping to the ever-more distant sounds of Al calling, "Beautiful? Beautiful?" from the restaurant sidewalk.

Chapter 16

By the time Phil arrived in Columbia, it was past nine o'clock. The breakfast rush was underway, and the lobby was an obstacle course of bodies, queued at registers or informally hovering around the condiment island and trash receptacles, flowing to and from the bathroom hallway, entering or exiting through the glass vestibule doors. Phil struggled to see beyond the counter as he navigated through the crowd, looking past the careless heads and shoulders for visual confirmation of the chaos his son's abandonment had wrought. A man moved unexpectedly in the direction Phil had chosen to pass by him and he was forced to abruptly recalibrate his path, croaking irritably. He touched backs and arms in a declaration of his intent. He crossed behind the counter, and his pace quickened as if stepping out of deeply muddy terrain onto solid, dry ground. He rounded a corner and entered the kitchen. And there stood David Samuel, a hamburger bun to his nose, inhaling deeply.

David Samuel saw his father and said, "Oh, hello, boss man. Does this smell off to you?" He took a step toward Phil, holding the bun in an outstretched arm. "Yeasty, that's the only way I can think to describe what I'm getting. But disarmingly so. What say you?" Two male employees stood behind him as if awaiting an imminent pass/fail decision on the product.

"What the hell's going on here?" Phil demanded.

David Samuel considered the bun in his hand as if to confirm that it was what he thought it was. "QC is what I would call it," he said, a question in his voice. "Interrogating the fidelity of your foodstuff." Like a ventriloquist, he raised and lowered the top bun in unison with the syllables of 'foodstuff.'

"I mean, what are you doing here?"

"Managing my restaurant," David Samuel said with a look of confusion. Then he threw his head back with understanding. "Oh, I see. Someone called you about the incident here this morning. This ship has a rat." He turned in the direction of the drive thru window. Phil turned too and saw Wanda back her head out of sight. "Well, you heard correctly: we had an incident here this morning with a 'regular customer,' a characterization that I'm invoking in the past tense. He attacked me, I insisted he leave, and then he began to chase me, his eyes full of madness and hepatitis-b. But, it was my great fortune to spot a squad car at the laundromat next door whose driver was more than receptive to my recounting of the thing. Long story short, I find it doubtful that filthy creature will be joining us for a cup of coffee tomorrow. Unless he had enough nickels left in his pockets to cover his bail."

Moved by the churning in his gut, Phil staggered slightly. He felt sweat on his brow. He peered at David Samuel, wanting very much for him to let go of the bun he was holding. It seemed perverted, the way his fingers dimpled and sank into the soft white bread, the roundness of the bun in his outstretched arm, dwarfed by the roundness of his body behind it. A classroom model of a planet and its moon.

"Far be it from me to overstep," David Samuel said to Phil, dropping the arm with the bun, its new proximity to his groin doing nothing to ease his father, "but you look like death."

An employee of dark complexion—one of the two who'd been awaiting David Samuel's appraisal of the hamburger bun—said, "él se ve como la muerte," with a wipe of his hand down his own face, his eyes stern and solemn.

This demonstration of David Samuel's concern had the odd and immediate effect of steadying Phil, as if his son had breathed against what was roiling inside him and provided him with stability. Phil stared at David Samuel for a long moment. David Samuel who'd proven the maturity to handle a problem customer by involving the authorities. David Samuel, whom he'd caught leading his team in a quality inspection of the store's product. David Samuel, who'd shown concern for his father's wellbeing. The feeling that resulted from this new clarity—while not quite as charitable as gratitude or self-recriminating as guilt—was nevertheless powerful: it was a feeling of pride. Fatherly pride, sure, but also a pride in himself, the pride of seeing that the course he'd taken to rehabilitate the boy had been correct. What he'd set out to do, he appeared to have done. Moved by this feeling in a way that was meaningful and insistent, Phil smiled up at his son. It was an awkward and unpracticed gesture that led David Samuel's face to screw.

"You're losing it, Dad," David Samuel said.

Phil voiced a single pulse of genuine laughter and turned away without another word. His sense was that all was fine now, but that he also needed to sit. He moved toward the office with visions of a new future opening up to him. A future of respect. A future where he could laugh off detractors and lame Phil Ochs jokes with the security of knowing he was accomplished enough not to care one bit. But, before he could even consider a plan to show off his accomplishment to the Chamber of Commerce, his phone chimed. Phil pulled the device from his muffler pocket and squinted at it. A new text from Jerry:

you heard?? The chamber done released the winner. them gd dog nuts. srry bud!!!

This time, the wave of sickness was in his head, a crash against Phil's temple that devoured all those flowery images of his new future and washed them to sea when it receded. Phil propped his hand against the drive thru partition wall, hope like topsoil eroding from his mind, exposing that familiar bedrock craving for respect.

PART TWO

Chapter 17

The Parent Area was long and narrow and populated with mothers who sat elbow to elbow in mismatched chairs. The mothers discussed leotards and gorilla gyms. They judged one another with passive smiles and overdone compliments. The chairs were clustered around a window in a partition wall that separated them from a studio space. In the window, a snowdrift of indistinguishable white children kipped and piked and saltoed into view.

Eddie Ellis sat with his chair turned away from them, his face in a book whose title might as well have been, *Fuck Off, Ladies.* The room recalled, for him, the makeshift set-up of a church basement on the night of a substance abuse meeting, but without the good stories.

"That's awesome," two mothers said in near-unison to a third's revelation of a new doggy daycare that had broken ground in her neighborhood. Their voices stepped in front of the passage Eddie was reading and deflected its meaning from his brain.

Some Saturdays, he couldn't concentrate at all, this ninety-minute wait pushing his mind to fantasize about that small swatch of studio space he could see through the interior window glass. Its landscape of mats and pads and projecting balance beams becoming an alien forest on some cushiony planet inhabited by regimented, somersaulting children. When viewed in long duration from the Parent Area, the studio could seem cozy, like a womb specially planned to gestate society's affluent physically fit, and Eddie sometimes longed to break into it, away from the mothers, to curl, fetal, on its foam floor, its nurturing climate his last chance at a fresh start.

A girl with a raised finger marched out of the studio now, yelling directionless to her unseen mother, something urgently concerning a boogie. Eddie slapped his book shut, tried politely to look away from the mother as she wiped at the girl's face and hand with what appeared to be a Target receipt. He prayed silently that this girl might be a sign: the avant-garde gymnast who presaged the return of all those children still leaping and tumbling on the studio mats.

Some minutes later, the outpouring finally came, and so began the chaotic rise and scatter of mothers pairing with children. The tiny gymnasts were let out by an older teenaged coach in high-cut shorts that revealed a tract of muscular thigh. Eddie wished for the sight of this tanned, womanly leg to fill him with regret, a lust that was inappropriate by twenty years, but his eyes passed over her and he had nothing to be ashamed of. Instead, he began his search for the dirty-blonde bunned head of the child who belonged to him.

He found her sitting on the floor, changing her shoes at a network of cubbies. "How's it going, Worm?" he said.

"Good."

"How was gymnastics?"

"Good. I'm ready to go now." Penny rose with youthful ease and started ahead of him. "What's that book?" she asked skeptically, as if literacy were a skill she had never presumed in her father and that she was not immediately prepared to believe from so passive a sign of it.

"I know him," Eddie said importantly, pointing to the man on the cover photo. "He was my mentor back when I worked in politics." He held the door for her.

"You work in logistics."

"Right, because I failed at politics. This was before, when I hadn't failed yet. Ask your mother about it. She'll tell you."

"It looks old."

"It *is* old. They don't even make it anymore. He was way more successful than I ever was and, still, everyone has forgotten about him by now. What do you think about that?"

Penny shrugged. She walked ahead of him through the parking lot. Eddie reflected that, in this arrangement, she appeared somewhat like a captured prisoner from an opposing army. When they arrived at the car, he attempted to lighten the mood by asking, "Hey, what was the deal with that one kid?"

"Which one?" she said, pulling open the backdoor of the sedan.

"You know, the one with the...face-thing. You have to know the one I mean." With his hand, Eddie pantomimed a vague snout-shape over his own mouth and nose.

"Who?" she demanded with a screwed expression. "What's wrong with her face?"

"I couldn't begin to describe it," Eddie said. "I've never seen anything like it before. Has anyone said what happened to her? Or was she born that way? There has to be a rumor. You can trust me, you know," he nudged. "The mothers will never get it out of me." Then, he leaned into the car as if to receive a secret.

Penny's face darkened, and in her mother's scolding tone, she said, "Don't be strange. Who are you talking about?"

Eddie dropped his head. He stared at the blunt edge of a coin that had become lodged between the backseat and the car door. "I don't know," he said, defeated. "I didn't see a kid with a weird face. I just assumed, in all those kids, there probably was one." He opened the driver's door and got behind the wheel. "Are you hungry?"

"Are you cooking?"

"God, no."

"Then, yeah, I guess so." She limited her gaze to her knees and the view through her window.

Eddie backed out slowly, paying careful attention to the children and parents who trickled into the parking lot then bloomed in all directions. As he did, the unwilled image came to him of what it might feel like to roll his rear tires over pedestrians in his blind spot. He heard the perfectly dramatic and unaffected ways Penny might present such an incident to her mother: *"You'll never guess what dad did at gymnastics yesterday..."* or, *"Guess who ran over Sally K. and put her in a body cast for the rest of third grade..."*

"You know," he said, as he turned the car onto the street, "I was still working with him when you were born." He raised the book into her sightline from the passenger seat, keeping his own eyes on the road. "Linwood Barth, that's his name," he said, waggling the book. "Did I ever tell you about him?" Penny said nothing. "He was a campaign manager; I was his advisor. Just local races: Adjutant General in 2007, we won that one; and Commissioner of Agriculture in 2009, another win; and Inspector General—that one we lost three times in a row, although the last time was contested and recounted. Guess how many we lost by."

"One?"

"Twenty-six hundred and fifty-three."

With a tiny, long-fingered hand, Penny enacted an explosion at her temple to indicate her young mind being blown.

"I was positioned to rival this guy to run state races until those losses and then, I guess, the well just kind of dried up. I got close, though. I really got close." He caught his eyes in the rearview mirror and looked away. "Hey," he called, "when your mother brings you to gymnastics, does she wait like I do? Is she friendly with those other mothers?"

"I don't know. I'm mostly taking gymnastics, so I'm not sure what Mom does. Or you, really. Some weeks, Gail brings me, but I don't know what she does either."

Gail was the child abuse attorney for whom Cindy had left him. It was she who had devised the argument against Eddie's drinking that had led to this reduced, bi-monthly, weekend custody of Penny—drinking which had only resurfaced as a problem when Eddie began to fear that his wife was having an affair with a child abuse attorney. The three of them—Gail, his daughter, and his ex—now all lived together in Gail's big Dorchester house, an arrangement that he privately referred to as a 'clit-ocrasy,' though only when the vodka icepicks had settled in his gut and found themselves capable of laughter and applause.

It had been eighteen months and now, when Eddie saw Penny, they demonstrated exactly what a thirty-eight-year-old man and an eleven-year-old girl have in common: precisely nothing. He suspected that it was only through daily interaction or the civil agreement of two people who share a bathroom that a man could manage any true connection with a daughter.

They arrived at a strip of fast food restaurants near Eddie's house, a neighborhood that had once belonged to her. From a stolen glimpse in the rearview, he judged that the tragedy of this was lost on her. "What are you feeling? Wendy's or Fry Buddy?"

"Fry Buddy."

"Rally's or McDonald's?"

"Fry Buddy."

"Fish-Head Express or Mutton King? Slop Shack or Sweetbread Hut? Stinky Tofu Garden or Schnasty's?"

Her reflection was stony. Eddie pulled into the Fry Buddy drive-thru.

At their turn, a tired voice on the intercom said: "Welcome to Fry Buddy. Vote Phil Ochs. Would you like to try a value meal today?'

"Excuse me?" Eddie said.

"Our value meals are a sandwich, drink, and fry. Or you can buddy-up to sweet potato fries for an additional forty-nine cents. Vote Phil Ochs."

"No, I mean—who's Phil Ochs?"

The speaker sighed, then said, "He owns our store. He's running for state Senate. Vote Phil Ochs."

"But—does he make you say that every time? To vote for Phil Ochs?"

"Yes. Vote Phil Ochs."

Eddie was silent.

"Dad?" Penny prompted.

"Wait, sorry, Worm," he said, waving her off with a distracted flitter of his fingers, then to the intercom, he said, "Is he related to that folksinger-guy? The 'love me, love me, I'm a liberal' guy?" His brain tried for more of the lyrics but found none.

The voice responded in the stilted cadence of one reading prepared remarks: "Phil Ochs is a job creator. Phil Ochs is a committed conservative. Any association you make between him and his liberal, suicide-case namesake in any form—be it accusation, question, or thought—is baseless slander and will not be permitted on these premises. Go ahead with your order, please. Vote Phil Ochs."

Eddie turned back to look at Penny with a 'can you believe this?' widening of his eyes. Her expression suggested hunger and annoyance and that nothing about this was any more ridiculous than what the grown-up world imposed upon her daily. He turned back to his open window. "Okay," he said, "uh—give us—two number ones with Cokes."

"I want sweet potato fries," Penny said.

He turned again to look at her. "Have you had sweet potato fries? They're bitter and gross."

Hunger and annoyance.

"But we want sweet potato fries," Eddie called. "I mean, buddy them up, or whatever. That's all." He paused, then said, "Hey, is he here now, Phil Ochs?"

"Phil Ochs will not be available to shake your hand or kiss your babies. If you want to donate to his campaign, please do so at the first window. Your total is eight twenty-seven. Please pull forward."

Then, in perfect unison with the voice, Eddie chanted, "Vote Phil Ochs."

Chapter 18

Later that evening, Phil sat in the breakroom of his Irmo store, snickering at the newspaper obituaries. He was alone at a table, his feet propped on a pulled-out chair. Sam Stopper was dead. Big Sam Stopper, bully of the class of '75. Sam Stopper, large in body and cruelty, small on brains, who, along with his toadies, used to warble the folksinger's, "Draft Dodger Blues" while lifting Phil's legs and flushing his head in the boys' room toilets. Old Sam Stopper, survived by a wife and three grown children, had boarded that highway to heaven the previous afternoon, ending his sixty-three-year theft of the world's precious oxygen, may he rot in peace. Probably alcoholic too, though the obit didn't say as much.

Phil felt a swelling in his chest, the rare, carnival excitement of having survived another one. He recalled Sam's giant frame, wondered if people were like dogs, their size inversely proportional to their lifespans, and fancied that he might live past one hundred if so.

The newspaper had been lifted from the restaurant dining room, one of three that was delivered daily and draped over wooden dowels for the benefit of the AM discount-coffee crowd. Or possibly only for the benefit of Phil, who took pride in doing things as they'd always been done, regardless of the Jitterbug phones that now predictably occupied space in his senior-citizen-patron's pockets, phones whose wireless connections could order-up these newspapers' same stories with a call of their oversized buttons.

He laid out the newspaper on the table, flattening it with his palms. Then he began the work of incrementally tearing out the obituary in a sloppy square, holding it aloft once freed from its source, then folding it into the jacket pocket of his tracksuit. "Good riddance, Stoppers," he muttered as he secreted away the clipping.

Phil turned back to page two: Politics. It had been six days since he'd announced his candidacy for state Senate, and it was only today that this city paper had finally written it up. Beneath the federal and the international, his eyes found the article. This was his fifth time reading it:

Fast Food King Throws His Hat in the Ring

Gilda Cranston, Democratic candidate for the 5th district Senate seat vacated by the death of Ernie Holcomb, finally has a challenger: local restauranteur, Phil Ochs. Ochs is running on the Republican ticket. Reached for comment, Ochs said: "Do not associate me in print with that pinko songwriter, do you understand me, bub?" presumably a reference to the liberal folksinger, Phil Ochs, who hanged himself in 1976. The special election to replace Senator Holcomb will be held on Tues, December 22.

'Restaurateur' affected importance, but Phil found himself frustratingly unsurprised by the article's reference to the folksinger, even after his instructions to avoid it. Goddamned liberal media.

"Phil," called a voice from the breakroom's doorway, "you have a phone call."

"Tell them I'm busy," Phil said, his eyes taking an inventory of his article's size in relation to those that shared its page.

"He said it was about your political thing," the voice clarified. "He said he was with the Republican Party. He spoke real proper."

"Real proper, huh?" Phil said. "Well, tell him I'll be there when I can be there, then see what he says. And, if he doesn't say anything, just lay the phone down on the counter and walk away." Footsteps receded behind him. Phil re-read his article.

Sometime later, in the restaurant office, Phil picked up the abandoned phone receiver and said, "Yeah?"

"Phil Ochs?" the voice asked, sounding startled out of boredom. "Is this Phil Ochs?"

"Yeah?"

"Mr. Ochs, my name is Eddie Ellis. I recently became aware of your campaign for state legislature."

"Yeah?"

"Well, sir, I wanted to introduce myself. I've been involved with South Carolina Republican politics for some time: I devised the winning campaign of the Adjutant General in 2007, Commissioner of Agriculture in 2009. I've worked on behalf of the Inspector General."

"So?"

"Well, what I was wondering, Mr. Ochs, is if you've considered taking on a campaign manager?"

"Campaign manager?" Phil repeated dubiously, as if the caller had asked if he were on the market for a Feng Shui consultant or a Sherpa guide.

"Yes, sir. I mean, with respect of course, using your restaurants for political messaging is quant—real down-to-earth-blue-collar-man-of-the-people-type stuff. But it hardly suggests the efforts of a serious candidate. If you'll allow me that observation."

With his pinky nail, Phil began to work at a poppy seed that had wedged between two of his teeth. "And what's not serious about it?" he asked.

"Well, soliciting contributions from a fast food drive thru window leaves an awful lot of available money on the table, for example, is what I mean. That is, when you're the legitimate Republican candidate running for this office."

"Legitimate, huh?" Phil said, liking the sound of this.

"Of course. You're the only Republican brave enough to have a go at Cranston in this thing. And I think we can win."

"We?"

"Oh, well—yes," the voice laughed, "I got ahead of myself there. It's just that I've been reflecting on it, and I can see your potential so clearly, as such an obvious thing that is, that I can't help but to envision myself as being a part of how you attain that brass ring. If you'll allow me that fancy, I mean."

"What you fancy is none of my business, buster, but that doesn't change that this thing doesn't concern you."

"You're exactly right. It doesn't, of course. Unless, that is, I mean, you want to win."

"Hey," Phil said, "what did you say your name was?"

"Eddie Ellis."

"Well, let me inform you of a short list of things that burn my ass, Eddie Ellis: grown men with little boy names, pushy know-it-alls, and strangers that call me at work to tell me my business. Now, knowing all that, how would you say you're coming across to me as concerns first impressions?"

There was a moment of silence before Eddie said, "Well, I couldn't say. But, let me ask you something: have you filed your SICPP? Do you even know what that is? Because, if you don't, I have news for you, Mr. Ochs: you're not running for anything. Except, maybe, the most foolish fast food restaurant owner in South Carolina. Have you interfaced with anyone from the state party? Would you know how to reach them if you wanted to? What about a PCC? Have you set up a PCC to get a campaign bank account? Or are you violating finance laws? I know how to do all that. And, let me ask you this: do you know the name, Jim Maythorn? Of course, you don't. Nobody does. Who would? He's a pill-popping, jug-eared hillbilly of a redneck hick, but he's been your City Ward Councilmen since 2004. Is that an election I was involved in? Maybe. Maybe not. It doesn't matter. Because I know who he is, while you, when I said his name, were thinking, 'wait, who the heck is this Jim Maythorn he's going on about,' and that's the point here, isn't it? I know Jim Maythorn right down to the condition of his jug ears and so, yeah, I'm a pushy know-it-all. In only the sense that I know it all, at least as far as you'll ever know from your current position of knowing really very little about any of this, if you don't mind my saying so. I can meet with you tomorrow about running your campaign. Don't say no, because we can't afford to have a Democrat win this thing. I have to trust you know that much."

Phil thought for a moment, frowning at a motivational photo he'd printed of the Faux-Gnads boys accepting his award at a Chamber of Commerce dinner. "The most foolish restaurant owner in South Carolina, huh?" he said finally, perturbed at having been called such a thing, but feeling grudging respect for this man for having had the nerve to do so. "Tomorrow at six in Irmo. You get five minutes. And, Mr.—I can see a picture in my head of what a campaign manager ought to look like. Do yourself a favor and resemble that picture."

"I'll see you at six, Senator," Eddie said, and then he won Phil further with his abrupt termination of the call.

Chapter 19

Phil Ochs was nobody. His campaign was a joke, and he had no chance of winning. Eddie knew this, even when he called to verbally prostrate himself before the man. But Eddie also knew that being nobody was a trait they had in common. So he'd made the four impromptu phone calls to local Fry Buddy restaurants until he'd found him, then hit him with his pushy-passive act—a communication style he'd honed in his second-act career in the seedy world of freight brokerage—just to see what reaction it got. He'd have been hung up on if Phil Ochs knew anything at all. But, instead, he'd secured this meeting, a clear sign of the candidate's weakness.

Eddie stood in his kitchen now, feeling like he'd discovered a secret vein of gold or spout of crude oil on land that others had overlooked as barren. His slick dress shirt was unbuttoned to his belt buckle, his tie loosened at the neck and slung back over his shoulder. It was rare for him to wear a suit these days and, standing half-clad in one now, it felt like the very costume of his midlife crisis.

He pulled a ribbon of paper towels from a roll on his countertop, counting out six sheets before tearing them off. He separated the ribbon into equal halves, then folded each half into a thick bundle of three sheets each and inserted them between the skin of each armpit and the fabric of his undershirt.

There was no end game to what he was planning, no real planning at all, really. He was being driven by a simple, opportunistic need, a why without a how: he needed to be better than the freight brokerage; to play, even if temporarily, the role he still felt was his life's calling; to be a star in the eyes of his daughter; to achieve a moment of success to rival that of the woman for whom his wife had left him. How he might manifest that success remained unclear.

He tested the paper towels with a subtle flap of his upper arms. This was not a try at comfort. The obstruction of the bundles was a constant reminder of his pituitary condition, much the way the brush of clothing across the protrusion of a tumor keeps cancer on the minds of its victims. Eddie's condition was not nearly so serious. His body's aptitude for sweating through two or even four layers of clothing with no correlated stress or exertion had been his private, daily struggle since adolescence. For most of that time, it had been an uncomfortable reality that he had characterized simply as 'swamp pits.' Following his divorce, however, he'd entertained a fleeting interest in self-maintenance, in finally sanding off his rough corners, in achieving a spiritual second-virginity. It took a trip to the dermatologist to learn that he suffered from hyperhidrosis, and from that same professional, to learn of his condition's only treatment: monthly injections of Botox into the folds and creases of the underarms. He'd left that appointment wiser, his paper towel tumors seeming not so bad a compromise.

On an average day, in the air-conditioned office of the freight brokerage, his underarm bundles would last four hours before they began to bleed moisture into the fabric of his clothing. Often, due to slippage or his own failure to appropriately freshen them, his shirt would stain with dark half-moons, forcing him to retire to the restroom, enter a stall, and remove his dress shirt. He would sit, pants-up, on the toilet, scrubbing the dampness away with toilet paper, aware that if someone walked in and heard this exercise, the observer might likely assume he was in the stall furiously masturbating.

Eddie buttoned his shirt now and righted his tie, then he stepped into the bathroom to study himself. Phil Ochs had told him to look the part. He wondered if he still did. There was a time when his good cheekbones, strong nose, and dark features had led Eddie to be cited by more than one educated woman at drunken campaign parties as having a face that could inspire intrigue on the national stage, the silent man behind the man. It was a face he liked to think he still had—though, at thirty-eight and with no romantic partner to reaffirm this, he couldn't be sure.

He checked the time on his phone, gave his reflected eyes a killer's stare, then scooped the keyring from his pocket, snatched up his suit coat, and headed out the door.

Fifteen minutes later, he slid into a booth at the Irmo Fry Buddy. As he waited, he clandestinely tugged the folded corners of his underarm bundles. A flowery, deodorant scent arose from his fingers.

"So why do you think I need a campaign manager?" a voice asked from a distance.

Eddie stood and smiled at the small man walking toward him. "Phil?" he said, extending his hand in a practiced manner that kept his upper arms clamped to his body.

"Yeah." Phil appeared to consider the hand before accepting it.

"How did you know it was me?"

"Look around you."

Eddie did so, and he saw that he was the fittest person in the dining room, save perhaps for Phil himself; the only patron wearing a suit; and possibly the only one in closed-toe shoes. He smiled his understanding. "Do you want to sit?" He began, himself, to sit, but then froze and resurrected himself when Phil remained immobile.

"Not necessary," Phil said. "I'm a busy man. I gave you five minutes. So? Why do I need you?"

A bead of sweat escaped the towels and ran coolly down Eddie's side. "Well—because you're running a major campaign. Because you've never run for office before. Because I know tricks you don't know."

"I'm a Republican in a red state. I'm a job creator."

"Phil, please sit," Eddie offered again, this time providing an example by reclaiming his place in the booth.

"Sorry, bub," Phil said, stretching his body as if to take the greatest advantage of towering over Eddie's seated frame. "Not if that's the best you got." He turned to walk away.

"Wait," Eddie called. Phil stopped.

Twenty minutes to the south, there was a freight brokerage. In a township to the north, his daughter had a bedroom in a home where Eddie didn't live. Two blocks from this restaurant, there was a liquor store where they knew him by name.

"Why do you need me?" he said "Because no one knows who you are. You own a burger restaurant. So, what? That doesn't move voters. And I've got news for you about this district—yeah, it's historically red. But, we've got purple bleeding in on all sides. And by every measurement, this election—*your* election, Phil— could be the one where that purple stains this seat blue. All we need for that to happen is the wrong candidate, the candidate who didn't take that threat seriously. You think it's a coincidence that no career Republican is running? They're afraid. They know what I know, and they said 'no, thank you.' Have you seen the data, Phil? Do you even know where to find it?"

Eddie paused here and took stock of how Phil had turned his body away from him, taking apparent comfort in the bustle of his cash wrap: white smiles, bills being broken and changed. He transitioned into his pitch: "I look at you, and do you know what I see? I see a maker. I see the American dream. I see eagles and flags and all that wholesome nonsense. I see a man who, unlike all those, quote, real politicians," here, he raised and dipped his fingers in imitated punctuation, "was willing to have a go at this thing. Who was brave enough to put his reputation on the line to do what he thinks is right for the state of South Carolina. That's what I see, Phil. And I can make voters see that very same man. The you that I see. The Phil Ochs that can inspire people to get up off their couches and turn out to cast their vote for a conservative future. You're a singular, virtuous man. The change candidate. A change back to what we haven't lost yet. A change back to what's the same. To apple pie and Uncle Sam and hard work setting you free."

Phil slid his eyes toward the speaker.

Eddie leaned closer, his voice cooing seductively: "But what I need right now, Phil—what the state of South Carolina needs right now—is for you to sit down and talk to me. Because otherwise—*otherwise, Phil*—this state's babies—*its babies, Phil*—are going to be born under Democratic rule. And I'm no fan of abortion," he said, clutching his chest to invoke authenticity, "but that might be a merciful alternative to being represented by some liberal who's on course to be elected if you and I don't hash this out. If you don't take a seat at this booth and help me save the children. They need you, Phil. *We* need you. So…what do you say?"

As Eddie waited for a response, Phil slowly turned his head, first one way and then another, as if in an appraisal of his fast food dining room, the public courtyard of his empire. He raised his hand to knuckle-away a tear. Eventually, he sat. Both men were silent for a moment, Phil staring at the tabletop, Eddie staring at Phil. "Seventeen," Phil said.

"Excuse me?"

"I own seventeen franchises, not one. Seventeen."

"Remarkable."

"All right, so I'm interested. What can you do for me that I can't do on my own?"

"I can get you on TV. News, ads, the whole thing."

"They'll interview me just because I'm running."

"In an off-year local race? Don't count on it. I can also put you in touch with some of the richest Republican donors in South Carolina. Stances on ballot measures, the whole game." He leaned in and whispered, as if telling a secret, "Did you know that right now, there's a measure being considered that would prohibit eminent domain in private use? Do you have any idea what that even means? I do. And I know what side of that line a Republican should be standing on."

Phil rolled his eyes and blew a short, dismissive raspberry with his lips. "And what do you get in return? What's your price?"

Eddie brushed away the question with a toss of his hand: "Nothing, as far as you know. My fee comes out of campaign contributions, and it's my job to make sure those come in."

"Selling me everything and it costs me nothing, eh?"

"If you like."

Phil stuffed his hands into his tracksuit's muffler pocket. He sat back and puckered his lips to one side, studying Eddie as if he were a riddle whose answer was not immediately clear. Finally, he said, "I'll think about it and let you know."

"I could come up with a slogan," Eddie said, his tone having transitioned to one of dreamy determination. "I have experience there. Maybe even commission a campaign theme song—nobody does that anymore. It might be a sign to the traditional voter that they're in good hands. Real old-guard conservative stuff." Forgetting himself, he chuckled out loud at his next thought before vocalizing it: "We could even play-up your name. Make it a mock-sixties-folk-thing."

Phil abruptly slammed a hand down onto the tabletop. A screw from the table's underside gave and dropped to the floor, and the tabletop slapped. Its metal legs reverberated. A child at the condiment island dropped from his mouth the plastic cup of coffee creamer he'd been sucking. "Is that a jab?" Phil demanded. "No one jabs me, boy!"

Eddie's eyes communicated confusion.

"I'm a job creator. A conservative man. Phil Ochs was a goddamned socialist muckraker and you will not make that association, do you understand me?"

There was a lightbulb-shaped stain on a ceiling tile just above Phil's head. Eddie studied it, feeling suddenly and woefully out of his depth. "But, people are going to make that association," he said, gently, as if explaining the simple profundity of death to a child. "It's your name."

"You don't know the misery," Phil sneered, "of living with a name like that."

Eddie knew he'd lost control of this meeting. "Okay," he tried, spit-balling, "so, we rebrand it. Take it back for the good guys."

But it was no use. He could see that Phil was lost, recoiled into some deeply-held, lunatic victimhood. He could explain to Phil that most voters had likely never heard of the folksinger, Phil Ochs. Or, that they would be unable to place the familiarity of the name even if they had. He could assure him that a three-week avalanche of primetime television ads would kill whatever legacy remained of the folksinger, imbuing the name, instead, with a Pavlovian craving for sweet potato fries. Instead, he leaned in, demanding Phil's attention, and heard his own voice as if from outside himself, another booth or body, detail a solution to the problem of Phil Ochs's name—a solution that burst suddenly to life in his own imagination and that would surely be the greatest stunt of his disappointing political carrier.

Chapter 20

"David Samuel, it's coming on," Lillian called from the bottom of the stairs. On the television behind her, a bellowing Nissan dealer gave over to the confessional whisper of the latest Playtex woman. "I made French fries." She tossed the plastic bowl to lift sea salt that had settled at its bottom. Above her came the faint groan of box springs followed by the heavy padding of her son's footfalls. Lillian moved to the sofa, nibbling one fry and then a second. Onscreen, a rainbow butterfly now put insomniacs to restful sleep. David Samuel appeared and sank into the sofa beside her, silently accepting the bowl when she passed it. Lillian crossed her arms in her lap to settle her nervous hands. "Can you believe he's doing this?" she said in as bright a voice as she could manage.

"Phil Ochs in a popularity contest? It does strain the imagination."

With a swell of synthesized horns and strings, an animated graphic moved across the screen reading, *Channel 5: News on Your Side.*

"Well, here we go," Lillian said.

At the news desk, Mercedes McLeod—orange

skin against bleached hair and teeth—began the segment with a profile of the recently-deceased Republican Senator, Ernie Holcomb.

Lillian whispered so as not to interrupt the broadcast: "When he told me he was doing this, I thought it was just a promotion for the restaurants. Pretend to run to get customers in the door, you know? The foo-foo intellectual crowd that wouldn't normally eat burgers. But then this campaign manager got onboard, so who knows?"

"That man sounds like a flimflammer to me," David Samuel said, chewing a fry. "Who else would take this seriously? Today he's a campaign manager, tomorrow he's the long-lost love child of some rich widow's dead husband, come to steal the pennies off his eyes, any old cadaver will do."

"Your father isn't a cadaver," Lillian scolded mildly, "but I do wonder what he's thinking." Phil had been so flippant when he'd brought it up to her, as if it were an aside: *Oh, by the way, I'm disrupting our lives for something I've never previously expressed interest in and for reasons I can't seem to ever fully communicate.* She'd held her tongue. Most likely, it was a benign and fruitless late-life whim. She'd only step in if she had to, should the threat warrant it. "Phil was so excited after meeting with him. He said this campaign manager had an idea that gave him a real shot to win."

David Samuel grunted.

"I don't know either. He said to watch and see. So, we'll see, I guess, when we watch."

Onscreen, the tuned-out mumble of Mercedes McLeod's introduction sharpened to coherence with the words, "Phil Ochs, welcome." And just like that, Phil was a person on the television. "Now, 'Phil Ochs,' why does that name sound familiar to me?"

"I'm a community leader," Phil said.

Lillian nodded her approval.

"I'm sure that's true. But our older viewers may

know the name for a different reason, wouldn't you say? There used to be a celebrity Phil Ochs, right?"

"No," Lillian protested. "Don't let her talk to you like this, Phil." She'd taken a fry from the bowl but now absently held it near her mouth like the physical exclamation mark signaling her alarm.

"Yeah, there used to be," Phil said sourly. "A liberal folksinger."

"So, not a Republican as you, yourself, are?" Mercedes said with a complicit smile.

"Not even close," Phil agreed, displaying none of that same merriment.

"I think we have a clip."

Several seconds of black and white footage began of a guitar-wielding young man in a leather jacket and tie singing sweetly to a horseshoe of teenagers seated on carpeted bleachers.

"What's he doing?" David Samuel asked.

When the broadcast returned to him, Phil was shaking his head. "That bastard," he muttered.

"Mr. Ochs!" Mercedes chided before demonstrating a refined but scolding nasal snort. "That clip seems to have stirred up some emotions."

Lillian tightened the knot of her crossed arms and clenched the fabric of her shirt in each fist. Was this a hit job? The Phil she knew wouldn't allow this.

"I'm self-made," he explained, "a successful business man. You don't know the burden it's been to drag that hippie's weight up the ladder. It got me no respect, I can tell you that."

Mercedes smiled. "But that's where your campaign comes in, isn't it? Why don't you tell our viewers how you plan to disassociate yourself from those comparisons? It's a very interesting thing that you're doing."

"What interesting thing is he doing?" Lillian said, placing a grip on David Samuel's arm as one might when anticipating impact.

"Well," Phil began, "the thing of it is this: on my birth certificate, there's no middle name. Phillip Ochs II, that's me. Phillip Ochs, that was my old man's name—and he was a drunken, abusive clown, himself, so I never felt comfortable to call myself Phillip either. My campaign manager, though, seeing how crippling this whole thing would be for bumper stickers and yard signs and that, he came up with a sort of gimmick to get around it."

"Tell us the specifics," Mercedes encouraged.

Lillian rose from the sofa. "What gimmick, Phil? What gimmick?"

"Well, as of today, we've got a website. And you all," Phil said, making a half-hearted hand gesture toward the camera, "the voters, I mean, can log on, or what have you, and suggest a middle name for me."

"David Samuel!" Lillian chirped.

"He's lost his mind," David Samuel said. She didn't turn to see it, but still registered a smile in her son's voice.

Mercedes asked, "And you'll let voters choose the winning name, right?"

"I'll pick my top five," Phil confirmed. "But they'll decide which of those is the winner."

"And this is real?" The anchor performed a showy skepticism. "You're committing to legally making this your actual middle name: 'Phil Whatever-Gets-The-Most-Votes Ochs?'"

"I'm legally doing it. Win or lose, it'll put an end to the worst burden of my whole life."

"That's showing a great deal of trust for the voters of South Carolina. You're a brave man."

"Well, I'm asking them to trust me in this election. So it's only fair that I should trust them too."

Who was this man? Lillian thought. Her Phil would never say that.

Mercedes McLeod turned to the camera. "Well, for now, his name is Phil Ochs. Maybe 'Phil in the blank Ochs?'" To Lillian, the little wink she gave felt bullying. "He's running for state Senate. If you have a name to suggest, visit his website. Mr. Ochs, it's been a pleasure."

The rainbow butterfly returned to the screen and resumed casting its sleepy spell. Only half-aware of it, the creature worked for Lillian like the harbinger of what felt to her like a dream: Phil on television, allowing a familiar news figure to break it to Lillian that Phil would no longer be Phil. He was changing careers and names, and then what else?

David Samuel was speaking, but she didn't catch it. Numbed in a way that felt almost drunken, she floated toward the foyer and her car keys and the explanation that was due her.

Chapter 21

"You did good, Phil," Eddie was saying. "You sold that 'trust' line just like we talked about." They were driving from the television studio to the Irmo Fry Buddy where Eddie had picked Phil up. "You came off as real though, you know? And we can play that up, really speak to people, run against that usual slick politician thing, like they were born into the arms of men in powder wigs. And swaddled in legal writs. And raised by personal injury lawyers." Eddie laughed at himself. Since the interview, he'd been animated by a high that had rendered him, in Phil's mind, irritatingly chatty. "What did you think, Phil? Are you feeling good about it?"

They were moving through a small shopping district, and Phil was passively distracting himself by appraising the fullness of the fast food parking lots. "How many more of those things do we have to do?"

"Televised interviews?" Eddie said. "None, probably. State legislature races are mostly low visibility: speeches, maybe a few ads. That's about it. Why? Didn't you like it onstage?"

Phil didn't answer. He was pleased to be ridding himself of the folksinger, but he had no interest in exploring that process through probing personal interviews.

"On the other hand," Eddie continued, "maybe this naming stunt could end up being a human-interest story. Fox News and The View all wrapped up together. It's...Karl Rovian, if you'll allow me to toot my own horn by saying so. So, who knows? Maybe it will get some traction and you'll be in demand."

Phil firmed his grip on the plastic garment bag in his lap. He'd insisted on wearing his tracksuit to the studio, changing into his uncomfortable dress suit only for the duration of the interview and then immediately out of it again in the news station's bathroom.

For the rest of the drive, Phil feigned sleep, offering the occasional back of the throat snore to dissuade Eddie from engaging with him, a deterrent that successfully prevented questions but that did nothing to stay Eddie's excited yammering. When they arrived at the Irmo store, Eddie pulled into a handicap accessible parking space beside Phil's Lexus. "We're here."

Phil opened his eyes. He blinked and smacked his lips for affect.

"Hey," Eddie said, "is that a vanity plate on your Lexus? I didn't make it out. Did it say 'king-*something*'?" He swiveled his body to peer through the back driver's side window. "KNG...what, SHT?" Eddie straightened his body and raised his eyes to the roof, his mind trying out pronunciations.

As if groggy from sleep, Phil said, "Hmm...the plate? No, it doesn't say anything. Don't bother with that."

"King Shit?" Eddie asked and turned to Phil.

Phil met his eyes for only a beat, then he gave a slight shake of his head and said, "Nah." He opened his passenger door, gripping the garment bag at its middle, then stepped out into the parking lot.

"Oh, well okay," Eddie called through the open door, "never mind. Good job today, Phil."

Phil nodded and slammed the door. He walked to the back of his Lexus where he stood stock-still until he saw from the side of his eye that Eddie had pulled out onto the street. Then, he unlatched the trunk with his keyring remote and threw the garment bag inside, taking care not to glance directly at the license plate.

It had seemed like a good idea a year before, when his malaise had first set in. This was before he'd opened his seventeenth location, when a last-minute hiccup with the zoning board had temporarily cast doubt on that store's future, when that lifelong sense of being beaten no matter how hard he fought had finally started to crack him. But Phil was of a generation which was taught to manifest their destiny, and so he'd gone to the DMV and requested the personalized KING SHIT plate with the hope that displaying it would make it true. The girl at the counter said it wasn't allowed. He'd argued, and something he said had started her crying—a misfortune that likely prejudiced her manager against his case. And so, the truncated, KNGSHT. Now, even this had begun to strike him as too bold a message, too easy a contrast between his hopes and his reality, another mote of failure to be mocked. He slammed the Lexus' trunk.

Phil walked into Irmo's glass vestibule and peered through the interior glass to count the patrons who were queued to order: three, not counting children. The fast food business was one that moved in predictable meal cycles, but he nevertheless felt tense during these off-hours when his registers had lines of fewer than five. This was the optimistic capitalist in him. It was an obese nation, he reasoned. Regardless of the time of day, there was no excuse why more people weren't eating.

He opened the interior door then moved across the lobby and behind the counter. As he cut through the kitchen to the office, he noticed something that stopped him, a sight so unexpected that his eyes momentarily swam with confusion. "Lillian?" he called.

She didn't hear him. She was leaning over the commercial bread griller, apparently rapt in conversation with the boy working the bun station. His gesturing suggested an in-depth explanation of the device's utility.

"Lillian," Phil called again, louder.

She turned to him with the held-over grin that the bread griller had given her, and then her face stiffened. She touched the bun station worker on the arm with gratitude, then navigated past the kitchen staff and equipment and came to Phil.

"What are you doing here?" he demanded.

"I was waiting for you."

This was no answer. Phil didn't restrict Lillian anything—she filled her days as she saw fit, spent their money as it pleased her. But it had always been an unstated rule that she wouldn't interfere in the business. It was strange enough now having David Samuel running loose inside his operation. He didn't need Lillian around, confusing his staff about who was in charge of this thing. Phil felt imposed upon, the way he might if she had walked in on him medicating a hemorrhoid or checking for testicular lumps.

"Phil, we need to talk." Her tone was curt and insistent.

"Did someone die, Lillian? Because, if not, now isn't the time. We can talk at home."

She took a deep, performative breath. "No, Phil. We're going to talk now. I don't know what you were thinking making this kind of a decision without talking to me first. But I simply will not have it. This is my life, Phil. I like it, and I won't stand by and have it destroyed."

Noticing the nearest patty cook grinning and making a poor show of concealing his eavesdropping,

Phil made a displeased grunt and signaled for Lillian to follow him. He led her through the drive thru cubicles to the office but found Jen there on a barstool counting register tills. Without answering her greeting, Phil directed Lillian to the back of the kitchen. Looking around and finding no better place, he pulled open the door of the walk-in freezer and invited his wife inside with a roll of his hand. He propped the door open with a bag of chicken nuggets then turned to find her momentarily awed by the tall shelves of frozen product. She had one arm extended, hesitating to touch a box of hash browns like it was the robe of some heavenly savior. "All right," he said with a clap of his hands, "do you mind telling me what exactly has made you lose your mind?"

Lillian turned to him and exhaled two shafts of visible white steam from her nostrils. As a statement rather than a question, she said, "You're going to let strangers change your name. And you let me find out about it from the television."

"Oh," Phil said thoughtfully.

"Oh?"

"I mean, yeah. I see what you're saying. But I guess—what's the problem exactly?"

She took a step toward him. "The problem is that I'm Mrs. Phil Ochs. Phil Ochs, the fast food king. That's who I agreed to be twenty-five years ago. And suddenly, without any warning, I'm some politician's wife whose name I don't even know."

The hurt he detected in her voice made Phil feel trapped. His response walked a line between her clear expectation to be comforted and his own frustration at being tasked with doing it: "Well, if it distresses you to think about it, then…don't. It'll all be fine." He waited to see if this landed with his intended tenderness.

"No, Phil," she said, "You won't dismiss me, not about this."

He was beginning to feel the narrowness of the freezer's walls, the lowness of its ceiling. "Lillian," he said, "I don't know what to say to make this better for you. I've got a hell of a lot of balls in the air right now, and maybe I didn't cover all the bases. You want to be part of it? Pick the final name, I don't care. But, I find the topic upsetting. I just had to watch film of that tree-hugger, and talk about him on television and all, and I'm just not quite settled yet. We can go all through this later." He made a move toward the door.

Lillian slid around him and blocked his way out. She raised her arms and held them out as if prepared to tackle him should he start forward. "Phil, we need to talk about this now."

He reached past her and pushed the door open. The frozen nuggets fell onto the kitchen floor. He began to duck beneath one of Lillian's arms, but she reached behind her for the edge of the door and pulled it closed.

A moment passed before Phil could speak. He simply stood and watched how the cold circulation of air dulled her features. Eventually, he said, "You're aware you just locked us in here?"

Without turning away from him, Lillian's fingertips reached behind her and gave the door a discrete push.

"Yeah," Phil said, "try it. Get a running start, maybe, and barrel into it. See what happens." He stepped out of her way to provide her room to do so. "But, it won't make a difference. This is where we die."

"Well," Lillian began, "maybe it's good I did lock us in, because now you have to hear me out." She stepped away from the door and looked at the impression of her body in melted frost on its surface. Something about it seemed to rock her resolve. "How often does someone come in here?" she asked.

"Whenever they need to," Phil said, settling onto a stack of French fry boxes. "Every few hours. It may be we won't freeze to death," he admitted. "That bag of nuggets on the floor ought to clue them in that something's up. But, then again, I'm not exactly employing society's finest minds." He pushed his hands into his muffler pocket.

Lillian held herself.

"So," Phil said, "why don't you say what it was you wanted to say? It'll be handy to know in case the cold gets you and I'm the only one that makes it out alive. The authorities will have questions."

"You just should have told me first."

"It's my name!" Phil said. He felt bolstered by the knowledge that, even though her point was sound, their current situation robbed her of some right to indignation. "And it's been the biggest burden of my life."

"You said that on television."

"I shouldn't have to say it at all. You know the deal."

Lillian leaned against the freezer wall, then moved away from the coldness of it. Phil had rarely known her to be so confrontational, and it seemed to exhaust her. "I don't want to seem like I don't understand," she said. "But it isn't right, all these changes." Her words formed with a white fog that rose and pillowed her head like a halo.

"Times change. The only thing that doesn't is the predictable fact that I work hard and achieve big things and then get no respect for my trouble. I even turned that little nut into a not-so-bad store manager, and what did that win me?"

"Don't call him that," Lillian said quietly. She was noticeably shivering, a sight that caused Phil vague discomfort. "*I* respect you, Phil. That should be enough."

"I know that, but it's not the same," he explained. "I probably should have talked this all over with you, fine. But I jumped on the opportunities as they presented themselves. It was all just an accident of timing."

Lillian nodded at the freezer's floor. After a moment, she said, "You're unhappy in fast food?"

"I'm unhappy with being laughed at."

"Who's laughing, Phil?"

"Oh, you know. *Them*. The ones that always make a joke of a guy until he does something big enough to shut them up. Which, on the subject of jokes, they'll have a good one about you showing up here and murdering me in this freezer."

Lillian paused to take all of this in. After a moment, she calmly asked, "Are you unhappy at home?"

Phil stared at her. She was pale and pitiful. Her normally straight posture had become hunched, and she was wiping her sleeve across her running nose. She met his gaze with eyes that were glassy. "Nah," he said, "it's the world that's under my skin, not you."

Lillian took a step forward and leaned into him for warmth, like some sad, withered succubus in floral-printed leggings. Phil wasn't prone to physical demonstration, but he was freezing, and so he didn't pull away. After a moment, they even wrapped their arms around each other in a tug of war for body heat that left them at a comfortable draw.

"You'll let me pick the name?" Lillian said into Phil's chest.

"Mm-hmm," Phil muttered.

And this was how they were found—in each other's arms, silent and shivering—when the boy working the fish station pulled open the freezer door and startled at the sight of them. A smile grew across his face and he raised a thumbs up. "All right, Phil," he encouraged, "get some."

The Ochses instantly separated.

"Sorry, man," the boy said. "I don't mean to interrupt. But can you hand me some fish? If you can spare it, I mean." He hit Phil with a baffling wink.

"This is my nightmare," Phil said to no one. Then

he and Lillian stepped past the boy, Phil kicking the bag of nuggets deeper into the kitchen for one of his cadre of geniuses to pick up and throw away.

Chapter 22

"Bear Freight, this is Ron."

"Ron? It's Eddie."

"Where are you, man? Don't tell me you're sick. Bret got a DUI last night driving his girlfriend home from that Arianna Grande concert, the dumb prig. I was going to have you cover his loads."

"I'm not sick. I feel really good, actually."

"Cool. What's up?"

"Well," Eddie said, pausing for a moment to order the information he wanted to communicate, "I wanted to let you know that I won't be in today, or anymore at all; that I didn't enjoy a single day working for you; that you're a creepy slime ball; and…there was something else…oh, yeah: go fuck your mother. Thanks, Ron. See you, man."

Eddie disengaged the call and tossed his phone onto the couch beside him. He took a long pull from a vodka icepick. It was ten-fifteen in the morning.

The previous afternoon, a donation from the South Carolina Republican Party had swelled Phil's campaign account to an operational size. An additional several hundred dollars were trickling in each day from visitors to the website. Not a fortune, but good enough.

For most of his adult life, it had been Eddie's dream to be an important person in a campaign, to unshackle himself from the eight-to-five clock and do politics full-time. The election was in only four weeks, so Eddie's would be a temporary freedom to be sure. But freight brokerages were like roach holes, and it would be easy enough to skitter back into one of them when the money ran out. For now, though, he was free.

He decided to take off the entire morning to day-drink and watch old war films. After a nap, maybe, he would roll up his sleeves and get properly to work. However, during the opening credits of Sergeant York, the texts started coming from Ron:

> *10:21 AM*
> *f.u. eddie*
>
> *10:23 AM*
> *Im gonna fk YUR mother, prick!!!*
>
> *10:34 AM*
> *u r going to fail like u failed yur lezzy wife, cuck!*
>
> *10:35*
> *go to hell drunk ass*

Eddie's mother was dead and buried, so the pursuit of intercourse with her would require a greater commitment of time and physical energy than Ron was likely to invest. However, the rest of the texts stuck. He sipped his icepick.

Onscreen, Gary Cooper was making a speech about Christianity and war, how a man was only a man if he served his principles and his country. But what happens when those forces are at odds, Eddie wondered. Joan Leslie would never cuckold Gary Cooper. And whatever he chose—service to God or service

to country—Sergeant York's would be right. Howard
Hawks would see to that. The good guy couldn't fail,
not in the old days anyway. Ice cubes struck Eddie's
teeth as he drained his glass, and he wondered, not for
the first time, if he was the protagonist of his own life
or just a supporting character who, if he were lucky,
would get to make a memorable speech as he bled out
on the battlefield, a speech whose only purpose was to
bolster the real protagonist for their ultimate win. But,
who might that protagonist be? Penny? Cindy? Phil?

He tried to settle himself by thinking of the tor-
ment he was avoiding at the freight brokerage: his
conmen coworkers, lifers or cocky twenty-something
post-frat bros, the fraternal cultural wang that they
lent the place.

Unexpectedly, though, he felt a growing anxiety
thinking of the brokerage. The loss of a steady pay-
check, of a workspace that was predictable and familiar.
Eddie began suddenly to feel isolated. The other bro-
kers were together at that moment, knocking against
each other. What if the very spark of life came from
the friction of those exchanges in all the offices and
worksites and family homes that surrounded his own
lonely little house? A cynical whisper bullied through
his thoughts, telling him that the world was continuing outside his door while he'd forced himself into
entombment, sentenced to the solitary acts of writing
speeches and checking metrics and waiting on return
calls from political players who would never ultimately
call. No one ever would again. He was unloved and
doomed to fail.

A bead of sweat rolled down his side.

Another icepick was the answer. He put the drink
together, watching the chemical swirl of the vodka and
iced tea as he drained half the glass.

He came back to the sofa and abruptly turned off
the film, stranding the doughboys in their Germanic
hell. The walls expelled that familiar heavy silence that

had moved in with him when his wife and daughter had moved out.

In those early weeks without them, that judgmental silence had pushed so strongly on all sides of him, had seemed so prophetic of a lifetime spent alone, that he'd briefly weighed the option of killing himself. But death was an ugly business of fluids and loosened bowels, and it seemed unnecessarily cruel to force his daughter to dress for her future prom in the bathroom where she found him hanging. Of course, it was unlikely Cindy would keep the house after his death, and even less likely that Penny would be the one to find him—his body would certainly be discovered by the cat, who, bitch that she was, would be a long way into devouring his corpse before anyone noticed he was missing. Still, he'd found that memories of his absent family somehow made them more alive in the space then when they'd been there to take for granted. He didn't want his blood to stain the floor where Penny took her first steps or for his bladder to evacuate on the mattress where he last woke up beside his wife. And so, to borrow from a popular conservative bumper sticker, Eddie had chosen life. Such as it was.

Realizing that he was slipping into a too-familiar self-pity, Eddie reached for his laptop to distract himself with work. It had been three days since the Local 5 news announced the "Rename Phil Ochs" competition, and Phil's website's traffic had swelled to an average of three hundred hits per hour, thirty-seven percent of which resulted in a unique contribution of a suggested middle name.

The webpage was set up like a partially-complete game of hangman, with Phil's first and last name on either side of an empty line: Phil _____ Ochs. A user could type on the line, then make it public by tapping 'Enter.' A simple content moderation algorithm automatically took down overtly offensive submissions. Eddie's admin folder already boasted hundreds of iterations of *Phil Fuck Ochs, Phil Tit Ochs,* along with unique suggestions, such as *Phil Pussyfart Ochs.* But the algorithm was programmed only to catch offensive words and phrases, which left Eddie with the daily task of manually moderating other categories of joke submissions.

Many of these were restaurant themed—*Phil Fry-Buddy Ochs, Phil Tater Ochs, Phil Pickle Ochs*—others focused on his age—*Phil Mummy-Fart Ochs, Phil Dinosaur Ochs, Phil R.I.P. Ochs*—and then there were those that subverted the point of the contest, drawing attention to Phil's namesake—*Phil The-Sixties-Folk-singer Ochs, Phil I-Ain't-Marchin'-Anymore Ochs.* There were other themes of course, dealing with Phil's height or spiky haircut, or his face's resting scowl.

Eddie had just deleted the puzzling entry, *Phil Buttafuoco Ochs,* when his phone rang. It was Cindy.

"Cindy," he said coldly.

"Hey, Eddie," she sighed, as if it were he who had called her, and she felt put out by the intrusion. "Do you have a minute to talk?"

"Only if it's about Penny," he said, both of them knowing he'd stay on the line even if it wasn't.

"It is. I mean—yes, it is. Gail got a call this morning from West Virginia."

"Okay."

"Her mother's sick. They don't think she has more than a couple of weeks."

"Okay."

"So, Gail's packing up now to go spend those weeks with her. In West Virginia." After a pause, she added, "And I was thinking I might go with her." She delivered these last words quickly, like she had crumpled them into a ball and pitched them at him.

"Why?"

Her pause suggested that she was puzzled by the nature of the question. "Because…I'm in a relationship with this person and I want to be there for her?"

"And you're taking Penny with you? What about school? Who'll sit in my chair at gymnastics and fend off those awful mothers?"

"Actually," Cindy said, "I was thinking maybe she could stay with you while I'm gone. I mean, if you're okay with that."

Eddie was a gentle bum when he was drunk, a loving simpleton, but he was not quite drunk yet. "Me? Well, I think that would be great. Honestly, though, I'm surprised that *you* do. Since I'm legally unfit for shared custody, I mean. But, otherwise, yeah, I'm all for it."

"Eddie, don't do that. You know I don't think you're a bad father. I never said you were. You were just so miserable with your job and everything, and you took the separation so hard, and you were drinking and drinking, and it seemed to me that the best thing for Penny was to not have her around that so often, not until you got straightened out."

"Cure the depressed man by taking everything from him."

Cindy's sigh was static in Eddie's ear. "You're right. Maybe I overreacted. I was messed up too. We can think of this as a trial run."

Eddie had the feeling that this conversation was wearing thin for her. "Fine," he said, "but I'll hold you to it."

"Yeah, fine. Will you be able to get her to and from school? Will it be okay with work?"

He took a sip from his glass, delighted in hiding it from her. "It so happens I just set myself up to where I can make my own hours."

Cindy was silent for a moment before asking, "Eddie, did you lose your job?"

"No, Cindy, I didn't lose my job. I took something new. In politics. It's good."

"Oh…wow," she said after another considered pause. "Congratulations, that's—I mean, good for you,

Eddie. Honestly."

It was a killer, that warmth she could still make him feel. "Thank you, Cindy. Hey, why don't we get off here while we're both nice people? And you can just let me know about Penny, okay?"

"Okay," Cindy said. "Thank you for doing this. She'll be excited."

"She won't, but I appreciate you saying so."

"Hey, Eddie?" Cindy said, just as he was preparing to hang up. "Whatever this political job is, whoever it is you're working for—they're not, like, super anti-gay, right? I mean, I know you do Republican politics, but promise me it's nothing hateful like that. Nothing where you're enabling prejudiced assholes in some messed up attempt to get back at me because we didn't work out." She laughed before pausing, as if to dismiss the idea as ridiculous. When Eddie didn't respond, however, her tone became nervous: "That's not what this is, right?"

Eddie, tipsy and emotional, found himself momentarily unable to speak. He was overcome with gratitude for this opportunity to confirm to her that, beneath the wear and tear from his many mediocre years, he was still, at his core, a good guy. "This isn't that," he said finally. "I would never help people like that."

Once they hung up, Eddie tossed the phone onto the sofa. There was a hummingbird flutter in his chest. The thought of Penny coming for an extended stay acted immediately on his home's oppressive silence like a crucifix repelling a vampire. The ice in his glass coughed but he pretended not to hear. He returned to his content moderation with a new determination to do something impressive with this campaign—with Penny in the front row to watch him do it.

A second after *Phil Dingle-berry Ochs* went public on the website, Eddie was there to delete it, with all the deftness of a man who was winning at life.

Chapter 23

Les Escarabajo performed for two hours. Ruzanna knew two of the songs they played. Coming out of the show, Collin's recent sullen strangeness seemed overtaken by the mania of a roided-up madman. When he'd repeatedly asked her what about the guitar solo in such-and-such song and what about some other attribute of another, Ruzanna had merely smiled politely.

In the car now, Collin asked, "Where do you want to eat, babe?"

"No," she said, "I need to get home." Ruzanna was not allowed to be out with Collin at night, her father having recently opined that her young man had 'a stink on him,' so her attendance at the show had required subterfuge—explaining why she was now outfitted in her Fry Buddy uniform. Ruzanna didn't like this band, or live concerts at all, really. She felt guiltier, somehow, that she'd lied to do something so joyless, and worse still, all for a boy.

"What? No, babe, I got to eat. Come on, we're having a good night, right?" He touched her knee in a way that didn't suggest sex. This was a new and notable maturation they'd recently achieved in their eight-month relationship.

"Fine," she said, annoyed, "but something quick. Anything but Fry Buddy."

"No," he whined, "a real restaurant. A sport's bar or something."

"Radish."

"Babe, you don't know how much I needed this night." His fingers pulsed on her kneecap in a succession of tickling squeezes. "Come eat with me."

"No, I'm going to get in trouble. Anyway, I didn't bring any money."

"You don't need money, babe. I've got you."

Ruzanna found it frustrating not to be heard. "Oh, yeah," she said, "I keep forgetting: the mystery money."

Collin drew back his hand from her leg and slapped it onto the steering wheel. He grunted unhappily. "God, what's your deal?"

"Hmm, I don't know. Maybe it's that I told you I wasn't allowed to do this, but you pushed me until I said okay. And now I'm going to get in trouble because my shift ended twenty minutes ago, and I'm late, and you still won't stop pushing."

Collin leaned into his car door and draped one wrist over the steering wheel in a performance of unaffected cool. "Whatever," he shrugged. "I wanted to treat you is all. Sorry to be so selfish."

For two highway exits, they were silent, Ruzanna staring out her passenger window, Collin brooding and quietly ringing his hands on the steering wheel. She considered saying something to him, not an apology, but something about how she appreciated his intentions.

Before she could, Collin undercut her with a quiet mumbling to himself: "Sucks…wish your attitude wasn't always so shitty."

"Excuse me?" she said, her temperature set to an immediate boil. "Did you say something? Maybe I couldn't hear you because my ears are still ringing from those deafening guitar solos that for some reason went on for-*fucking*-ever."

Collin harrumphed.

"No, you know what? I think my favorite part of you 'treating me' was the way they kept holding their guitar necks out in front of them like they were cocks. God, that was hot! Is that what it's like having one? Do tuneless, meandering musical riffs blare out when you beat it off?"

"I shouldn't have brought you."

"Oh no, but I'm glad you did. How else would I have learned—what was that line they kept repeating—'my baby only likes it in the backdoor, backdoor'? I mean, good for her. That's some third-generation fem shit. I'm inspired, Radish, and I say that as a woman."

"Just…stop talking," Collin said in a hurt whimper. He seemed to her like a cat who'd lain some dead prize at his owner's feet, only to be scolded for tramping blood into the house.

Ruzanna did stop talking. She leaned away from him and cracked her window. The sound of the wind rushing in and the cool ripples of it against her face felt like a mediating entity had entered the car, one whose constant tries for her attention allowed her to shift her focus away from her anger.

"Will you please close that?" Collin said, unable even to let her have this.

"I like it."

"You can't drive on the highway with the windows open," he said, each word slow and measured.

"Just, whatever. Give me a minute."

Collin said no more, but Ruzanna became aware that he was monitoring the dashboard clock, his finger on the steering wheel ticking off the seconds. When the clock changed, he said, "Okay. That was a minute. Roll it up."

"Why are you being a dick?"

"Why are you? Is this about the money?"

"Oh my God!" Ruzanna said. "Who said anything about that money?"

"You did! You brought it up." He closed the passenger window himself with a button on the driver's door.

"Dude, you're, like, obsessed," Ruzanna said in the new quiet of the car. "I mean, what did you have to do to get that money? Are you ashamed or something?"

Collin recoiled. "What do mean, what did I have to do? What did you mean by that?"

"I don't know, you're just weirding me out. I mean, did you have to, like, blow a guy or something?"

He flattened his lips and nodded manically. "Nice."

"No, I just mean, if you earned the money by helping a guy to…I don't know, clear a stump from his yard, you'd say, 'Babe, I earned this money helping a guy clear a stump from his yard.'" Feeling somewhat dickish herself now, she added, "Although, I guess there's more than one way to clear a man's stump."

"Fuck you."

"Fuck you back."

For the rest of the car ride, they were silent. Collin exited the highway and turned onto Ruzanna's street, parking the car away from the house as he'd done a dozen times before. Ruzanna sat for a moment, anxious about the time on the clock, but unable to move from the car. The gravity of this argument felt like a bowling ball placed in her lap, pinning her legs to the seat. In her most grown up voice, she said, "Radish, it really was nice that you wanted me to go. I'm sorry I didn't like it. I hope you still had a good time."

"I want to break up." He never stopped staring straight ahead into the darkness of her sleeping street.

She wouldn't have expected it given her anger, but her tears came quickly. She nodded—only nodded— and let herself out of the car. She walked a block to her house, those first tears now hesitating below her chin, building the courage to jump. And, as if this evening wasn't devastating enough, when she turned up the driveway, there on her porch were Mr. and Mrs. Singh, awaiting her arrival with poison in their eyes.

Chapter 24

David Samuel was hanging a sign for eggnog sweet potato pie, a seasonal Fry Buddy menu item that, at only ninety-nine cents, was a predictable annual boon. This was his third sign, hung strategically throughout the dining room with the aid of a corporate marketing map, and he felt he'd finally gotten the hang of the step stool. "Firmer on the left," he said to one of the two kitchen staffers who braced him on either side from the floor, his previous solo experiences with the ladder having led to several backward spills to that same floor tile. A shoulder pushed harder into the small of his back and an upwardly-extended hand squeezed his left shoulder.

From this vantage point, those previous signs were in his line of sight, swaying slightly in the dining room's circulated air, their ripped borders mocking him. After a steeling breath, he declared, "I'm going to raise my arms now. This is when things get serious." His eyes shut protectively as he raised the sign by its two plastic clips. Fumbling, he failed to engage the left clip with the edge of the tile's border strip. It slipped from his hand and the string that secured the right clip began to unravel. The sign sliced, guillotine-style, left to right, through the air, striking the right-side kitchen staffer in the face. Abruptly, the staffer released David Samuel who began to wobble and tilt backwards, only to be saved by the wounded man's hand pressing firmly into his manager's right buttock, pushing him back to plumb. In the aftermath, the three of them were still for a moment, as if in reverence for tragedy narrowly avoided.

"Courage, gentlemen," David Samuel said.

"Este hombre blanco está jodidamente loco," said one staffer to the other.

David Samuel turned, indicating the left clip to the speaker with a meaningful shake of his hand. "This time," he said, "is our time. Ready yourselves. Here. We. Go." He thrust his left arm above his head again, punching a hole in the ceiling tile, before recalibrating and finding the border strip, trying again and again until the clip's teeth sank into it and the sign was secured on that side.

"Shoo," David Samuel respired. For the first time since embarking up the ladder, he was able to take his hands off the sign. The registers were at his back. He swiveled his head for a peak at his crew, the bulk of which had congregated behind the counter and now turned away or knelt and busied themselves as if their attentions had been directed toward something other than the big man on the two-foot stool and his quest for seasonal signage. "If there's time to lean, people…" David Samuel reminded them. It was after three o'clock, deep into that middle period between lunch rush and dinner rush when the minutes ticked slowly, and the restaurant affected the expectancy of a held breath.

David Samuel reclaimed the right-side clip. He winked at one of the men who supported him and, upon receiving no response of solidarity, repeated this gesture with the other. Then, in a single, blind motion, he raised his arm and affixed the right clip. It connected easily, expertly. And when he opened his eyes, the sign was secure, swaying with considerable agitation, a long crease down its middle from the struggle, but the most pristine sign of the three.

With an air of pride, he said, "You may return to the kitchen, gentlemen. I'm coming down."

The staffers peeled away and ambled back into the kitchen. David Samuel bent and gripped the rounded handle of the stool with both hands. A sudden cool spot down the divot of his lower back alerted him that his shirt had come untucked. He stepped down onto the tile then partook of the deep, restorative breath of one who's faced adversity and lived to tell the tale.

While he worked at folding the stool for storage, a man in a deep yellow suit coat entered through the vestibule and made his way to Wanda at the only open register.

"A good afternoon, young lady," he said with a bellowing good humor. Miles of teeth below his black moustache. "How does this afternoon find you?"

Wanda responded with an uncharmed cluck, like the weariest of skeptical chickens. "You was a baby sooner ago than I was young and I don't know what you think you're playing at with that 'lady' business."

"I would never presume to play with your lady business," the man said. "And we are all children in the eyes of the Lord."

"Mm-hmm," Wanda said, frowning. "What can I get you today?"

The man was momentarily distracted by the stuttering of the stool's rubber feet on the tile floor as David Samuel dragged it behind him. David Samuel watched the man's eyes following him as he came with the stool behind the counter. The man's gaze returned to Wanda as David Samuel passed behind her. "I'm sorry, young lady: what was it you were asking me?"

"I say, you come here to eat? Or you come to evangelize?"

"I've got time for both," he said with another full-toothed grin. "Now that you mention it, may I inquire as to the status of your here-after planning?"

"Oh, here we go," Wanda said loudly to herself, then she leaned toward the man, her arms resting on the register's display monitor. "Let me tell you something: I spend four afternoons a week in this uniform, plus I cut hair three nights at the pagoda down the way, and that don't count the side hustle I got cleaning houses on the weekends. So, Jesus ought to know I ain't got time to play hide-and-seek with him. So, if he ever needs me, then his all-seeing butt ought to know where to find me." Then, to David Samuel, she called: "Hey, little boss man, we got us a live one."

David Samuel was fitting the step stool into the tight space between the industrial ice cream maker and the wall. By the time he arrived at her register, Wanda was walking away. "Break time for me, baby. I'll let you take care of Colonial Mustard here. I don't get paid enough to listen to this kind of horseradish." As she crossed the lobby, Wanda passed Ruzanna who arrived behind the counter for her shift with a face that was puffy and red-eyed.

"Can I help you, sir?" David Samuel said, his attention taken by the devastated look of the girl coming to his side.

"You've got yourself a bit of a firecracker there, it seems to me," the customer said of Wanda.

David Samuel made an oh-brother-you-have-no-idea sound of solidarity. "Order when you're ready." Ruzanna took a place at the register beside his. "Are you okay, pretty girl?" he said.

"I'm fine," said Ruzanna.

"Mercy," the man said, eyeing the big, lighted menu board that hung above David Samuel's head. "What's a Number One?"

With rote delivery, David Samuel said, "It's the Best Buddy combo. The Best Buddy is a Regular Buddy with tomatoes, lettuce, and a second beef patty, and it comes with fries and a drink." Then to Ruzanna, "Are you not feeling well?"

"Fine. It's…just…my boyfriend," she said with delicate, controlled heaves. "He…broke…up with me."

Unaware, the man continued, "And how's that different from the Number Two?"

"Cad!" David Samuel said.

"Me?" said the man.

"The boyfriend, of course. The Number Two is the Secret Buddy combo. The Secret Buddy is the same as the Best Buddy, but with no tomatoes and you get our secret Shush Buddy sauce, and it comes with fries and a *wink*. Corporate makes us say that. It's really just a medium drink." To Ruzanna, he continued, "Are you okay to work? You don't look terribly well."

"Let me ask you this," the man interrupted.

"The descriptions are all on the menu, sir."

"Oh…Yes, I see," said the man, squinting.

Ruzanna whimpered, "I…have to…work. I lied… to…my parents and…they're making me pay them emotional damages. They say…it will build my character." Here, she collapsed into David Samuel's chest.

"Okay, give me the Number One, but hold the tomatoes. Oh, and add that secret sauce."

"Hey, hey, hey now," David Samuel said. "Don't do that. You're a beautiful soul and so much better than some boy from this armpit town."

The man looked to a male patron who had gotten into line behind him, and then back at David Samuel. "Me?" he asked.

"A Number Two for you," David Samuel snapped, reaching around Ruzanna to hit the appropriate register button. "Would you like an eggnog sweet potato pie with that?"

The man responded with a hand placed, splay-fingered, on his chest, as one might who's earnestly touched. "I appreciate you asking, brother. Could I have two?"

"You can have as many as you want."

"No, no. I'm not greedy. Two is more than fair. I'll take my order to go, please."

"Okay." David Samuel confirmed the order from the display monitor, then said, "That comes to six forty-eight." He returned his attention to the girl, gently repositioning her so he could hold her shoulders at arm's length. "Listen, do this for me: say your name," he told her, and she did. "That's right: you're Ruzanna. Ruzanna who's too darn good for that boy anyhow. So, Ruzanna, I need you to smile, honey. Because this dark world needs that light. And I need you to do something else: I need you to go ahead and clock out and take the day off. You need a Me Day."

"You...want me to...go?" the girl sniveled.

David Samuel nodded, having not thought this through, but savoring his role as a giver of graces.

"You're...like...the best boss."

David Samuel responded with a benevolent bow of his head, then shooed her off with his fingers. His look of satisfaction transferred to the yellow-suited man when he returned his gaze to him.

"That was real sweet, boss," the man said. "But you've given me a question: you suggested my total to be six forty-eight. The Number Two is only four fifty. If I'm reading that menu correctly."

"Four fifty, plus the two pies."

"The two pies that you offered me?"

"The two pies you said you wanted."

"Correct," the man said.

"So...six forty-eight."

"And that total includes, if I'm keeping up with you, the two pies you offered me?"

"Yes, the pies you said you wanted."

"I see," the man said. "Let me ask you this: what do you think Jesus would do in this situation?"

"Pay for his pies, I'd presume."

"Mm-hmm. Well, as it happens, I enjoy a close personal relationship with our Lord and I'd posit to you that He would want you to let me have my combo, along with the pies you offered me, for four forty-six."

"Well," David Samuel said, eying the two-person line that had formed behind the man, "then I'm afraid Jesus has a poor understanding of restaurant waste logs. So…you can pay me for your food, or I can delete your order and you can go." From the corner of his eye, he thought he saw Wanda start around the corner, but duck back at the sight of the man.

"Why be stingy, brother? Pies for Jesus."

"Did I tell you I enjoy a close personal relationship with Sheriff's Deputy Slattery, and I'd posit to you that *he* would want you to pay for your meal? Should we call him and find out?"

The man took a step back from the counter and put a hand into the interior of his mustard suit coat as if to retrieve a wallet. Instead, he extracted an empty hand in the flat-palmed gesture of peaceful supplication. "We appear to have arrived at an impasse," he said, "so I believe I'll go." Then to the line behind him, he said, "How are you all doing this fine afternoon?" and hurried away.

David Samuel jammed his finger into the series of buttons necessary to void the order then looked up at the next customer in line.

"Hey, fella," the customer said in a cartoonish, lyrical voice. "That was pretty impressive work you did there, you know? Mighty strong handling of a hustler." His brow wrinkled, and he asked, "You're Phil's son, aren't you?"

"If one is to believe my mother. Your accent sounds Northern."

"You have a good ear to boot." The man smiled seductively.

David Samuel returned the expression, leaning confidently on the counter. "Your name doesn't happen to be Jim Trebek by any chance?"

The man extended his hand. "My reputation proceeds me, eh?"

"Oh, it does indeed. I've been waiting for you to come around since I took this position. Why don't you sell me on the exciting next phase of my career in this industry?"

Chapter 25

Phil sat in a dining hall in a private mansion that made his own big house look like a young couple's modest starter, scratching and pinching at the crotch of his pants beneath his cloth napkin. Eddie was seated to his right, occasionally touching Phil's elbow to stay his arm, but it was Eddie who had forced him into this getup, so Phil considered his opinion moot.

The donor dinner was a two-hundred-dollar-per-plate affair hosted by Rog Gypsum, co-owner or advisory board member of thirteen of Grant Thornton's Top 100 businesses, putting his hand in, among other cookie jars, South Carolina software development, logistics consulting, wallboard manufacturing, steel fabrication, and waste collection. He was a decades-long top private investor in state Republican politics, and he was generally understood by insiders to be a big fucking deal. Phil had never heard of him.

As Eddie explained it, Gypsum was a ghost, a force whose money worked so quietly through back channels and charity groups and benignly-named PACs that it was impossible to know the actual extent of his reach. If Gypsum was the tallest and most rec-

170

ognized figure in the local business world, his political dealings were every bit the broad, murky shadow such a figure would cast.

Phil glanced around the table now at suits with interchangeable heads. It was just these sorts of old-moneyed elites who'd turned up their noses at him for years, keeping him at the margins of respectability for being a mere fast food magnate, and he struggled to find their snobbish refinements impressive. He was self-made, after all, and should be venerated alongside others of that ilk—Harlan Sanders, Dave Thomas, God—who began with nothing and ended-up ruling a world of their own creation. But Phil didn't make the rules, so he'd come with the good-faith intent to smile at jokes, lick a reasonable number of boots, and drag himself one rung higher up the social ladder. The reception he was receiving, however, put his magnanimity in peril.

"So, Phil," Gypsum called from the end of the table, "what's your take on S980?" The question caused the suits to turn toward Phil, smiles blooming above their collars. Phil glared at his host. Eddie leaned nearer him to whisper an answer, but before he could, Gypsum clarified, "protecting the right to work, I mean. Are you for it?"

"A man's got to work," Phil said.

Gypsum's face grew a puzzled smile. "That's not really an answer, Phil." Dusty, old-money laughs arose from the table. "Does that mean you're for it or against it?"

"For it. A man's got to work. What do you want him to do? Live off the government?"

To his right, Eddie whispered, "unions, unions, unions," but Phil paid him no attention.

"But—hmm, that's funny," Gypsum said, making eye contact with several of the suits. "I was thinking I read on your website that you opposed S980 because of the power it gave to unions. But maybe I'm mistaken," he allowed. "That must have been some *Republican* website I was on."

"What Phil means," Eddie said, "is that he supports the spirit of the bill, as long as the language on union protections is stricken."

"I can say what I mean," Phil snapped.

"Can you, Phil?" Gypsum said. "Then, what do you mean?"

Phil was silent for a moment, the weight of the room's eyes depressing each answer he considered until he settled on: "I meant what Ellis said." He jerked his head to indicate Eddie.

"Of course you did," Gypsum said.

It was the last he spoke to Phil before the first course was served. Three waiters with rolling carts emerged from the kitchen. Quickly and efficiently, they presented each of the diners with a plate of steaming shells in shallow broth. The clatter of silverware and agreeable murmuring surrounded him, but Phil was consumed by the horror of the plate that was set before him. "What the hell is this?" he whispered.

"Mussels," Eddie said quietly.

"I know what it is. I mean, does he expect us to eat it?"

"It seems that he does?" Eddie said, the lilt of a question in his voice.

"What's wrong, Phil?" Gypsum called. "You don't have a shellfish allergy, do you?"

"I don't have any allergy," Phil responded, volleying this clear suggestion of weakness. Quietly, he studied how the others were approaching this problem, then he emulated them by lifting his fork in one hand, a shelled slug in the other, and set about prying out the slick meat.

As soon as he pulled the fork from his mouth, Phil's tongue alerted him to an emergency. *I can send this forward or back,* it said, *but it's not welcome here.* He attempted to swallow it whole, and this proved to be the wrong decision. His throat constricted and tossed it back up with a force that nearly broke the dam of his clenched lips. His cheeks puffed with air and mollusk. His interception of the regurgitated bite was accompanied by a brief hocking sound. The suits leaned toward him, hopeful to see him shit his metaphorical bed.

"Phil," Gypsum said, as to a child, "if you don't like mussels, you don't have to eat them on my account." He added, "If you'd like, I can have someone run by Fry Buddy and pick you up a, what, Number Three?"

More laughter from the table.

With watery eyes, Phil stared at Gypsum, who stared right back, and then he swallowed defiantly. First, the mussel cooling on his tongue, and then each of those remaining in his bowl.

"Nice job," Gypsum said, then made a show of slowly savoring his own portion.

As Phil patted briny sweat and broth from his lips with his napkin, his phone began to vibrate. It took effort to extract it from the narrow pocket of his slacks. A glance at the screen found that it was only Lillian, but Phil used this call as an excuse to leave the table. "I have to take this," he said. He rose and navigated the tangle of chair legs, then answered importantly, "Phil here."

"Phil? I need you to come home right away." She sounded breathless and pained.

"An emergency, huh?" He bellowed for the benefit of the table.

"Oh, Phil, it is," Lillian confirmed. "Can you come?"

"Well," Phil said, his mouth fishy and slick, "that poses a bit of a problem." He wandered from the dining hall as if for privacy, then continued through a hallway, peering between mocha-stained doorframes until he came to a bathroom. He went in and shut the door behind him. "What's all this about?"

"It's David Samuel, Phil. I just—I can't."

"What's he done?" Staring at this rich asshole's toilet bowl, Phil lamented that he didn't have a good sturdy dump in him, a movement that was epic and scandalous.

"No," Lillian said. "He needs to be the one to tell you himself. I'm out of this. I'm staying out of all of it. I'm done."

This was intriguing. What could the boy have done to stay Lillian's motherly helicopter blades? "Well, the thing of it is, I'm at this donor thing. If I go, Ellis will have to suck off all these stiffs by himself, and he's only one man." He was crouched above the toilet paper roll, whipping a turban of its luxurious sheets around his hand.

"Suit yourself," Lillian said, "but I'm through worrying about it. You two can learn to get along or you can kill each other. It's up to the pair of you. I'm out of it."

Phil wadded the turban and flushed it. It hung momentarily in the drain but found its way through. He began work on a larger wad. "Lillian, you sound… troubled. Not like yourself," he said distractedly. "Anyway, why would we kill each other? Things have been okay lately, no?"

There was a pulse of laughter in his ear. "Oh, you'll be troubled too, Phil. Troubled at the very least. Trust me: killing is not so unlikely."

When he flushed again, the toilet paper twisted in the mouth of the drain then caught. Water rose to the rim of the bowl and stopped. Phil smiled, taking a mental picture of this handy work. "Well," he said, "I better come then and figure out whatever's going on. These boys will have to get along without me."

"Thank you, Phil. Don't be long."

Phil disengaged the call then wandered to the bathroom mirror and regarded himself in his uncomfortable suit. He looked like he fit in with this crowd, which made him feel favorably like a spy. A garlic and rosemary belch rose in his throat. Phil straightened his tie and pulled at his lapel in the mirror. Then he unzipped his pants and pissed into Rog Gypsum's marble sink. Kingmaker or not, no one talked shit about Fry Buddy.

When he returned to his place at the table, there was a beef dish awaiting him, raw-looking and thinly sliced. The sight of it made the mussels in his stomach swim. "Look," he said to the group, "this has been real nice, but I've been alerted to an emergency that I'm specifically needed to take care of. It's something I have to go see about, so Ellis here can answer your questions." To Eddie, he said, "Ellis, represent the team."

"You're leaving us, Phil?" Gypsum said. "What's the trouble, did someone clog your milkshake maker?"

"Phil," Eddie protested, "that isn't how—"

"It's a family emergency. My hands are really tied here." He patted Eddie on the shoulder. "Thanks for everything, fellas."

Twenty minutes later, when Phil stepped into his foyer, Lillian called, "Phil? We're in here." He tossed down his keys in the ceramic dish, then walked into the living room. Lillian was on the sofa. David Samuel was spilled into Phil's recliner.

"Out of my chair, bub," Phil said, prompting David Samuel to roll his shoulders and tent his fingers over his stomach. "Do you have any idea how important that donor lunch was? I had to leave Ellis on his own. What's going on here anyway?"

"Eddie is a grown man," Lillian said curtly. "He can take care of himself. David Samuel, tell him. Tell your father what you told me."

There was an odd serenity on David Samuel's face, not a smile exactly, but a satisfied, carefree sort of a look. "Dad," he said, struggling out of the chair, "maybe you should sit down." He stepped away from the recliner and invited Phil into it with an outstretched hand.

The heat radiating off its plastic cover caused Phil to decline. "No, you just go on and say it."

"Dad, do you recall how for years you looked down on me and on my pursuits until you found yourself in a moment of vulnerability having lost Tony with no obvious replacement? Then you promoted me to the role, and I immediately demonstrated my fitness for the respect you'd so consistently denied me? Well, I've recently become aware that not everyone requires so high a threshold of proof as regards my basic competence. In a word: I'm a desirable commodity."

"Yeah?" Phil said. "Desirable to who exactly?"

"Well, let me set the scene: I was faced with a challenge that required a two-fisted managerial approach. Tenderness in this hand," he said, extending his left fist. "Mated with steely strength." He extended his right. "My successful resolution of the affair was witnessed and commented upon, and in the context of the praise that followed, an offer was extended to me. So, Phil, I thank you for providing me, however reluctantly, with this opportunity. But effective today, I'm presenting you with my two weeks' notice."

Behind Phil on the sofa, Lillian dissolved into hopeless sobbing.

"What the do you mean?" Phil hissed. "You can't quit on me." His necktie had become strangling. He worked its knot loose and dropped it on the coffee table.

"I can, in fact," David Samuel said. His smile projected a measure of sympathy. "It would be deceptive for me to say I feel no pleasure in this turn of events. But take heart that any malice toward you is minimal. It simply feels good to be wanted."

"Wanted where?" Phil shouted. "I gave you everything. I made you a manager."

Behind him, Lillian sobbed, "Tell him, David Samuel. Tell him who you're talking about."

David Samuel seemed to steel himself with a deep intake of air, then said, "I've been hired to apply my expertise in our industry by a supplier of restaurant parts."

"No," Phil croaked, working at the buttons of his collar to free his restricted throat.

"A charming Canadian gentleman named Jim Trebek."

"No!" It was a disbelieving exclamation, the full extent of expression his shock would allow. He tried again, but said only, "No!" And again, "No!"

"I'm afraid so, Dad. I feel ready for this challenge. And who knows? Maybe I'll even fly this coup, give you two lovebirds some privacy."

Lillian's sobs were quaking.

Phil had worked his shirt buttons loose and his restrictive cuffs, and he let the shirt drop to the floor, his body feeling overheated and feverish. "You…you can't," he managed. "Not with him."

"I'm not leaving you high and dry, Dad. I'm giving you notice," he reminded him. "There's plenty of time to find my replacement."

"That bastard," Phil managed. "Don't you see? He only wants you to jab at me. He's all the time jabbing me. How can you do this?" His breathing felt forced. He unbuckled his belt for the centimeter of freedom it allowed his diaphragm.

"Don't be petty, Dad."

"Look what you're doing to your father," Lillian wailed. "You're killing him."

Without realizing he'd undone their complicated series of fasteners, Phil's uncomfortable suit pants hit the floor. He staggered to his recliner and fell into it. "Still warm," he whispered of the chair, his face contorted in disgust, "it's still warm."

As if from a great distance, Phil heard Lillian declare, "I'm out of this. I've tried and tried, but this is the final straw. I'll be your mother, and I'll be your father's wife, and I'll keep happily ignorant of anything else going on between you. I mean it, David Samuel…"

Phil closed his eyes, and their voices receded, and it wasn't until his wife and son had left the room that he'd reconstituted enough to yell to no one, "It's about family. I had your back, bub. All these years. A home. Clothes. A job. I made you a manager." More quietly, he intoned, "How could you? How could you leave me?" But the only response was the stillness of the room.

Chapter 26

Lillian owned nice things: Swivel Sweepers, an H2O Dual Blast Steam Mop, two Bionic Steel Low-Volume Flow garden hoses, Hurricane Fur Wizard lint brushes, DLX Top-Fill Steam Humidifiers, Aqua Dog All-In-One Travel Bottle Bowls (in the event she ever took an interest in camping), Spin Spa Spinning Body & Facial Brush Sets. On and on. What she did not have she realized on the morning of Phil's debut speech, were nice clothes.

In her youth, she'd worn dresses. But, as she'd gotten older, her wardrobe had relaxed to a point that she now dressed almost exclusively in comfortable blouses and floral-patterned leggings. She found leggings to be nearly scandalous on young women, those with rounded thighs and youthful buttocks. Leggings on these women came off as a try-before-you-buy situation, showing men the landscapes that awaited them if they could ply their way in with drinks or charm, hinting at the warm private crevasses where they might burrow and curl and rest. Not so for Lillian who, at fifty-two, possessed the small, straight, curve-less body of a nineteen-eighties Nancy Reagan. She had nothing to show and nothing to sell: a simple, wholesome canvas for floral spandex.

Phil's speech was in three hours, and a thorough excavation of her closet had revealed only two choices. The light blue suit she wore to weddings and the black suit she reserved for funerals. Neither of these was entirely appropriate, but either of them, she suspected, would do. She measured the speech against these outfits' traditional functions: was this more of a marriage between Phil and his voters or the death of their lives before politics?

The death of their lives. The thought made her shiver. She still felt reservations about this turn of events, though she'd found a measure of peace with it since her heart to heart with Phil in the Fry Buddy freezer. It was, to her way of thinking, the duty of a wife to support her husband, presuming that husband was struggling for something noble, when the intentions behind his actions are pure and good. So, Lillian soldiered on.

The atmosphere had been icy in their Prosperity home in the days since David Samuel's bombshell, the organism of their shared space only limping along due to an untouchable aspect in David Samuel's demeanor following his professional victory combined with the private nature of Phil's pouting and Lillian's commitment to ignoring the posturing of both. The only real dust up had occurred the previous morning when Bernie the rabbit had been found scalped, his ears hanging by a narrow fuzzy tendril that ultimately detached in the physical passing around of the beast during the argument that ensued. David Samuel blamed Phil for an intentional act of vandalistic revenge. Phil blamed the unmooring on the unnatural stress that resulted from David Samuel's habit of goonishly carrying the rabbit around with him. True to her word, Lillian kept out of it. She had other concerns. Most immediately, what to wear to Phil's speech.

With the suits laid side by side on her bed, she grabbed her tablet from her nightstand and performed a quick image search for Janet Huckabee, the elegant wife of former Arkansas Governor Mike Huckabee. Reds and greens. Shoot. She searched again, this time for *attractive republican women*. The results that returned were a visual assault of image after image of Sarah Palin, bikini-clad and holding an oozy; S.E. Cupp, Photoshopped onto the body of a pornographic actress, firmly gripping a man's monstrous erection; Betty Ford, Photoshopped again, spread-eagle, opening her genitals in a two-handed tug, her posture like a bodybuilder captured in the middle of a butterfly curl. Lillian gasped and fervently backed out of the search. She cleared her throat and tried again, this time with more carefully considered search terms: *michele bachmann suit*. A gallery of images of the former Minnesota congresswoman returned, professionally dressed in reds and grays and greens and cremes. There was a single image on that first page of Bachmann in a black suit, none in light blue. Black it was.

Lillian returned the blue suit to the closet and slid into the black one, mindful to address every button and zipper to avoid a wardrobe malfunction.

She'd never been on a stage before. Her duty today, Phil had told her, was to simply stand behind him and smile. Still, she felt a flittering in her stomach. She wouldn't be alone, Phil assured her. Eddie Ellis would be standing at her side. Eddie Ellis, whom she'd yet to meet in person and still thought of as the man who would steal Phil Ochs, if only in name.

Looking in the mirror now, she saw that there was something sad about her reflection in the black suit. She suspected that it might be the many souls she'd seen off while wearing it, the half-dozen dead, painted faces the suit's cuffs had brushed against as she leaned in to deliver her final goodbyes. Lillian interlaced her fingers and held her arms against her abdomen. She smiled, cocking her head as if intently listening to words that were awing and revelatory. The effect was not that of a political candidate's supporting spouse. Rather, it was of a woman who was overly-excited to send off a departed loved one.

Lillian wished she had a campaign button, but Eddie had advised them to be cost prohibitive for a truncated, off-year race. An American flag brooch might work, but a search of her jewelry box found nothing along those lines. She opened each of her dresser drawers—other than the top drawer which held nothing but underwear on one side and rolled pairs of floral leggings on the other—then stepped back to appraise them for accessories. She had no elegant gloves, no strings of pearls. Glancing into the bottom drawer, she saw a blush of red amongst the matchless socks and button-less or ripped garments that she'd stowed away expecting to one day drum up the itch to mend them. She stooped and hooked the item with her finger and it came and came as she pulled, with a subtle, satisfying resistance.

A lightweight, bright red polyester belt scarf in satin and sheer net. She'd forgotten she'd bought it.

Lillian returned to the mirror and tied on the scarf, first tucking its ends down into her white blouse, then freeing them to hang loose along the slight protrusion of the black jacket's bust. She pawed it. Red, like Janet Huckabee. The difference it made was remarkable. She smiled, reached out to shake a spectral hand, waved to an enthusiastic voter. She turned her back to the mirror, then slowly and dramatically reached toward the mirror, like Jackie O grabbing for the discharged fragments of her husband's skull. Appraising herself in the mirror again, she giddily reached out for another hand, purring, "Vote Phil Ochs," in the husky, seductive voice she typically reserved for telephone customer support agents.

Downstairs, Phil's crotch was sweating, and something kept tapping him on the jaw. With each occurrence, his head jerked only to be reminded that the culprit was merely the sturdy collar of his new dress shirt. He was standing in his office, his suit pants being too uncomfortable to sit in when not forced to do so, talking to Eddie Ellis on speaker phone. On his laptop screen was the speech Eddie had emailed to him. He appraised it from the distance demanded by his myopia. "What's all this in red?" he said.

"Anything in red is just stage notes," Eddie said. "You don't read it out loud. Just pause or inflect or whatever it tells you to do."

"Mm-hmm. In this, whatever, *accomplishments* part, what about adding that I won Fry Buddy franchisee of the year in 2003 for the Southeast region? Lou Becker gave me the certificate himself." He glanced to where the prize was mounted on his wall beside a photo of the Fry Buddy CEO shaking his hand.

"Just trust me on this one Phil," Eddie said, then pacified him by adding, "we'll have more speeches to give. Maybe we can work that into one of those."

"Mm-hmm. How many people do you expect will show up to this thing?"

The location of the speech was Bobby's Original Mountain Music, an autumnal bluegrass festival that was held on five acres of barren farmland owned by Bobby Blue III, native son, former professional picker and grinner, and increasingly alarmist amateur conservative bloviator.

"Well," Eddie said, thinking, "I got you a prime space on the grounds, right between the cornhole super bowl and the hillbilly pig drop, which Bobby says are two of the most popular attractions on Saturday afternoon. Also, I had some stationary made up and some of those little golf pencils stamped with 'I Renamed Phil Ochs.' I figure we can set up a table at the back of the audience and let people suggest a name while you're speaking and drop it into the box. We're past five thousand entries online, so we don't need them, but it should draw some people in."

"What's a hillbilly pig drop?"

"Oh, well, as I understand it, they sell people numbered pieces of paper for a dollar each. Then a pig walks around on a giant bingo card and whoever bought the number the pig shits on wins a prize. But, I mean, classier than that. A real game of chance."

"Mm-hmm." Phil heard a child's voice and a rustling on Eddie's end of the line.

"Sorry about that, Phil. Listen, we should meet out there in about ninety minutes. Are you feeling good?"

Phil only shrugged, the question pushing his thoughts into the uncomfortable territory occupied by David Samuel's defection.

After a pause, Eddie continued, "Well, you're going to do great. I'll see you there, all right?"

"Yeah," Phil said then tapped his phone to end the call. As he stood reading the speech, his laptop screen darkened, and he had to wipe his fingers across its oily touchpad to restore it. Eddie had drafted the speech in an oversized font with tall, white spaces between each line that he said would help Phil keep his place in front of the crowd. He was halfway through the third page when he heard three crisp knocks on his office door. "Yeah?" he called.

The doorknob turned and in stepped Lillian, dressed in her funeral best with a red scarf tied around her throat. She entered in a way that could best be characterized as a reveal. "Well?" she said.

"Are you mourning the death of my political campaign?"

"No, it's a fashion. With the scarf, see?" she said, flittering it with her hands. "I think I once saw Libby Dole dressed in something almost exactly like this."

"Mm-hmm." Phil returned his attention to the

speech and, just as she turned to leave his office, he said, "Do you think I'm making a fool of myself?"

"No," she said, then added what he suspected to be a serviceable lie for his benefit: "I think you're trying to do a difficult thing for a wonderful reason."

"Mm-hmm," Phil said again, weakly.

Chapter 27

When Eddie and Penny arrived at the fairgrounds, she informed him, "It stinks here."

"I know," Eddie said. He'd sold this to her as a South Carolina Disneyland. And it was. If Mr. Disney had only six hours to set it up. And if he only needed entertainment enough for three wet days in November.

"It stinks like bung," Penny clarified.

"I know," Eddie said, "but I don't think you used that word right."

"I did. What word should I use?"

"An eleven-year-old girl? 'Poo.'"

"Ew, there's already mud on my shoe!"

"Maybe it's bung."

"I wouldn't be surprised."

When Cindy had dropped Penny off for her extended stay the previous afternoon, the girl's body language could have only better communicated her reluctance toward this arrangement by affecting a visible storm cloud above her head. She'd held onto her suitcase for a long time after her mother had gone, as if her preparedness for a change in plans might nudge that change into being. Soon enough, though, she'd seemed to accept her fate, if not entirely warmed to it.

They walked toward the festivities now. Eddie didn't do her the disservice of making her hold his hand. "After the speech, do you want to stick around and play some games or listen to the music?"

"Country music? No. What kind of games?"

"I don't know. There's corn hole and face painting…"

"Face painting isn't a game."

"And there's a pig that—never mind," he said, discouraged by the scowl she'd adopted. "Just be thinking about what you want to do after."

"What about during?"

"What do you mean?"

"What do I do?"

"I already told you. You do nothing. You just stand upfront until it's over."

"How long will it take?"

"I don't know. Twenty minutes?"

"Are you going to vote for him?"

"Of course, I'm going to vote for him. Are you going to vote for him?"

"No." She wrinkled her nose.

"Why not?"

"His sweet potato fries are, like, what is it, like, bitter?"

Did she remember that it was he who'd told her this? Doubtful, but it warmed him regardless. "That's true," he said.

"And I can't vote."

"Felony on your record?"

"What?"

"Nothing. Hey, I think this is us."

Past a sea of corn hole boards, there was a folding table and, set back against the tree line, a small plywood stage with a podium. On the table, Eddie threw down a bag and from it produced a cardboard box with a slit in its lid, four small tablets of paper and a box of golf pencils. He arranged the items on the table, then turned to Penny and said, "Do you want a pencil?"

She took one from him and studied it, then read "'I Renamed Phil Ochs.' What does that mean?"

"He doesn't have a middle name, so he's letting people pick one for him."

"What names can they pick?"

"Well, anything. At first. Then he chooses a few that he likes, and people vote for one of those. And then he makes that his real middle name."

Penny strained to understand. "So, wait—if people all vote for Beyonce, he'll change his name to Beyonce?"

"Well," Eddie said, "I don't know that Beyonce would be on the list he'd pick, but that's pretty much how it works, yeah."

"That's dumb."

"It isn't dumb. It's a gimmick."

"What's a gimmick?"

"A fun way to win an election. Here, do you want to suggest a name?" he said, handing her a tablet of paper.

Penny hesitated, then took the pad from him and scratched something onto it with the pencil. "Now what?"

"Now, pull off that page and fold it and stick it in this slot." She did as instructed. "See? Wasn't that fun?" Penny said nothing, her critical gaze had moved on to study some attraction in the distance. He noticed, however, when she secreted the pencil into the pocket of her pink pants. Eddie made a mental note to check the box tonight for an entry of 'Phil Bung Ochs.'

They passed an hour sitting on the wooden stage, eating corndogs and drinking Cokes. When Phil and Lillian arrived, Eddie stood and held out his arms, making a show of greeting them. One paper towel bundle jostled down his sleeve. "Who are these people?" he asked showily. "Have I told you, Senator Ochs, how well you clean up?"

In response, Phil barked, "My taint's so swampy I'm afraid an alligator might bite me in the ass."

It occurred to Eddie that, should he win, Phil might bristle when he learned that the uniform of the South Carolina state legislature was not a polyester tracksuit. "Lillian," he said, "you look lovely. It's nice to meet you."

"And you," she said, walking toward Eddie. In a fluid motion, she took him by the elbow and led him away from Penny and Phil. When they were a short distance away, she turned Eddie to her and said, "Eddie, he seems nervous to me. That's not common. Are you pushing him too hard?"

"Well, I mean, no, I don't think..." Eddie stammered.

"Keep an eye on that, would you? He's like a dog with a bone, and I love him for that, but if this were to get out of hand... Well, let's say I'll step in if I have to." She smiled warmly.

"Oh, well, right. No I agree," Eddie said.

"Good. That's all from me. It's very nice to meet you." She took his arm and led him back toward the others. "Is this your daughter?" she called sweetly.

"Uh, yes. Penny, this is Mr. and Mrs. Ochs. Mr. and Mrs. Ochs, Penny."

"My goodness!" Lillian said in a tone that was as excited as it had previously been scolding. "You are just the prettiest little thing." She walked to Penny and took a seat beside her on the stage.

"Thank you," Penny said.

Noticing the corndog in her hand, Lillian asked, "Do you like corndogs, honey? You know, I have a home corndog fryer—well, it's for corndogs and taco shells—but I make the best corndog you ever had in your life." She leaned in close to the girl. "There's a secret to it, you know."

"Okay," Penny said, tossing her eyes to the left, Eddie noticed, the same way her mother did when she was lying or in an uncomfortable situation from which she could not extract herself.

"You'll have to bring her over for my corndogs, Eddie," Lillian called. "She's a little angel."

"Thank you," Eddie said, thinking how earlier that morning his little angel had told him his homemade pancakes tasted like sadness. Then, hoping Lillian would hear him, he turned to Phil and asked, "Are you doing okay?"

"Not a lot of people here," Phil said, looking over the grounds.

The area between the stage and the folding table was large enough to hold around two hundred standing adults. Presently, the space was one-quarter filled, mostly with disinterested festival-goers taking advantage of the shaded space to drink their beer or bottled water or neon blue snowballs of shaved ice.

"Well, it's early still. We'll be fine, don't worry," Eddie said. And it was in his own appraisal of the grounds that he saw what his credulity at first dismissed as a mirage. He squinted and blinked, but the image held: a cameraman whose equipment was stickered with the logo of a top-three national news networks. "Holy shit," Eddie said.

"Daddy!" Penny scolded.

"Sorry, Worm," he said, moving toward the logo as if beckoned by it. Over his shoulder, he said, "Sorry, Lillian."

On more than one occasion, Eddie had awoken from dreams whose plot had simply been a national crew showing up at one of his candidate's events. He moved toward just such a camera now, awake and sweating cold beads down his sides. In the meager local press pool, the logo had the effect of a whale in a fishing pond. "You're here for us?" Eddie asked as he came upon the man who was twisting and calibrating his camera's various knobs and dials.

"Yup," the man said, staring through his viewfinder.

"Slow news day?" Eddie joked in a lame attempt to sound unaffected.

The man said nothing.

In response to this non-reaction, Eddie asked soberly, "Why are you here?"

"Politics is kind of our thing, man," the cameraman said in reply.

"But, I mean, I'm the campaign manager. I didn't know you were coming."

"Look, brother," the man said, lowering the camera to his side. "I've seen this before, so let me give you some advice: don't get excited, all right? Whatever I record here is probably never going to air. I've recorded weeks' worth of this kind of b-roll stuff and almost none of it even gets edited. It's just in case."

"Just in case what?"

"I don't know, just in case they need to fill three minutes somewhere; just in case a rival network airs something about it and we want to have our own footage in the can; just in case your guy goes full Budd Dwyer and shoots himself in the head on stage. You know, just in case."

"Did they send a reporter?"

"Talent don't come just in case. I'm all you get. If they decide to use it, the wizards will put a narrative to it later on. But, like I said, they won't use it, so don't worry about it."

"Why Phil, though? Why this race, I mean?"

The man sighed and flattened his lips before saying, "Who knows, brother? They get tips from local affiliates. Something somebody said got somebody's interest. I just aim and shoot."

"Okay," Eddie said and smiled. "Thanks." Behind him a crowd was beginning to form, likely hoping for a glimpse of a recognizable on-air personality. The cameraman noticed the crowd and, in Eddie's last up-close look at the man, he was deep into an I-hate-my-life roll of his eyes.

Eddie walked briskly back to the stage, making a mental note to send an arrangement of flowers to Mercedes McLeod.

Chapter 28

Once again, Penny was stranded. This had been the way for her in the last long year and a half: stranded at her grandmother's when she and her mother had moved out; at Gail's big house when they had moved in; stranded alone with Gail—who would be fine if she would just back off—and with Gail's dogs she didn't know, all in the name of what her mother called settling in; then stranded two times a month in her own bedroom in her old house, which she'd once confused with the safest place in the world. This time, she was stranded in the front row of a crowd between a big man in bibs and a woman who held her hand on her hip, and whose elbow kept grazing and lifting strands of Penny's hair.

Her dad had planted her here when it was time for the speech to start, telling her, "Don't worry, Worm, I'll be right up there. You'll be able to see me the whole time." Seeing him and having him were, of course, not the same thing. But then he'd left her. He stood, now, at the back of the stage, beside the old man and his wife. The wife waved at Penny secretly, and Penny returned the gesture half-way. Another man with a round belly and a tall, floppy, train conductor hat came onto the stage and shook hands with the woman, then with Penny's dad, then with the old man. He walked to the microphone and said:

"Welcome everybody. If you don't know me, I'm Bobby Blue, and I am so happy to see y'all out here with us today. Who here's looking forward to some live bluegrass music this weekend?"

As the crowd responded, he rubbed a palm over his belly, which made it look to Penny like he found their applause to be mouthwatering.

"That's just great," he continued. "It does my heart good to see all the little runts out there, come to hear real and traditional American roots music. You all mamas and daddies must be raising your babies right, I swear."

Penny was close enough to the front to be the subject of the man's hammy wink. She shot her eyes nervously to the left.

"You know, this is the fifth year that we put on this festival, and we got a real treat for you this time around. Ernie Holcomb, God rest his soul, was a friend of mine, a friend and a darned fine public servant too. And after his passing there wasn't anybody willing to step up to fill his shoes. Not one Republican—until we got the man standing right there behind me. And it's my honor that our little music festival has been chose by this man to make what I believe to be his first speech in this political campaign. If you care about wholesome family values, then you ought to thank this man, uh, Phil Ochs, for volunteering to be the only thing that stands between you and Democratic representation."

There was a smattering of boos from the crowd.

"Now, Democrats, you know I love you. If you're out there, I encourage you to stay. Stay and spend your money with us. Heck spend it all with us. And all I ask in return is one teensy favor: stay home on Election

Day, would you?"

A weak current of laughter rolled toward him.

"But I'm not going to take up any more of your time. I just wanted to stop over and welcome you and introduce this man. Before I go, though, just remember we got two more days packed full of music and fun. But, now, here he is, your next senator, Mr. Phil Ochs."

Bobby Blue stepped back from the microphone and shook the old man's hand with enthusiastic pumps, then he took a single step down from the stage and Penny watched him disappear through a maze of corn hole boards.

The old man came forward. He looked pale and dead, like a goldfish Penny once overfed: the same giant, wet eyes. He came to the microphone like he didn't really want to, and then he pulled folded white papers out of his coat pocket. But his hand shook and he dropped them. The pages scattered. One went over the edge of the stage close to Penny. He stared down at the pages like they were nasty bugs or a dog that had bit him. Her dad stepped forward and knelt to grab them, but two more pages went over the edge then danced off to play corn hole. Beside Penny, the man in bibs snorted. Her dad stood up with a bright red face, then backed up beside the old man's wife while the old man frowned at him—her dad, maybe, a second dog that had bit him.

Penny had never seen anyone give any kind of a speech, except at school assemblies, but this was clearly tragic.

"Thanks," the old man said. "How's it going?"

"Fine," a voice said from the crowd, and people laughed.

The old man dusted something off the podium with his palm. Behind Penny, the crowd felt quiet and full, pushing toward her with something other than their bodies. The old man's wife seemed nervous, looking over to frown at Penny's dad too.

"Do…uh…do you folks know Dave Thomas?" the old man said.

Her dad's smile looked fixed and fake and was partially covered by a hand over his lips.

"He was…err…he was the founder of Wendy's. I don't know if he was a Republican. I know his daughter was adopted, so he had one of those alternative lifestyle situations, but he was a great entrepreneur. But, Dave Thomas, he was the founder of Wendy's, like I said. I bring him up because Dave Thomas is a man I respect. A great job-creator, Dave Thomas. And, you know…I've always been proud to be one too, a job creator. But…you know…a guy like Dave Thomas, he created jobs all over the world. Me, I spent my life creating jobs right around here. Your jobs, maybe, and your kid's jobs."

Penny didn't clap at this, but some of the other people did, and that seemed to make the old man relax a little.

"You hear about this deal to give me a middle name?

"Rename Phil Ochs," the woman beside Penny yelled and held up a little pencil.

"It's a hell of thing to go through life with the same name as a guy like that. A hell of a hard time. But I overcame it. Because it's all about winners and losers. Life is, I mean. And you can believe me, I'm a winner."

This triggered applause that was rounder, more filled out.

"I don't always get credit for it. It's always been like that for me. But now I'm running in this thing against a Democrat," he continued, prompting a light hissing from some of the crowd. "Aren't we all? Running against Democrats. I don't know much about this one I'm running against if you want to know the truth of it. But, as it happens, her brother-in-law works in the same industry as me. He's this Canadian clown that's always stealing my people away to work at his outfit. So, I don't know, but when it comes to stealing jobs, I'd guess that's a trait that runs in the family."

The crowd liked this, and the old man now appeared to Penny different from when he started, happier to be there. Her dad, too, had started to look less like throwing up. And that, for Penny, was when it got boring.

She dropped her head and studied the differences in the toes on the sandaled feet of the man and woman she stood between: hers prim and polished, his overgrown and gnarled. She noticed a tear in the red, white, and blue paper skirt that was taped to the edge of the stage, tried for a while to make it tear more with only her mind. She looked at her father with a how-much-longer-do-we-have-to-do-this stare, but he didn't notice her. Then, she looked at the old man's wife, whose eyes were also wandering. She was fingering the red scarf around her neck, trying and retrying arrangements for her hands.

While Penny was watching her, the wife looked across the audience and met her eyes. The wife smiled. Penny looked away, and then back. The wife's hands were now one over the other on her belly, and she lifted the top hand slightly to reveal the fingers and thumb of the other, then quickly opened and closed them like a talky mouth at the expense of her husband. Penny smiled, and so did the wife. They each looked at the serious man who'd brought them, then back to each other. Penny feigned sleepy eyes and a head too heavy not to topple. The speech made applause, and this time Penny joined in, properly, with her chin up, delicately smacking fingers to palm. Lillian laughed, and Penny saw her dad notice, but they each pretended nothing was up, and he returned his eyes to the podium.

The speech went on, and the old man sounded angry now in his voice, and the crowd got angry too. The wife was watching the speech again, so Penny's eyes resumed wandering. She made patterns out of the holes in the distant corn hole boards, looked again at the toes, the torn stage skirt, the folded speech papers gently flapping in the grass. But her eyes kept coming back to the wife, checking to see if she was watching. Finally, she was again. She rolled her eyes just a little for Penny's benefit. Penny returned the gesture, bigger and more dramatic. The wife looked at Penny's dad, and then out into the crowd, and when she seemed sure no one other than Penny was watching her, she stuck out her tongue at the girl in a brief, darting motion. And it was a video still of that split-second of exposed pink tongue that hovered beside the national news anchor's head as she finished the C-Block of Monday evening's seven o'clock news broadcast.

Chapter 29

Lillian Ochs making faces, that's what got them on the big stage. The renaming contest had been interesting, Eddie supposed. Interesting enough to send a network camera to cover Phil's speech. But it was the candidate's wife's dry, pink tongue that proved to be the shriveled cherry needed to top it off.

Eddie wasn't bothered. Since the network's number-three pundit had run the video as a *Lighter Side of the News*-style commercial bumper—a broadcast that was re-aired for a second and then a third time during the overnight hours—Phil's website had repeatedly crashed under the strain of national curiosity. Upgraded web hosting had been required. Eddie's phone rang with congratulations from state politicos who would never have taken his calls the day before. Their website saw an immediate and measurable increase in donations. Most unusual, a producer for *Chat!*—a national afternoon talk show featuring a kettle of career B-list and one-time A-list female celebrities—had called to pitch the idea of profiling Phil on the day of his legal name change, culminating with a remote live interview with the newly rebranded man.

Phil Ochs had become an overnight minor national oddity. And in a popularity contest, Eddie reasoned, this was a better pedigree than the low-key career in civil service that Gilda Cranston could boast.

Just before noon, sitting cross-legged on his sofa, his laptop propped on a pillow, Eddie refreshed the site's Admin page for an updated total of contributed names: eighty-six thousand validated entries. When selling this stunt to Phil, Eddie had committed to personally winnowing the full list in pursuit of the best fifty names. For the sake of time, however, and because Phil would never know the difference, he now copied the latest fifty into a Word document, deleted the rest, then shut down the contest to new submissions. He linked the document in an email to Phil, then pounded out a request that he promptly narrow it to his top five so the finalists could be published and made open to voting.

As he hit *Send*, Eddie's phone began to chime. The name that appeared on its display screen was so unexpected that he experienced a momentary sense of vertigo when he read it—a swimmy, doubled-vision feeling as if from the glitch of his reality being overlaid onto one in which this call might reasonably come. He hadn't heard from his political mentor in nearly a decade and, having assumed he never would again, it felt like a lie when he swiped the screen to signal his acceptance. "Linwood Barth?" he said, incredulous.

"Ellis, you fucking shitbird. How are you, my friend?" The Louisiana melody in the voice was like hearing a song pick up at just the moment Eddie had turned it off all those years before.

"I'm fine, Linwood. It's been…years. Why are—what's going on with you?"

"Me? Oh, I'm just calling to shit in your Toasty Oats. But, I figured we could visit for a minute before I take a squat on your table—that's the gentleman in me. How's the wife?"

"Gone," Eddie said, perplexed.

"Hell's bells, you don't say. What about your son?"

"She's fine."

"Roger that," Linwood said.

Eddie waited for him to continue, but soon enough realized that they were engaged in an artful silence, one that was meant by Linwood to discomfit him. Bewildered as he was by why this ghost would call to impose this on him, Eddie understood that the position of strength would go to the man who waited out the awkwardness longest. He eyed the drinking glass from last night's vodka on the television tray and absently wished it full. After barely a minute, he broke and said, "So, Linwood, about my Toasty Oats…"

Linwood performed a victorious chuckle. So fixed was this man in Eddie's past that he couldn't help but visualize his own younger self sitting across from him, smiling at his rhetorical win in whatever bygone year Linwood was calling from. "So, you want to get right down to it, eh Ellis? I can respect that," he said. "Well, we got us a situation, you and me. Seems your little project has created a bit of a stir in the inner circles—a few of which circles, believe it or not, I've yet to be ejected from. You done good with that naming thing, I'll hand you that." If he meant to communicate sincerity in this comment, the sentiment was muted beneath his accent's cartoonish embroidery.

There were only a few places this conversation could go, and Eddie dreaded them all. He pictured a Republican establishment panicked by Phil's novelty, rushing to install a rival candidate, and hiring Linwood to run the campaign against them. "What is this, Linwood?" Eddie said.

"My hand to God, man," Linwood continued, unfazed, "I've signed on to my share of stinkers, but the sweet potato man? That's the best you could find? You're going to have to put a second mortgage on that house to pay for all the turd polish you been waxing this clown up with."

"He's a good candidate."

"He's a polished clown turd."

"You have someone better? Is that what this is?"

In response to this question, Linwood pulled back, his tone softened and slyly casual. "That's a way of looking at it, I guess," he said.

"Meaning what?" The stress of this game was pulling Eddie's body forward on the sofa, his chin now resting on the upper edge of the laptop screen, lowering incrementally with the screen as it slowly collapsed under the weight.

"Well, young man, it's just that with Mr. Potato Head in the mix, Gilda Cranston doesn't look like such a sure thing anymore. Of course, looks can be deceiving, as you and I both know. There isn't any real jeopardy for her here. But, nevertheless, she's concerned. I made sure of that even before your little media blowup. Made her see the soundness of investing in a campaign manager."

"You're managing Cranston?" The laptop screen snapped shut and Eddie sat up with alarm.

"Eight days on the job already." Linwood confirmed. "How are them Toasty Oats tasting?"

"But…you're a Republican." Eddie heard how naïve this sounded, but the sentiment behind it was genuine.

"Yeah, but more than that I'm an old fuck," Linwood said with a new philosophical dreaminess in his voice. "And as much as I hate to say it, over the years Ella got to be an old fuck too. And sometimes we old fucks get pancreatic cancer, which happens to be the kind of one Ella turned out to be. Regardless of my actions here, your Fry Guy will fizzle and Cranston will win. The only variable is do I make a move to take possession of every dollar I can snag riding that sure thing to the state assembly. The answer is: yes, I do. Which I have to assume, Ellis, is a plan that sounds familiar to you?"

From Eddie's freezer, the vodka bottle cleared its throat, suggesting that it could stand to lose a slug in sympathy with this trouble.

"Ellis?" Linwood said. "You still with me, Gravy? Tell you what: what's a good email address? I got something I want to debut for you. A coming attractions sort of thing."

With a rote detachment, Eddie recited the address, to which Linwood responded, "Giddy up," and disengaged the line.

Within five minutes, the email arrived. Its subject line read, 'Toasty Oats,'" but the link it contained was titled, "I survived Phil Ochs." With a trembling finger, Eddie tapped the link and the rectangle of his video player fitted itself onto the screen.

The scene opened with a medium shot of a wiry, scarecrow-like man standing in front of what was recognizably a Fry Buddy restaurant, though no identifying signage was visible. "My name is Tony," the man said. "I used to be a manager at Fry Buddy. But then I survived Phil Ochs." There was a cut to a similar shot, a similar parking lot, where a woman who called herself Margaret delivered this same message. Again and again, in parking lot after parking lot, the script was repeated by Phil's former managers. A succession of anecdotes followed, delivered in their various, overlapping voices, detailing threats and outbursts and breakdowns, each casting Phil as a mad king. Their stories came faster and faster, overlapping into an ultimate unintelligible muddle of rising and falling emphasis as a shot tightened on a lone French fry, abandoned on parking lot blacktop, one end stepped on and exploded and strangely affective as an emblem of emotional pain. Then abruptly the voices shut off and the screen went black. "I'm Gilda Cranston," came a voice from that void, sounding powerful in its relative crispness and clarity, "and I approve this message."

Chapter 30

They needed a counter to Gilda Cranston's attack ad to be on the air by the week's end, and Phil insisted that the testimonial to his character be delivered by his restaurant supplier, Jerry Tatum. When Eddie gently pointed out that Jerry was missing two teeth in the front and had a lisp that made half of what he said completely unintelligible, Phil had said, "No, not completely. Sometimes, you can't get it the first time, but if you ask him to repeat it you can usually figure out what he's saying. Once people see it a couple times, they'll understand him, probably." Eddie had then suggested one of Phil's employees instead, possibly someone pretty and young and sympathetic, a hot single mother type. Preferably from an abusive relationship. A hot, abused, single mother opioid addict—prior to coming to Phil and Fry Buddy, of course—one who managed, under Phil's tutelage, to turn around her fortunes. But Phil wouldn't have it: "That Canadian brother-in-law of hers is trying to put Jer out of business and he stole my staff away and put them in that damned commercial. And now he's gone and taken…" Phil continued, then he abruptly stopped and reddened. "Never mind that. Jerry gets it. He's the one I want." So, Eddie re-signed himself to Phil's wishes, attempted to convince himself that Jerry Tatum would play as a genuine, salt of the earth type, and then he set about the challeng-ing work of writing a script that included no iteration of the letter S:

~~Phil Ochs is a,~~ ~~I've known Phil since,~~ I've worked with Phil for ~~years~~ a long time. ~~He's~~ I've never known a man to work ~~so, as,~~ harder. I've never known a man ~~who's~~ to be ~~smarter~~ more intelligent than Phil. He ~~loves, cares,~~ can ramble on about ~~his~~ family and ~~his,~~ our community. Don't believe the attack ~~ads, commercials,~~ commercial ~~lies~~ narrative. Phil ~~is, expresses, embodies, shows,~~ will ~~always represent~~ be the epitome of good judgement with a ~~strong,~~ firm but affectionate demeanor. ~~He's my,~~ ~~We're friends,~~ I'm ~~his~~ a good friend ~~of his~~ to Phil and I know ~~his,~~ ~~the man's,~~ the character of the man. In the upcoming election, I'm proud to vote for him. You ~~should,~~ can too. Do the ~~best,~~ right thing for your family: ~~vote for our friend, Phil for Senate,~~ vote for our friend, Phil, a ~~business,~~ job creator and a ~~decent, respectable, wise, sympathetic,~~ okay guy.

"Lordy, that wath fun!" Jerry beamed after com-pleting his testimonial with the videographer, "Thith ith a real honor. I ain't never been on video before."

"Don't mention it, Jer," Phil said.

From there, they were to travel to the Columbia store to get silent footage of Phil in his element: inter-actions with customers and staff that would play him up as a serious and respected business man and limit the amount of screen time devoted to Jerry Tatum's toothless face.

In Eddie's car, with Phil in the passenger seat and the hired videographer in the back, Eddie said, "That went okay, I thought. Right?"

"Yeah, Jer's all right."

"What do you think? Do you think it went well?"

Eddie called to the backseat.

The videographer shrugged.

"Oh, Phil, I got your five names posted and open to voting this morning. I'm excited to see where it stands tonight." Upon receiving Eddie's list of fifty names the previous afternoon, Phil's response had been surprisingly prompt. "Since we have some good momentum right now, I only left the voting open through the end of the week. I figured we can work it out with *Chat!* to record you filling out your petition with the civil court sometime next week. Or maybe we'll just do it at the DMV; maybe that's more relatable. What do you think? I'm guessing they'll probably just arrange for a camera crew from their local affiliate, rather than fly someone out. Either way, it'll look good. That's all that matters. The pageantry of it. The optics. Sound good?"

Phil said nothing.

Eddie's phone began to vibrate in the cup holder where he'd stowed it. It was Cindy. With an awkward, apologetic snicker, he said, "Sorry, Phil, I have to take this. Penny's mom."

"Mm-hmm."

"Cindy? Is everything okay?"

"Yeah," she said in a voice that seemed to him thin and intended to communicate some form of minor personal grief.

Perhaps Eddie had grown with this recent period of success, or maybe his refusal to immediately follow up by asking her what was wrong was in service to his passengers. He wasn't sure. But, in either case, he remained chipper: "We're driving. We're going to get some b-roll for a campaign commercial. Is that right?" he called to the back. "B-roll?"

The videographer shrugged.

"Who are you talking to?" Cindy asked, sounding imposed upon.

"The camera guy, he's here. Phil's here." He turned toward Phil and tilted the phone from his ear thinking

Phil might greet her, but he said nothing. "Phil says hi."

"Okay. Hi," she said and sighed audibly in his ear.

And with that sound, his resolve crumbled. In as cheery a voice as he could manage, Eddie said, "You good? You sound a little off." Ahead of them, Columbia's porcelain Fry Buddy sign came into view on its tall pole.

"Fine," Cindy said. "Just a little homesick, I think. I miss Penny. Has she straightened out at all?"

"Yeah, she's great. I mean, you know, difficult still, but great. Actually, we have a speech at the Elks Club tomorrow night, and Phil's wife said she'd watch her while we're gone. She's mad about Penny. You'd like her." He looked at Phil and winked, but Phil missed it, his eyes fixed on his porcelain sign.

"For how long?" Cindy asked, her tone of self-pity transitioning to one of accusation through that practiced mechanism they'd built together when their marriage had started going wrong.

"It'll only be for a couple of hours, and we'll be back early. That's okay, right?"

"I mean—yeah, sure. I trust your judgement, Eddie." In spite of himself, his chest warmed at this slight reassurance. "It isn't that."

"So then, what is it?"

"I don't know. I'm just thinking I should come home early."

In a risen, hoarse whisper meant to disguise confrontation from his passengers, Eddie said, "Cindy, if it's a problem to have someone you don't know babysit Penny, just say so. Don't do that passive thing though. It doesn't help anything."

"No, honestly Eddie, it isn't that. I just—I feel like coming home."

Eddie turned into the largely empty Columbia Fry Buddy parking lot and turned into a space, then sat with her revelation for a moment. "Okay," he said.

A thread of suspicion remained in his voice. "Then, let me know what you decide, I guess. But we're here now," he continued hurriedly, "I'll have to let you go. I can call you later if you want."

"Oh," she said, seeming surprised to be dismissed, "okay. No, that's fine. I'll call you and let you know what's happening."

"Sounds good," he said, employing this modern, casual, catchall phrase to punch her slightly, an illustration that he could leave her feeling as marginalized and inconsequential as she'd made him feel these long months. A verbal power grab. "Bye, Cindy," he said and disengaged the call. He knew that later this evening, with vodka in him, his mind would be compelled to theorize on what this call had really been about. To his passengers, he turned and smiled showily and said, "We all ready?"

It was two-thirteen when they walked into the restaurant, just after the lunch rush had subsided. Phil led the group behind the counter and the registers to the open area behind the kitchen where there was room to confer on a plan of action. "So, what do I do?" he said, but then the trio's attention was taken by the sounds of footsteps and heavy breathing echoing up the back stairs.

"David Samuel!" Phil spat when his son appeared on the landing. "What the hell are you doing here? You don't work today."

"The shift manager called off," the big man said, huffing from exertion. "I'm store manager, aren't I, for the time being? It was my duty to come in."

"Nobody called me," Phil said suspiciously.

"He did call you, actually. More than once, I'm told. You just didn't answer. And, anyway, I have it handled."

Phil pulled his phone from his pocket then turned it to Eddie, glaring at him over his three missed calls. It was Eddie who'd suggested that he mute the device during Jerry's taping.

"And what exactly are you doing?" David Samuel said, sizing up Eddie and the videographer with narrowed eyes.

"A campaign ad," Eddie said.

"I'm sorry, you are?" David Samuel said.

Eddie extended his hand. "I'm Eddie Ellis," he said with a professional smile. "Nice to meet you."

"Oh," David Samuel said, "the campaign manager."

"Right. And who are you?" he asked, dropping his unwelcome hand but not his smile.

"David Samuel Ochs," he said with offense, as if a reputable person would have known without being told. "I'm the son of this one." He thumbed acknowledgment toward Phil, who winced as if the flicking gesture had splattered him with something vile.

Eddie noted this reaction, but trudged ahead saying, "We'll, it's nice to meet you, David Samuel Ochs. Are you excited about your dad's campaign?"

David Samuel snorted.

"Well," Eddie said after giving David Samuel a few unclaimed beats to clarify, "Okay then."

"None of this intimidates me," David Samuel said, indicating the camera and the videographer and Eddie, himself.

"Right," Eddie said, confused.

"Knock off the goony act, traitor," Phil said to David Samuel. "This guy's going to tape me walking around, talking to customers and that. All you need to do is stay out of the way, got it?"

"Fine," David Samuel said, pushing between them. "Just keep it brief and try not to get in the way of my staff. This is a place of business, after all."

Eddie moved beside Phil and together they watched David Samuel lumber around a corner and disappear. "Impressive kid," Eddie said.

"'My staff,'" Phil repeated. "The Judas." Then to

Eddie, he said, "Let's get this over with."

Having arrived after the lunch rush, the dining area was two-thirds empty, and the guests who remained were largely older retirees who were not bound to the rigid eating schedule of Columbia's working class. The camera captured Phil interacting with several of these older patrons, standing and shaking their hand, or sitting across from them at their booths, chatting. Eddie had assured Phil that it didn't matter what they talked about, since these clips would be silent, laid over the monologue Jerry had recorded earlier. Phil took this as an allowance to silently move his mouth while staring the perplexed old folks in the eye, nodding his head and, on occasion demanding they do the same. "Nod," he would say unexpectedly while silently exercising mouth shapes, "smile."

While Phil was seated across from one grandmotherly customer, the camera targeting her face caught David Samuel strolling slowly and unnaturally into frame, through the windows behind the bench, straight-backed on the store's sidewalk, arms held stiff at his sides, in an Alfred Hitchcock-style cameo, left to right, then gone again. The same happened when Phil was pretending to council a young man at the grill press: David Samuel, right to left, posture straight as an arrow. When David Samuel bombed a third scene, his father broke character and turned to his son and shouted, "Creeping Jesus, you back-stabbing spook! Why don't you give it a rest?"

"Phil," Eddie said, pulling him aside, "why don't we do a scene with him? He seems to want to be in the thing."

"You're out of your mind. The kid's got a head like an ugly fruit. The TV channels would have to censor the goddamn thing."

"Aw, that's not fair, Phil. He's interesting. I mean, the hair and everything. What is he, like a goth or something?"

"It's not a movement he's a part of. He's just a moron."

Eddie was struck by Phil's harshness, but it only made him push harder. "Let's try it, Phil. Maybe we use it, maybe we don't. But we're here, we have the camera…"

"We won't use it."

"Fine. But let's shoot it anyway. David," he called quickly, before Phil could protest, "we want to get a scene with you and your dad."

"Oh, do we?" David Samuel said, gliding toward them. "It's David Samuel, by the way."

"Sorry. But, yeah, come over here and stand beside your dad. That's the way. Phil, you two just…improvise. Whatever you want to do."

David Samuel shouldered up to Phil at register four. "Dad," he said in greeting.

"Let's make this clean and quick, kid. You and me, we'll look down at the register here, then I say something funny and you laugh. Got it?"

"Look down and laugh," David Samuel repeated, shaking his head as if to inspire an accidental perfection in his hair. "I'm sure I can manage."

"All right," Phil said to the videographer, "do it."

Phil and his son stared down at a common point hidden from the camera behind the counter. Phil adopted unique and varied mouth shapes while continually murmuring to his son, "Don't screw this up, don't screw this up…" David Samuel was excellent: looking down, interested, then up at his father, back down and up again like he was truly learning from him. It was by far the best shot of the day, until Phil whispered, "Now," and David Samuel's face twisted with confusion.

"Now what?" he said.

"Laugh, dummy," Phil instructed from the side of his mouth.

"But you didn't say the funny thing."

"There isn't a funny thing. Just pretend there is."

"Oh," David Samuel said with an expression that looked to Eddie like repulsion. "Okay." Then he let out a laugh so forced and fake that Eddie called cut.

"That was great guys, until the end. Are we clear now on what needs to happen?"

"This time tell a joke," David Samuel said.

"I don't know a joke. Just pretend I said something funny," Phil said.

"Just pretend, Dave," Eddie repeated.

"David Samuel," David Samuel corrected.

"Sorry, David Samuel. This will be video only, so it only has to look good."

"I know that," he said in a bitter tone that Eddie found reminiscent of his father. "But, I can't just laugh if nothing's funny. It won't look real."

"Just smile, then. You don't have to laugh. Hey, there's no pressure here. You two just need to be on the same page. Phil, David Samuel is just going to smile, okay?"

They repositioned themselves. But before filming resumed, David Samuel said, as if breaking bad news, "I think it would look so much better if it ended with me laughing. Just give him something funny to say."

"We don't have anything prepared for that, David Samuel," Eddie said.

"Oh, don't you?" David Samuel said as if cataloguing this as proof of Eddie's incompetence. "And you?" he asked the videographer, who shook his head once. "Good team, Dad."

"That'll do!" Phil said, slapping the register with finality, "We're through beating this horse. Cut," he added, slicing his neck with his finger and eying the videographer whose camera was already resting on the restaurant counter.

Eddie also felt done: with Phil and with David Samuel and with their shared familial strangeness. More so than fatigue, what he felt in that moment was spite toward the wreck of them. He hadn't fully appreciated how everything with Phil had to be done the hard way until that dilemma had been compounded with the entrance of David Samuel. As a man with an estranged family, Eddie found it upsetting, the volatility evident when he stood father next to son. And it was with a peevishness toward them both that he smiled then and sweetly pleaded, "No, David Samuel can do it. He wants to do it, right David Samuel? It's easy—ha, ha, ha, see? Ha, ha, ha—easy, right? Come on let's do it one more time."

"Nah," Phil said. He'd taken several steps away from his son. "He won't do it. He'll screw it up. On purpose, probably. The kid's got it in for me. Make it work with what you have."

David Samuel eyed his father angrily.

Eddie paused, accepting that it really wasn't important to push this further. "Okay," he relented. "Let's pack it up."

"Fine," said David Samuel. He took a sideward step toward Phil. "Pick up the camera," he snapped impatiently. "Let's get it done."

The videographer glanced quickly at each of the three men, found no evidence of instruction in any of their faces, and so raised and aimed his camera.

"If you're doing something here, boy…" Phil said into his son's chest.

"Break a leg, Dad."

"Are we ready?" Eddie said. "Okay, I guess let's try it again."

So, again they began to pantomime, and again David Samuel was excellent. Looking down, he feigned interested. Looking up, understanding. The time came, and Phil's face brightened in a clear invitation to put his on-video pupil at ease. It was not a friendly look, so much as an expressive adjustment from stern to stern and crazed. But David Samuel took the cue to laugh, or to silently pretend to do so, opening a half-moon of blackness across the lower third of his face, shaking his shoulders up and down, jiggling the various parts of himself that hung loose inside the front of his shirt. At the sight of this, Phil seemed to soften too, briefly, if only from the relief of it being over—until David Samuel abruptly threw an arm around his father's shoulder, pulled him in close, and planted a real and audible kiss on his cheek.

"Creeping Jesus!" Phil shouted, pushing his son away.

David Samuel tossed his head cattily and walked away from the group of them. As he did, he called, "I guess you were right, Dad: I screwed it up after all." And then, he disappeared into the kitchen.

Chapter 31

Collin felt like shit.

It wasn't like he hadn't broken up with girls before. Obviously. But, when he'd done the deed those times, he was legit over them. This wasn't even the same thing at all. He hadn't thought about it until he shot off his mouth and dumped Ruzanna, but thinking about it ever since then, he saw they could have stayed together maybe even as long as senior year.

His mom and dad were being nice about it. But weirdly, like, courteous? Professional, like it was their job to be distantly polite to their son who was all fucked up over a girl. He knew how they really felt, though. Their thing was always grades and sports and scholarships. No girls in that equation. Girls were bad news. "No offense intended to that very sweet girl," he could picture his mom saying of the very sweet Ruzanna.

It was Family Night Out and they were at Cheddar's, which is what Tom picked. Mom and Dad's politeness that night was in the form of ignoring Collin outright, even though he slumped in his chair, stretching his legs straight out under the table, raiding everybody's personal leg space. Collin brooded into his phone. Mom and Dad and Tom were all watching the same basketball game on three different screens that hung on the walls. Being invisible was better than a lecture or a heart to heart, he guessed. Or maybe not really, but whatever.

A waitress brought two plates of loaded potato skins and set them so everyone could reach. When Collin just sat there, his dad was like, "Come on, Coll, dig into these," and then he kept that grin on his face like he took Collin ignoring him to mean, "Sure, Dad! Sounds great! Gosh, I love you guys!"

Then Tom started being a shit. Like, forking a potato onto Collin's little app plate and pushing it toward him, going, "Here you go, buddy! Nothing like Vitamin C to cure a broken heart. What? You don't want it? Well, okay. Thanks, man," and shoving the whole thing into his mouth.

"To-om," Mom said with that two-syllable thing.

Tom did that throat-sucking, voice-changing giggle he had lately, which who could eat after that anyway, right?

"Oh, can you believe this clown?" Dad said right then all spiteful. Collin thought he meant Tom, which was a weird enough thing to make him look up from his phone. He saw that everyone else took it that same way, both Mom and Tom, himself, staring at Dad too. But Dad was shaking his head at the TV, which made it pretty obvious that that's what had made him yell out. When Collin looked where his dad's eyes were, his face went numb like that time at A.J.'s when they made Irish Car Bombs.

It was a picture of Ruzanna's boss. On the television. At Cheddar's.

Collin tried to read the commercial's closed captioning, but there was no way his brain could fuck with deciphering words right then. "What's this a commercial for?" he said, and his voice must have been screechy or loud or whatever because it was all of a sudden his turn to have the whole table staring at him.

"It's that fast food joker that's running for Senate," Dad said in his calm 'talk to your children like respectable adults' voice as if he couldn't see that Collin was bugging out. "If you ask me, I'd say a man that works for Fry Buddy isn't fit to cater the Senate, let alone serve the legislature."

As much as his head was swimming, there must have been a part of Collin that kept track of what was going on around him, because he registered Mom's cold stare at Dad like, 'Fry Buddy equals the girl that shall not be named,' and then Dad's face back at her like, 'Lordy, Lordy, I'm a bumbling fool.'

"Collin, honey," Mom said in the soft voice of damage control, "are you going to get some ribs? Did you need to look at the menu?"

But Collin couldn't answer. On the commercial, there was now a black and white picture of some old lady with her tongue out, and it was legit ominous. Like, mocking-him-from-all-sides-of-the-restaurant ominous. Because the thing of it was that Collin had already been thinking about karma the last couple days in the sense that Oswald Park had been uncool, and maybe that's why the universe made him dump Ruzanna when that wasn't really what he wanted to do. Seeing the old man on a television at Cheddar's, and then that old woman looking at him with her tongue out? It was like his distress had conjured up a poltergeist that had gotten outside of him, free and flying.

The commercial ended, and Collin looked over to Tom like he might get it since he'd been at the park too. But Tom obviously hadn't made any connections between the commercial and Ruzanna's boss. And he didn't know about Collin taking out the man's journal every night and reading it like some kind of obsessed fanboy.

"You're losing your shit, bro," Tom said.

"Thomas David Radaszewski!" Mom said.

But Tom was right: all shit was lost. Right then, Collin knew his secret was too big. He needed someone to forgive him, or at least for someone to know in detail exactly why he was unforgivable. He wasn't stupid. He knew it might be his teenaged broken heart talking. But when it told him that absolution could only come from Ruzanna, he didn't question it was true.

*   *   *

He got out of basketball practice by lying about a dentist appointment. He'd forged a note, but Coach didn't even ask for it. It was still in his pocket when he pressed up against the brick wall outside the east entrance, out of the way. It was two-fifteen: end of the day for non-athletes. The bell rang and they came like a pipe had burst, on and on out the doors. No one saw him where he stood, which was the point. When he saw Ruzanna, he came off the wall and called, "Ruz! Ruz!" until she heard him.

She got out of the stream and asked him why he wasn't at practice, and he told her he had something to say that might take a minute. She was like, "I'm not allowed to talk to you. You got me in so much trouble, Collin. You don't even know," which hurt on account of he didn't want to have gotten her in trouble and because she made a special point not to call him 'Radish,' which is what she would have called him before. Still, she leaned her backpack up against the wall like, "I'm listening." He told her he was sorry, babe—which was habit—and that it would only take a minute.

"Hurry up. I'm going to miss my bus," is how she gave him the go ahead to lay it all out for her.

"It's about the money. Where I got it from."

"I don't care, Collin," she said, which he didn't buy.

"It's not my business now."

"Your boss gave it to me."

The way she went all ridged said this was the stunner he knew it would be, even though it turns out she misunderstood. "David Samuel gave it to you?" she said. "Why would he give you all that money?"

It was a name that was hard on the ears on account of he knew it from a poem in the journal called, "I'm David Samuel, Hear Me Roar." So, right away, Collin disabused her, like, "No, your boss, Phil. He's running for Senate." He thought this would be another bombshell, but this time he was wrong.

"Yeah, I know. Everyone knows that."

"What do you think it means?"

"What are you talking about, Collin? Why would Phil give you all that money?"

He didn't answer because all of a sudden his gut said maybe this wasn't worth it after all.

"Collin," she repeated, "why did Phil give you that money?"

"It was for, like, a job. I thought it was no big deal. But I don't know now. I'm all fucked up about it. Remorseful, I guess."

"Remorseful for what? What was the job?"

He spit it out like here goes nothing: "He wanted me to, like, beat someone up. To teach him a lesson."

"Oh my God! And you did that?"

Collin exposed himself by opening his arms like when a magician shows you his hat is empty and on the level. Except that Collin's hat really was. "I feel terrible about it, Ruz. I feel really awful."

"Who was it?" she demanded.

Collin fished out his phone from his pocket. He got to the video and started it and turned the phone so she could watch. Over at the buses, air brakes were starting to puff and squeal to tell stragglers it was time to get on the stick.

He watched her squint at the jerking, blurry images of grass and sky, trying to make out the out-of-focus faces and too-close body parts. Then she went white in her face and Collin looked away.

"David Samuel?" she gasped. "He paid you to beat up his David Samuel? *You beat up David Samuel?*" In all his life, he'd never felt worse than right then, looking at Ruzanna's expression. His dumb ass had done something so bad it turned her pretty face into the ugly, angry one she was showing to him now.

Right when the first bus pulled away, she was like, "Oh my God, Collin," looking over her shoulder and stepping away from him. "Just—oh my God."

"I'm so sorry." He wasn't blubbering yet, but he was close.

"Wait," she said, like there was something even worse about it than she'd thought of at first. "You thought this was no big deal? But now you're freaking out—for yourself? Because you can't live with it?"

"Babe," Collin said.

"I have to go." She turned away and hightailed it toward her bus because the doors were closing.

"You have to help me figure out what to do," Collin called. "I need you." Pathetic, even at a time like this.

"You're sick," she shouted, then said, "send me that video." She rapped on the closed door of her bus with a flat palm and it opened. From its lowest step, she turned back and shook her head at him, her eyes wild with anger. "Send me that video, Collin. Today." Then the door closed, and the bus rolled forward, and she was gone. And Collin Radaszewski—power forward, number twenty-three—fell back against the brick wall and didn't even care who saw him crying because the only person who mattered already knew he was a monster.

Chapter 32

Lillian checked herself one last time in the hall mirror then rushed to open the front door. "Hello, Penny," she said, beaming. In an act of etiquette, she added, "And you too, Eddie." When one had a visitor in one's home, after all, a gracious host made that visitor feel welcome. Even if that visitor had planted ideas in one's husband's head encouraging his late life political whims as something more than benign fancy and best achieved through a publicity stunt that invited strangers to legally change his name. For example.

"Hi, Lillian," Eddie said. "Penny," he prompted, "say hello."

"Hi," Penny said, speaking to the carpet, the openness she'd managed with Lillian during Phil's speech having apparently hardened on its surface.

No matter, Lillian thought; she'd win her back. "Are you so excited?" she said, her breathless tone leaving them no need to reciprocate the question. "I have glitter glue and felt sheets and googly eyes."

"You didn't have to do all that, Lillian," Eddie said. "That's very sweet though."

"Oh, no, I had them already. You two come in, come in." She stepped backward and turned her body to allow them past. The pair stepped through the foyer and Lillian delighted at the sight of the little girl's head turning this way and that, taking in the enormity of her big house.

"I really appreciate you doing this," Eddie said.

"Oh, stop. I'll let Phil know you're here." She turned her head from Eddie. "Phil!" she called, loudly, "Penny's here! Eddie's waiting on you!"

There was a rustling from the hall, followed by a solid bump from the floor above them. Phil descended the stairs in a tracksuit. "This is what I'm wearing," he said by way of a greeting.

"Oh," Eddie said, some manner of judgement poking at the edges of his smile. "Okay, yeah. Well, I mean, it's just the Elks lodge. This will make you seem…relatable. And it's purple and white, which are their colors."

"It's Toledo blue," Phil corrected.

"Well, sure. But, you know, close enough. They'll get it."

"Phil, say hello to Penny," Lillian urged.

"Mm," Phil hummed, glancing and nodding at the girl, who kept her distance.

"We ought to get going, Phil." Eddie said. "Basically, it's just same speech as last time. Not that you really had the chance to give the speech last time. I have a copy you can look over in the car."

Phil moved toward the door and Eddie followed.

"Bye hon. Good luck," Lillian said.

"Penny," Eddie said, "be good for Mrs. Ochs. Have fun. We'll be back in a few hours."

The expression Penny returned to her father reminded Lillian of certain children she'd seen on television, that stance they took before telekinetically morphing an adversary into a jack-in-the-box or summoning to their aid the full powers of hell.

"Don't worry about a thing," Lillian said, shooing them toward the door. "We're going to have a ball." The two men stepped onto the porch and Lillian closed the door behind them. She turned to the girl and clapped her hands, then clasped them at her chest. "I plugged in the corndog fryer to make sure it was good and hot for us. Are you hungry?"

Penny shrugged.

"Perfect. The kitchen's this way." Lillian led her through the living room. "The first thing is, we have to decide on a batter. We can do traditional cornmeal, bacon batter, jalapeno bacon batter, maple syrup bacon batter… What sounds good?"

"Your house is nice," Penny said.

Lillian stopped and turned and saw the girl's captivated eyes move over the room, then halt on the bald rabbit on the living room coffee table. "Thank you for saying so, honey. That's our Bernie, by the way. He had an accident," she said, then asked brightly: "Do you live in a big house?"

"With my mom and Gail. My dad's house is small."

"Well," Lillian started, but then couldn't find appropriate wisdom in any proverb she could think of. She settled on, "it isn't the size that counts, it's the emotion." She led the girl through the broad kitchen doorway.

It was so rare she had visitors that Lillian couldn't help but see her kitchen through the eyes of the girl: its expanse of horizontal granite and vertical dark wood cabinetry. Straight lines inlaid in straight line inlaid in straight lines. When she moved behind the fan-shaped island, she fancied that Penny could lay on its surface and roll and roll before reaching the edge, such was its impressive width. It was a whimsical thought, she knew, particularly since the island's surface was presently obstructed by the futuristic metal box that hissed and spat hot oil in a viscous, circular splatter on the muted granite.

"Don't mind that," Lillian said, grabbing a wet towel to address the fryer's expelled oil. "That's just the moisture. It should calm down. Have a seat, maybe one farther away from the action."

"It is new?" Penny said after a moment.

Lillian looked up from her attempts to wipe away the oily slick to see that the girl had pulled out a chair at the island that happened to be the one Lillian had chosen to stow the fryer's cardboard packaging. The girl was holding the outer box, seeming to study the picture on its side—a pristine, benign version of the contraption that currently steamed and gargled hot oil across the counter from her.

"Oh, no, dear," Lillian said, charmed, "I've had it for years. I just take care of my things. Here, I'll show you." Lillian dropped the towel into the sink and maneuvered around the counter to snatch the box. Penny followed her to a narrow door at the back of the kitchen. When she opened it and switched on the room's row of overhead florescent lighting, Lillian revealed a virtual warehouse of consumer kitchen gadgetry, pantry space converted to hold row over row of boxed appliances, neatly warehoused with their red As Seen On TV stickers facing out. "Well," Lillian said, pushing the fryer box into an empty hole on a lower shelf, "what do you think?" She watched as the girl evaluated the merchandise shelved on one side of her, then the other, peering down the rows and then back up at Lillian's awaiting face. Penny shrugged her response—a shrug, Lillian presumed, of reverential wonderment. "These aren't the kinds of things you need every day," Lillian said, her own eyes moving over the boxes with accomplished satisfaction, "but when the need comes, you'll be glad to have the right tools. In a way, this is the room I'm most proud of."

"Where did you get it all?" Penny said, reaching out to lightly touch the colorful box of the Rapid Mac macaroni cooker.

"Television, mainly," Lillian said, watching the girl's fingers, which caused her to return them to her side. "How did we ever live without them?" she added, as if such a novelty warehouse was standard to every first world kitchen. There was a loud pop from the fryer then, causing the pair of them to start. "I think it's about time to get cooking."

Penny stepped out of the room and Lillian followed, lingering momentarily after turning out the light to take in the orderly, satisfyingly angular shadows of her collection. When she closed the door and turned to Penny, the girl was seated in her chosen chair, hands politely in her lap, eyeing the fryer warily.

"It sounds like it's quieted down, doesn't it?" Lillian said. "Did you decide what kind of batter you want?"

"I don't know."

"Well, I went ahead and made up some plain cornmeal batter. Let's just keep it as-is then." From the refrigerator, Lillian produced the batter in a large, clear bowl. She placed it on the counter and removed its cover of plastic wrap. Then, she produced a pack of hot dogs, a packet of wooden skewers, paper plates and paper towels. She folded the towels into fourths, thick and square. With her materials laid out, Lillian smiled at Penny enticingly and said, "Are you ready to get down to it?"

They sat side by side at the island, Lillian explaining that the secret to a great corndog was to slice the dog lengthwise before battering it and then filling the opening with a healthy stream of spray cheese. She led Penny in the proper technique, the pair of them opening, filling, spearing and dredging the whole pack of hot dogs. "It can be messy if you don't do it right," Lillian said, "but if you put it in the batter cheese-side-up, it will seal right up and hold the cheese in. Then, when you serve it to someone, the cheese is like a gooey surprise. Have you ever had a corndog with cheese inside?"

"No."

"Surprise!" Lillian smiled, wiggling her jazz fingers.

Penny smiled at this. She seemed more comfortable now that her fingers were satisfyingly gross and wet and grainy from the cornmeal and giving off that appealing dogfood smell of raw hotdog. Lillian could confirm this pleasure to be ageless.

"Do you think we're ready to fry these up?"

Penny nodded.

Lillian rose and walked around the island then produced two thin baskets with rounded bottoms, long enough to hold three dogs end to end. After wiping her hands on a damp dish towel at Lillian's instruction, Penny filled the baskets with their creations. Lillian took the baskets by the handles and moved them to the fryer, dribbling two paths of batter on the countertop which caused them both to giggle. The baskets continued to drip as Lillian held them over the fryer and, when the droplets hit, the oil hissed hungrily.

"Okay," Lillian said, "you say the word and I'll drop these beauties into the fiery depths to meet their fate."

"Okay."

"Do it now?"

"Now," Penny said.

Lillian lowered the baskets until they were just over the oil, then sent them off with a final prayer: "From wieners," she said, "to dogs." She dropped them in and the fryer screamed and bubbled. This startled Penny, who was laughing at Lillian and then laughing about being startled, and across the island from her Lillian was laughing too.

Soon the sizzle of the fryer reduced to a static burble and their laughter subsided. There must be something about forced waiting that encouraged awkward silences, Lillian thought, because, while the corn dogs fried, she felt the girl's eyes on her and suddenly couldn't think of an appropriate thing to say. "When I was a girl," she tried, "I didn't have things like this either. What's your favorite thing to eat when you're at home?"

"I don't know," Penny said. "Gail likes to grill. Gail's Mom's partner. Dad used to cook, but he can't do it now."

"Well, I'm sure he's very busy," Lillian said, careful not to project negativity on the subject of her father.

"No, he still does it. It's just, like, bad now."

"Oh? How strange," Lillian said.

"I think he forgot how when me and Mom moved out." She was rubbing at a stray eyelash that lay like a bridge across her tear duct, which Lillian could see but that the girl's fingers couldn't seem to find. It was an unconscious action that made her revelation seem all the more tragic, Lillian thought, for the casualness of its delivery.

"Well," she said with a sympathetic smile, "you're staying with your dad for a while, aren't you? Maybe with you around, he'll remember."

"Maybe," Penny said, distracted by the eyelash now adhered to the tip of one finger. Her cheeks puffed slightly as if she were desperate to blow it, but when she raised her eyes to see Lillian watching her, she instead secreted the lash in the pocket of her pants. If she were able to find it later amongst the lint and stray seam threads, Lillian wondered what she'd wish for. If she were in Penny's place, it would be for her parents to reconcile. But that seemed too simple for a modern girl like Penny who was able to discuss their arrangement so matter-of-factly. Lillian's would be the wish of someone who was scared of loss. But Penny seemed comfortable with the rebuilt version of her life. It struck Lillian then what a tremendous gift this was to give a child, the comfort of knowing that life can be rebuilt. She felt the full weight of her fondness for Penny in that moment, and for the girl's mother, whom she'd never met, but who was growing this girl to be a stronger woman than Lillian believed herself to be.

A loud siren arose from the fryer then, signaling that it was time to raise the corndogs. Lillian lifted the baskets and hooked them to dry on the rim of the cooler: golden brown and magazine cover perfect.

"Those look good," Penny said.

"They do," Lillian agreed. So good, in fact, that as she watched them cool she couldn't help but think of Eddie—too heartbroken or out of practice to prepare his daughter a meal as marvelous as this one Lillian made her. Enabled by the privilege of this victory over him, she allowed herself a measure of fondness for him as well.

Chapter 33

The election was in two weeks. Eddie felt good about their chances. In the only poll that was likely to be conducted for such a small race, local News 5 showed Phil three points behind Gilda Cranston, well within the margin of error, and with the rocketing potential of the winning name announcement and a national interview on *Chat!* still ahead of him.

It was ten-thirty at night. Penny had been in bed for hours. Eddie was looking at the current standing of the naming contest. Two days of voting remained and already there was a likely winner, a name that was ahead by eighteen thousand votes, one that made him laugh to himself when he thought of it. Several weeks ago, he'd taken a man who had no hope of winning even the base percentage of Republican voters and he'd turned him into a public interest piece, a novelty whose WTF factor alone could lead him to victory. From the walls of Eddie's imagination, this candidate had been rebranded, renamed, and now it was likely that the state of South Carolina would be imminently possessed of him. For better or worse and all Eddie's own doing.

He took a drink and thought more about what had been nagging at him for the last thirty-six hours: David Samuel kissing Phil's cheek. Penny hadn't kissed Eddie in nearly two years, even before her mother had moved her out of their home and set about the course that had made her a stranger to him. He would have given anything for her to want to hug him, to see in her eyes some feeling of security from his being near her, that when she was with her daddy there was nothing in the world to be afraid of. It was different with boys, Eddie imagined, and certainly different with a grown son. But, when Eddie witnessed Phil's reaction to David Samuel's embrace and cheek-planted kiss, it had left him with an eerie feeling he'd yet to fully shake. It was a moment he'd plucked from the raw footage and, by now, had re-watched a dozen times. The disgust Phil demonstrated when his son touched him stuck in Eddie's mind as something vile. A reaction suited to a snakebite or a mugging, rather than the touch of his own child. Never to the touch of your own child. Watching it now, sipping a neat Vodka, it was an image that brought drunken tears to his eyes. The flush of intoxication broke down the barrier between his thoughts and his words, and he stood up abruptly from the couch and declared: "A parent should love their child." For good measure, he saluted. It was a fine punctuation, it seemed to him then, for the heaviness of this insight. "No matter what?" he asked himself aloud, as if from the audience of his declaration. "No matter what!" he, as himself, confirmed.

But what if Penny grows up to be some big, weird, pudgy, goth boy?

It wouldn't matter, he answered, returning the dialogue to his thoughts. He would still always welcome her embrace.

He was down the hall now, having only the vaguest awareness of travelling from the sofa, standing outside Penny's bedroom door. As quietly as he could, he opened it, his glass tinkling against the wood. He stood, swayed, and regarded her sleeping face. It was difficult to admit to himself until he'd consumed a certain quantity of alcohol, but Penny at rest had always reminded him of photos of corpses he'd seen throughout his life: her thin contorted body, her open-mouthed face with the dark-circled eyes that were a trademark of his family line. When she'd lived with him, his deepest fear had been to open her door and find her with her earbud cord wrapped around her neck, the dumb internet video she'd fallen asleep to still playing on her tablet. Actually worse might be to find her missing, her cold body already planted in the woods by the time he checked on her, where it wouldn't be discovered until some redneck hunter tripped over his shotgun and found himself face to face with her tiny, fleshless skull.

But, tonight, she was there, neck untangled with cords, present and accounted for in the bed that, during their estrangement, he'd more than once passed out in. He stood quietly, his large, cartoon eyes fixed on her throat, until the rhythm of his body calibrated with the stillness of the room, and he was able to perceive the tiny movement of her breathing and was assured that she was okay.

It occurred to him to kiss her on her sleeping cheek, but he couldn't shake the thought that the gloss of vodka on his lips would leave a permanent sanitized mark, a bleached, diamond-shaped tag that would mar her face for life. So he closed her door and stumbled down the hall to the kitchen to pour himself another drink.

The refrigerator's ice maker knocked and rattled but delivered nothing into his glass. When he removed it, however, six half-moons of ice immediately tumbled to the floor. Eddie cursed and got to his knees and retrieved the ice, submitting to the pageantry of blowing off the first few cubes before adding them to his glass, but adding the rest without examination.

He realized, on his knees, that he could still hear the knocking, so he put an ear to the freezer door. The sound continued in the opposite ear, from elsewhere in the house. He rose and—because a man should finish what he starts—completed refreshing his drink before investigating. He took small, patient steps toward the sound, waiting between its bursts of three or five knocks, then moving a few more steps, like a game of Marco Polo. He was halfway into the living room when he realized the source of the sound was the foyer. Someone was knocking at his door. Eddie looked at his watch. He couldn't read its face but didn't really need to. Whatever the time, it was too late in the evening for good news. He moved back the curtain on the door's small window. There was no one on the porch. Perplexed, he waited several seconds then turned and was startled to see a face peering at him through the foyer's side window. He jumped and splashed vodka down his shirt. A single cube of ice escaped and spun on the granite floor.

A second look revealed that it was Cindy. She moved back to the front of the porch and opened the storm door to let herself in. "Did I scare you?" she said with a smile. "Sorry. You didn't answer, so I was trying to peek in to see if everything was okay. Are you drunk?"

"If I was," Eddie said, considering the cold, wet spot on his stomach, "I wouldn't be now. Why are you here?"

"I came back early. I told you."

"You said you were thinking about it. You said you'd let me know. But, regardless—why are you *here?*" he repeated, this time indicating the foyer.

"Am I not welcome?" Cindy said defensively. "I had nowhere to be, I guess. I thought it might be nice to hear how things have been going with Penny. Can I come in?"

Eddie moved into the living room and stretched out an inviting arm.

"What are we drinking?" she said, looking around the room, sweeping it for foreignness to the memory of when it was hers.

"The same old stuff. Do you want it over ice, or do you want to suck it out of a shirt?"

"Ice, please." She sat politely at the edge of a sofa cushion. "How's Penny?" she called into the kitchen, over the knocking of the ice dispenser.

"She's good," Eddie said. He heard footsteps and his daughter's bedroom door opening—that squeak it made when the knob turned—then closing again. "I'm happy to have her here." He appeared in the living room doorway with two drinks. Cindy was resituating herself on the sofa. "Are you going to take her now that you're back early?"

"Only if you want me to. I told you it would be a few weeks, so I don't think it would be fair to take her early. Unless you want me to," she said again. She accepted her drink and took a sip, and her face momentarily contorted at its strength.

"I don't want you to." Eddie took a seat at the opposite end of the sofa, adjusting his body to face her.

"I didn't think you would." She took another sip before saying, "You know, I really like that you two are reconnecting. I was never comfortable with how it was before. Anyway, with Gail still at her mom's, it'll probably be good for me to spend some time alone, get my thoughts together."

"Oh Lord, here we go," Eddie said, dropping his head.

"What?"

"Nothing, nothing. You show up here unannounced. You immediately lob a salvo like that. You came to tell me about your problems, didn't you? Relationship stuff? If so, am I too late to stop you? Or do you get to haunt me now because I invited you in?"

Cindy made vampire teeth with her fingers and they laughed together somewhat self-consciously. Once they'd settled back into a mutual silence and she'd taken another sip of her drink, she said, "Isn't it the worst though?" She paused to appraise the contents of her glass. "I mean, you spend so much of your life with someone and they become the person you tell things to. Dumb things. Anything. And then this happens—separation and everything—and it's like…who do you tell that stuff to? You know? It's the worst."

"Pretty bad," Eddie agreed, "but not the worst."

When she looked at him, her pity was evident. "I saw a story about Phil Ochs on a news show. Congratulations, Eddie. It's wonderful."

Eddie laid his head against the back of the sofa and stared at the ceiling. "I don't know if it is actually. The more I get to know him, the more I'm convinced he might be a nightmare of a human being."

"Ignore that voice. That's just you getting in the way of your own success. I remember that voice well."

"Why don't you say what you came to say, Cindy?"

She finished off her drink and set the glass beside Eddie's laptop on the television table. "Oh, it isn't anything, really. I just wanted to complain, which is childish and unfair."

"Yes, it is."

Cindy nodded.

"Buyer's remorse?"

Cindy nodded.

"Careful what you wish for." He rose with his glass and collected hers and refilled them both. "Well," he said with an acquiescent sigh, "I hope everything works out." He settled back onto the sofa. "I don't at all, of course, but it's important to me that you're the only one of us being childish and unfair tonight."

"I appreciate that," she said.

"Don't mention it."

She took a drink, her eyes lost in some distant

place. "I don't know," she said finally, "I think maybe it's not good to go from one person to another with no time in between. Aren't I too old not to have known that? I'm sure that's all it is. I just need to sort myself out." She gave a terse nod as if this were advice being offered her. She raised her glass and he raised his and they clinked them together. "You should really change that shirt."

"Eh," he said, running a palm over the dampness, "I think it announces me: what you see on the outside is the same as what's sloshing around on the inside." He sipped his vodka with tight, smiling lips.

"Aren't you cold?" she said. She touched the damp spot with glancing fingers, as one might a hot stovetop.

"No, the vodka's started to give me a soft blanket of fat across my belly to keep me warm against the elements."

"Oh, you look fine," she said. Eddie noted that the hand she'd lifted from his shirt had landed close to him on the sofa. "God, do you know how long it's been since I've had a drink?"

"I do not."

"I'm turning into a lightweight."

"You were always a lightweight. Do you want me to make some coffee? I'm clearly too far gone to drive, so if you get hammered we're going to have to wake up Penny to drive you home."

"I'm okay," she said. "I'll just stop with this one."

"Or, you could sleep in the bed and I can take the couch. It's pretty common that I sleep here anyway."

"Really? I'm sitting on your bed right now? That's so sad." Her frown was a measure too cute, Eddie thought, too hopeful it would be adored. "Is this spot for your head or your feet?"

He shrugged. "It just depends on which direction I topple."

"You drink too much Eddie."

"That's none of your business."

"You'll always be my business," she said. She leaned toward him. He felt uneasy but predictably excited. "That little girl in there means we're in this together, no matter what the arrangement. We're in this for life." She studied him, and he, her. It seemed to Eddie that, in her closeness, she'd cross a psychic barrier he hadn't authorized. Without speaking, she indicated the bedroom with a subtle jerk of her head in the direction of the hall.

"Cindy," Eddie said with a skeptical, almost paternal tone.

She took immediate stock of herself and leaned away from him. "Sorry," she said. "That was dumb. I'm just a little tipsy. God, I can see why you like this stuff so much." She laughed self-consciously then cleared her throat.

Eddie stared at his lap. Whatever this was, he reminded himself, it wasn't real. A miscalculation having to do with some unhappiness with Gail, or her loneliness without Penny, or a poorly-processed reaction to his recent success, and unless he forced coffee on her and sent her out the door, what happened next would be regrettable, and it could have far-reaching consequences for the lot of them. On the other hand, though, Eddie's recent successes had nullified several of his deepest regrets, and he wondered if he wasn't justified in taking on one more.

Without speaking, he rose on wobbly legs and started down the hall. A familiar groan from the sofa springs told him that Cindy had followed. By the time he stopped in front of the bedroom door, she was at his side. He turned the knob and quietly pushed the door open to reveal their sleeping daughter.

"What are you doing?" Cindy said.

Eddie swallowed and found himself unable to look her in the eye. Lamely, he feared, he answered her: "Saving myself, I guess. You should sleep here tonight. She'll love it in the morning. I'm going to bed. If you want to find me when you're sober and not so sad, I'll be here. Give me some signs—and I mean, like, the really obvious kind—and I'll be sober too."

He left her in the hall then, closing her out of what had once been her bedroom. And, whether in show or by the necessity of his sloppy, drunken fingers, he made a significant racket while locking the door.

Chapter 34

Ruzanna knew it was selfish, but the whole thing seemed worse when she recognized Oswald Park. She noticed it when David Samuel stumbled, and the phone camera tilted up to catch a corner of the cement bathroom on the hill beside the duck pond.

On their first proper date, last summer, Ruzanna had forced Collin to leave this park for a gas station with a bathroom. She had to go and there was no way she was touching her bare ass to any surface inside that stinking box. As they left, they had passed by it, and Collin had playfully nudged her toward the bathroom's entrance, and Ruzanna had giggled and squealed and clenched against the fullness of her bladder. It was the first physical contact they'd ever shared, Collin's flirtatious pushing and threats.

The camera came close to David Samuel's face, and the shadow arm of the camera man—A.J., she recognized by his voice—fell over David Samuel's cheek and his trapped, wild-animal eye. A hand entered the frame, pushing his face into the grass, a familiar class ring. Collin's long, elegant fingers spread over David Samuel's cheek and Ruzanna was reminded of the many times she'd seen him spread them this way to palm and lift a basketball. In the video, the fingers didn't lift; they pushed David Samuel's head down, the pinky finger dangerously close to teeth that clenched between screams, leaving no mistake they meant to bite whatever of that hand they could get a piece of.

It had felt special to Ruzanna that Collin chose to bring her to Oswald Park on their first time out together. At sixteen, her sample size was limited, but she'd come to know the hallmark of first dates as bad films—typically horror, as if planned with the expectation that she might leap in fright from her chair into the lap of her adolescent suitor—preceded with, or followed by, fast food. Last winter, her older sister, Saanvi, had confessed to performing oral sex on a date for taking her to dinner at New York's Gramercy Tavern. Saanvi had been nineteen and her date, forty-one. Ruzanna reacted to the story with horror. She wondered, if her own romantic life were subject to this transactional reward system, what would be the affectionate analog when treated to a $5.99 fast-food value meal? A punch on the shoulder? A quick, over-the-clothes squeeze of the testicular sack?

But, instead of the bad food and film, Collin had brought her to Oswald Park. Children came to parks for a safe place to play, and old, widowed people came for a safe place to remember, and his bringing her here had made her feel safe too. It wasn't a space that was tailored to attract them. It didn't proposition them as a cool teenage hangout. It was for everyone, real people, and his bringing her here made him seem more real too, somehow. More so than the other boys, anyway. It seemed brave to walk in a park with someone you didn't know because there was no avoiding them. This early appraisal of Collin's bravery and her belief in a distinguishing realness in their relationship had buoyed her through their rougher patches—when he was acting selfish, or when she considered evidence that he may be shallow. Selfish or shallow, perhaps, but it had never occurred to her that he might also be cruel.

Just as this thought came to her—Collin being cruel—the camera tilted up to capture him in profile. His gaze was low, his attention focused on the assault, all cheek and chin and flexing mandible. Behind the camera, AJ called to him to ham it up for the camera—to smile or wink or otherwise perform for the video's benefit—but Collin appeared set at his task. It seemed so cold to her, his steadiness in doing something so ugly. But after a moment he did turn toward the camera. Not prompted by AJ, but a natural, curious turn of his head. For the first time, Ruzanna had a clear look at his eyes. They were round and wet and frightened. He stared straight into the camera as if silently pleading with her to help him out of this. Ruzanna had to look away.

No, Collin Radaszewski wasn't cruel. He could be dumb sometimes. He was culpable and guilty, but he had hundreds of dollars of incentive. Greed, not cruelty, motivated him to do this. And that was above and beyond his also being a jock, programmed by school athletics to see aggression and intimidation as tools for success.

Ruzanna clicked the video player closed and stared across her room to a line of big-eyed stuffed animals who stared back as if in anticipation of her next move. "What will you do with this evidence?" those eyes asked. She wasn't sure how she could go back to work. Seeing Phil, knowing what he'd done, and acting like everything was normal? David Samuel had only ever been kind to her. How could she face him now and act like she hadn't witnessed his humiliation, seen him cry and beg and bite and—as AJ had made a specific point to document—soil himself?

She looked to her laptop screen, at the expanse of white in the email Collin had sent her with the video as an attachment, no message in its body, the subject line reading only, 'sorry, babe.' She thought of the wet, frightened eyes of the boy who had first taken her to Oswald Park, and then those of her innocent stuffed animals, all looking to her for an answer. Ruzanna didn't know what the right action was, but she knew she couldn't be complicit. She had college committees to think of and personal dignity and justice for David Samuel, and she could not allow herself to wind up on the wrong side of a moral or legal line. So, by the time her mother called her down to dinner, Ruzanna Singh was a firebrand. She slapped her laptop closed with the knowledge that her next move would be an important one, one that would ripple through political and legal and moral conversations all over South Carolina.

Before turning out her bedroom light, she looked back at her animals, who smiled at her gratefully—she, their girl, the one they could count on to do the right thing. And as her room switched suddenly to dark, she pictured Collin along with them, and Ruzanna smiled back.

PART THREE

Chapter 35

Phil Ulysses Grant.
P.U.G.
PUG Ochs

It was a good name, for sure. A moniker fit for a World War II general. The voters had done him right.

On the day before he made it legal, Phil felt like a bride on the eve of her wedding. Mundane tasks took on an air of gravity. *This will be the last time I create a regional sales PowerPoint for my managers—as Phil Ochs,* he thought. *This is Phil Ochs's last inspection of restroom tile grout for urine and semen and feces...*

He'd decided to spend this metaphorical last day in Columbia. Fry Buddy's familiar chaos proved a welcome inhibitor to the dyspeptic burbles that floated up his throat to signal his excitement. In this den of comestibles, he was not unlike Jesus at the Last Supper, Phil mused, trading the coming cross and cave for DMV licensure and Social Security Administration bureaucracy as the instruments of his resurrection. Though his Columbia crew didn't map onto this analogy precisely as disciples, this was his flagship store and he considered their presence serviceable for the role. Except, of course, for David Samuel. So, upon his arrival, Phil had ordered his son to the parking lot with a pair of gloves and a garbage bag for a thorough removal of cigarette butts.

"I may be leaving," David Samuel had hissed, "but I'm still the manager."

"Hit the parking lot, Judas," Phil had said.

He sat in the restaurant office now, leafing through files in a cabinet drawer, examining iterations of his signature. At sixty-three, Phil's was a predictable autograph—a self-consciously illegible, scribbly, looping mess of characters in two brief sets. How good would it feel to sign those three strong, uppercase characters—P-U-G—and have them legally represent him on new hire paperwork or franchise contracts or even, given recent successes, state legislation? How freeing would it be to sign his name without hesitation or that practiced sloppiness that suggested his hand to be less sure than it always actually was? To leave a mark that was purely and clearly his own, such that even a child could read it and know that it was the work of PUG Ochs?

In a group of papers in a hanging folder, he chanced upon Tony's employment contract. He pulled it and laid it on the countertop then frowned at the weak and frightened look of his signature beneath Tony's own. From the cup at the back of the counter, Phil removed a pen and appended Tony's scrawl with the word, 'asshole.' The pen's ink took a moment to flow and what was left on the paper was the curious word, 'shole.' Above his own signature, he signed his new name. The impact of those letters proved more eye-catching than the typed text they overlaid. In the contract's right margin, he signed the name again, first with periods behind each initial then without. The effect of the punctuation struck him as too hesitating, lessening the impact of the four big capital letters that resulted when their edges were freed to touch. On the border of the document, and then over its type, Phil tried the name again and again, delighting at the strength it communicated.

When he'd defiled all available space on the paper, Phil gave his graffito a final appraisal then crumpled the document into a ball and threw it in the trashcan below the counter. As his body turned with this action, he saw Ruzanna start around the corner then freeze at the sight of him. She was out of uniform, and her street clothes seemed to him improper attire for the private wake he was staging before laying Phil Ochs to rest. "Hey there," he greeted her anyway, feeling benevolent and forgiving.

Ruzanna's face tugged toward the ground. "I was looking for David Samuel," she said, then started past Phil in the direction of the breakroom.

"He isn't down there," Phil called.

Ruzanna stopped and paused as if steeling herself before returning to the office entrance. "Do you know where I can find him?" she asked.

"I sent him out for some air. You may not have heard, but that guy won't be around much longer. If there's something you need, though, I'm sure I can help you."

Ruzanna shook her head and turned to leave.

Phil tried on a compassionate smile he'd conceived of as arsenal in PUG Ochs' bag of rhetorical tricks, then called, "Hey! I know you're not working today, but in the spirit of some good news I'm celebrating, why don't you comp yourself a meal before you go? Or, if you already ate, take something with you for Radaszewski. I'm sure a kid like him has got to pack the calories in." He wasn't sure what he'd said wrong, but at the mention of Collin, Ruzanna's pretty caramel skin flamed red. The flicker of that same fire in her eyes burned his new smile down to a clarified pucker. "You all right there, kid?" he said.

She looked like she might be ill. When she finally spoke, there was a timidity in her voice that was perplexingly discordant with the accusation of her words. "I know about you," she said.

"Come again?"

"I know everything. I know, and I think you're disgusting."

Had Phil not been so consumed by the importance of this day, had circumstances with David Samuel not changed so dramatically since the occasion of his assault, Phil might have put together what she meant by this. As it was, however, he was utterly perplexed, though his face still blanched at the accusation. It was something to do with her innocence of tone, her surety of his guilt that made him presume it to be true, whatever it was. "I…don't know what you mean," he said, hoping to prompt her to explain.

"You do know," Ruzanna insisted. "I've seen what you did. You're a terrible man."

Seen what? Phil wondered frantically. "Look…I mean," Phil said, stuttering. "I'm not sure what the deal is here, but it might be that there's a misunderstanding. Tomorrow's a fresh start, I mean. And whatever it is you're talking about, that's the past. Today's my last day. My last day," he said again as if to clarify.

Ruzanna squinted at him, making a show of her confusion. "Okay," she said, "Well, it's mine too. I quit." She stood for a moment longer, challenging him. When she finally turned on her heel, she left him feeling uncomfortably stripped and exposed.

Alone in the office, Phil worked to steady his breathing and slow his pulse. From the trash can, he extracted Tony's crumpled employment contract, smoothing it on the counter and focusing his thoughts on that document's dozens of reminders that tomorrow he'd be a new and better man. That the trials of Phil Ochs would soon be at an end. That, before his resurrection, even Jesus had his cross to bear.

*　　*　　*

"Who's a good boy?" David Samuel asked, his lips puckered, the trash bag he'd acquired an hour before for cigarette butts, empty and flapping in the wind. He was standing in a parking space that was two down from a curly-haired retriever whose head was pushed through the narrow opening in the passenger window of a parked truck. It was as close as he could comfortably allow himself to the creature.

He stooped to grab an abandoned sweet potato fry from the blacktop. "Do you want this?" he asked the retriever, extending it toward him.

The dog sniffed the air and whined.

"If I bring it to you, will you bite off my fingers?" A mother and son cut between them on their way into the restaurant, the boy pausing briefly to accept the dog's extended tongue on his face. David Samuel turned away until they'd passed. "Are you a killer, boy?" he inquired when they were once again alone. He took a step toward the truck. "I'm going to throw this to you, okay? Are you ready?" He tried his arm in a few underhand passes, then flung the fry at the truck, hitting its passenger door well below the open window, the dog nevertheless trying and failing to catch it in its mouth. It tilted its head and gave the fry a sidelong glance, mourning it with a protracted whine.

"Terrible," David Samuel said, accusingly, "that was just terrible." He took several cautious steps into the empty space beside the truck. "Did you do that on purpose?" he said. "To get me close so you can bite my throat out?"

The dog panted happily.

David Samuel came to the painted line that announced the border of the truck's parking space. The fry had landed just on the other side of it. "I'm going to bend down now and get this for you," he said to the dog as one might announce their intentions to a police officer before reaching into his own pocket. He stretched one leg in front of him to scoot the fry closer with his foot, then he bent to retrieve it. The dog barked, and David Samuel shot away from the truck with a squeal.

"David Samuel?" Ruzanna said, and he squealed again, losing his grip on the garbage bag. It skipped away in the breeze. "What are you doing?" she asked.

"That beast," was all he could say, "that beast."

"This guy?" she said, massaging the retriever behind his ear. She reached down to pick up the fry, then fed it to him from her open palm. "So…I guess I just quit. And I might have told your dad he's a terrible person."

"That," David Samuel said, warily eyeing the retriever, "is a sentiment I've communicated to him on numerous occasions. If you think he's going to respond to it correctively, I'm sorry to disabuse you." To fully collect himself, he turned away from the truck and the obscene oral regard its retriever was paying Ruzanna's hand. For several seconds, he caught his breath. Then he turned to face her. "What were you saying?" he said. "That you quit today? Is this about your basketballer?"

"Collin?" she said with a blush. "No. I mean, that's all starting to feel…complicated, but no, that's not why." Sheepishly, she added, "Before I go, I actually wanted to talk to you about that."

Ignoring her, he said, "I find it very strange that you chose this moment to quit."

"I don't know," she said, "I mean, sometimes, a person should stand up and do the right thing, don't you think? Like, have someone's back when they've been nice to you? By the way, thanks for being nice to me about all that with Collin the other day."

He waved away the thought with a graceful toss of his hand.

"Sorry I cried."

David Samuel's eyes were on a cigarette butt at his feet that he had no intention of picking up.

"Sorry I hugged you," she said with a prominent rolling of her eyes. "I mean, get your shit together, Ruzanna. Right?"

"The softness of this body invites affection," he said with a sigh. "It's a burden I've learned to live with."

"Anyway," Ruzanna said, as a pallet cleanser. After a pause, she continued, "Now that I don't work here anymore, and you're not my boss, would it be okay if I talked to you about something important?"

"I'm sorry, Ruzanna, there's a thing here I just can't get past: you've worked here for how long? And you choose this moment to quit?"

"Yeah, but I mean, so what? It's not like I can't get another cashier job. My parents will be super pissed, but I just feel like I have to do the right thing, you know? I know something that would make it really hard to stay. That's what I wanted to talk to you about."

David Samuel pondered a cloud before responding. "Ruzanna," he said finally, "you sound upset, unsure of yourself. Is that fair to say?"

"Eh," she said, "I'm cool. It's all just kind of a lot." She'd turned her body away from him and was again allowing the retriever to lap at her with its tongue. David Samuel winced. "There's just something I need to tell you."

"Ruzanna," he said with a warm authority that left her no choice but to turn to him. He fixed a stare on her that immediately prompted tears in her eyes. "Ruzanna," he said again, taking a single step toward her. "You poor thing." He took her hands in his. "Forgive me for being blunt when I say this, but I'm getting the distinct impression that what you want to say to me is difficult?"

She nodded.

"Yes. Well, let me save you from having to say it then: I'm five years older than you and in a different phase of life completely. You are newly suffering from a break-up, and it's only natural for you to seek comfort elsewhere. In a figure of mature authority. But I, as flattered as I am, will never be that source of comfort."

"What?" The word sounded wispy and small.

"You've been throwing signs like daggers since you walked out here to speak to me. If you'll forgive me the vulgarity of putting it into words: the atmosphere of this parking lot is a stifling fog of lovesick hormones. But it's okay. I'm not embarrassed. Neither, though, am I interested. However, because I do enjoy your company, I'll tell you what we do: to celebrate your emancipation from the underside of Phil Ochs's orthopedic boot, and to celebrate my similar extraction, I'd like to extend to you an invitation for dinner tonight—not as a date, underline, but as former colleagues, a pair of food service professionals."

Ruzanna began to speak, but David Samuel stopped her.

"Don't think about it," he said. "Don't try to politely decline. Just answer me this: do you like corndogs and French fries?"

"I mean," Ruzanna said, "I guess."

"Then it's settled. You and I, sweet girl, are going to have a very pleasant evening. Your phone number is in the office, yes? I'll call you with the details. For now, though, just keep your chin up. And until we meet again, I want you to be thinking about two questions for me, okay? Who is Ruzanna Singh? And why is she fabulous?"

Chapter 36

Eddie was nude and drinking on a Sunday afternoon. Cindy had taken Penny out for lunch and shopping. She hadn't said a word to Eddie about their near-miss sexual encounter, and her silence had the effect of a river flood, a swelling to the borders of that moment's opportunity that separated it from him like a distant island. He'd come to feel regret for denying her, his lonely raft pushed ever further from her invitation by silent waters. So, he'd begun his day with three neat vodkas taken fast. They'd gotten his nerves throbbing and he'd become weepy and morose and, at some point, found himself wrapped in the bathrobe he'd bought for Cindy for their last Christmas together. The one she'd mindfully left behind as a token of just the sort of baggage she didn't intend to carry into her new life. He tried it first over his clothes, then stripped off those clothes to see what psychic impressions might enter his pores if the robe's light, knotty fabric touched his skin directly. There were none, of course, because he was being stupid; another drink told him that. She'd never even worn the robe, after all, so it was an unlikely repository for phantom smells or stray hairs or memories of better days. Had she been a missing person, and this robe a possession given to a cadaver dog, the poor woman's body would never be found. So, he'd pulled it off and thrown it somewhere and continued through his morning naked, hiding his shame beneath the computer in his lap. The device's warmth and the subtle vibrating hum of its hard drive left him with a passable erection, or at least the partially-swelled starting point of a man more generously endowed than himself. All things considered, he felt good.

PUG Ochs. Good Lord, what a name.

Tomorrow, Phil would make it official. Eddie needed only to choreograph the specifics: Phil arriving at the Irmo DMV, shaking hands with a few well-placed voters, submitting his documents and reemerging a new man, one built by the people. All of this would be videotaped and quickly edited for air on that afternoon's episode of *Chat!* Eddie would coach Phil for the remote interview with the hosts, but only for etiquette—if your politics are challenged by the well-known liberal actress-turned-talk show panelist, don't call her a derogatory name; if the celebrity attorney panelist points out that the name change isn't official until you receive updated documents from the DMV and Social Security Administration, don't call her a derogatory name, and so on.

This was a national daytime television program, so their interest in this tiny state race was no greater than their enthusiasm for some zoo's new baby panda or the irony of a genetically flawless actress preaching the restorative benefits of kegeling an ancient jade egg in her twenty-three-year-old yoni. All was good that kept the audience smiling.

Eddie's phone rang: Linwood Barth. His erection flexed.

"Linwood," he said, intending to signal a confidence he'd failed to bring to their last conversation.

"Ellis, you fucking shitbird. You're beating me,

kid. You're actually beating me. I mean—Jesus Christ, what's going on here, dude?"

A flush ran over Eddie's cheeks. "We're only ahead by one." This, a reference to new data by the race's only pollster.

"Right, which means you exceeded a three-point gap in a week. That name thing, brother. I mean, I got that it was good, but goddamn."

"It's a red state," Eddie said with a touch of humility.

"It's purple as a nut-sack vein. You know it. God knows it. And God knows I know it. So on account of the fact that my girl was a sure winner, you'll understand my surprise when we started losing ground to your sweet potato turd. I got no choice but to tell you, Ellis: over the last couple days I've started to develop a mighty strong dislike for you, young man."

This declaration caused Eddie a second blush of embarrassment. As deeply in Linwood's shadow as he'd always been, to now be the subject of his jealousy was, to say the least, complimentary. Still, Eddie felt a tinge of guilt for having achieved a taste of the national attention that had always eluded his mentor. It didn't help that this attention was cheap and novel. It was attention that PUG Ochs didn't deserve. As clever as he felt the naming contest was, Eddie doubted that he, himself, deserved it either. Feeling disgusted by the gooseflesh visible on his legs and arms, he pushed the laptop onto the sofa and began collecting and dressing in his shed clothing.

"Is he as short as he looks on TV?" Linwood asked.

Eddie attempted to project confidence, to speak Linwood's language: "He's 8'6" if he's a foot."

"And as old?"

"If so, the coeds he's going to bed with haven't noticed."

"Well," Linwood laughed, "we are what we eat, they say. Look, Ellis, I have a confession. I didn't call you just to shoot the shit. I have a proposition to make."

"I'm not going to rename your candidate," Eddie said.

"I want a debate. One night, open to the public."

"We're two weeks from the finish line and I have momentum. Absolutely not."

"Because you know your man can't win a debate."

"Because I can afford not to take the risk."

"Phil Ochs is an ass. Everyone who's ever met him knows it. Believe me, I've talked to them. You think if I put the resources on it, I won't find a story from his life that will sink him? And you right along with him?"

"If you had something, you'd have used it," he said, "You're bluffing."

"I got a donation today. From the DNC. Not the SCDC, the national party. Turns out, they have an interest in this little race of ours. They think a blue state legislature will soften up voters for a blue U.S. House and Senate candidate next year. I can't say as I disagree with them, either."

"Then use it. Check him out. If it was an option, you would have played that hand already. You wouldn't be pandering to me for favors."

There was a rattle at Eddie's front door. He made a quick, perfunctory check of his zipper and the buttons on his shirt.

"Look, Ellis—I'm sixty-two years old. Ella has the pancreatic cancer. You're a fox and I'm a fox. I don't want to run reconnaissance on your man. He's bad for this state and you and me both know it. I got a plan to pay myself off and get the hell out of Dodge, which makes you the go-to state strategist, the man who got a grease-trap turd on the national news. You're made, boy. You don't need to win this race. But I need to walk away from it with as many funds as I can possibly legally claim to belong to me for services rendered. Let that little freak hang himself in front of an audience.

You'll still be Goldilocks to the people that matter. I'll be out of your way. And the state will get a senator that's able to do the job."

As she came into the living room with Penny, Cindy called, "We got you a slurpy," before seeing that Eddie was on the phone. Eddie took a seat beside his laptop. As she ran by him, Penny smiled—actually smiled—before closing herself in her bedroom. Cindy sat in the chair opposite him and stared after her.

"Sorry, Linwood. You're on your own here. This isn't going to happen."

Linwood was quiet for a moment, then said, "Well, I guess I can't say as I blame you. One thing I will say though: you've grown some balls since the days when you was following me around with your nose up my ass. Once upon a time, you'd have stood in traffic if I told you we needed the distraction."

Cindy took a sip of his slurpy then offered him a smile at the transgression.

His chest warmed. Even if this was all there was, at least they were friends again. "You're mistaken, Linwood," he said. "I didn't grow these balls; I stole them from you."

"Oh yeah?" Linwood said with a laugh, "How do they fit?"

"They itch a little, to be honest. But I think I'm getting used to them."

Chapter 37

"I can't believe I'm here," Ruzanna said. She was seated on a stool at the granite island and eyeing the expanse of the Ochs's giant kitchen.

"Well, we're glad to have you," Lillian said, washing from her fingers the Icy Hot she'd applied to her shoulder after finishing with the Choice French Fry Potato Cutter, a preemptive gesture before the ache set in. The kitchen smelled of frying oil and starch and medical mint. "I can't remember the last time David Samuel invited a friend over."

"I'm a solitary creature," David Samuel confirmed. "One is born alone and must die alone. But, Mother, I believe what Ruzanna meant is that she never foresaw herself seated in the home of her iniquitous employer. It's a sentiment I've awoken to daily." He smiled then, and Lillian looked at him with visible displeasure.

Without a word about his betrayal, she returned her eyes to the swirling patterns in the oil, seeking signs of the perfect frying temperature. To Ruzanna, she said, "You and Phil don't get on?"

"Oh, well, I mean…" Ruzanna began.

"Ruzanna is a sensitive soul, Mother. An elemental light. Exactly the type your husband feeds upon. He's an emotional vampire. I assure you, they do not 'get on'."

He expected this to prompt a motherly scolding, the tut-tut invocation of his name, but Lillian remained silently committed to her frying oil, and to her stated position of being done with it all.

"You have a really nice house," Ruzanna said.

"Thank you, dear," Lillian said, and then: "Okay. It's time." To the accompaniment of sizzling burps and gurgles, she dropped a basket of corndogs into one well of the fryer and a basket of sliced potatoes into the other. "And now, we wait," she said, finally looking her son and his guest in their eyes, her forehead shiny with atomized oil.

"Where's your dad again?" Ruzanna said quietly. She had only agreed to this celebratory dinner at the Ochs house on the promise that it would in no way involve Phil. In truth, she'd also agreed because, once her parents found out she'd quit her job, she suspected it would be a long time before she was allowed out of the house again, so this had felt like a necessary outing to seize upon, such as it was. Despite David Samuel's promise that Phil would be out all evening, she couldn't shake her fear that he may burst through the door at any moment, that she might be forced to win her emancipation from his home by maiming him with whatever form of weaponry she could manufacture from this kitchen's various convenience products. *How long will that oil stay hot after these corndogs are done frying?* she wondered.

"He's at some political this or that," David Samuel said dismissively. "Forget him. Who needs him?" Then to his mother, he clarified, "Meaning no offense to anyone here who feels they do."

In response, Lillian said, "Golden brown! These dogs are barking." She pulled up the basket of corndogs and hooked it on the slot above the well. To David Samuel, she said, "Should we triple fry the fries in honor of our guest?"

"Oh, that isn't necessary," Ruzanna said.

"I'm going to anyway," Lillian said with the cadence of a naughty admission. She raised and rested the second basket.

Two more times, she dropped the fries. "I'm not going to stick around," she said finally, a corndog in each hand like divining rods tuned to navigate her to a place in the house where she wouldn't be in the way of her son and his guest. She'd taken a long time to wipe oil from the granite countertop then wash out her rag at the sink and wipe some more, the whole effort performed with a hurried, one-last-thing-and-I'll-go look of urgency that didn't seem to inform the speed with which she finished. "I have a phone call to make," she said as she left them. "But if you need anything, just let me know."

"Your mom is funny," Ruzanna said as she danced a French fry around her paper plate in a nervous, twirling motion.

"There are worse things one could be, I suppose," David Samuel said. "Well, here's to your taking wing and leaving Fry Buddy behind forever." He raised his corndog and held it aloft for several seconds before Ruzanna realized he meant for her to touch it with her own.

At the corndog cheers she involuntarily said, "Clink," then lowered hers back to her plate. To fill the silence that followed, she said, "What did your dad say when you told him *you* were leaving Fry Buddy?"

"What could he say? Something obtuse and laced with obscenity. But, he's kicked me around for long enough." With his teeth, he peeled the remainder of one corndog from its stick, trapping it inside his mouth. "This Canadian fellow happens to be related by marriage to Phil's political opposition. They asked me to star in an advertisement against him, but, while he isn't deserving of pity necessarily, I do have my reservations about going public with our little family squabble. The dirty bird, and all that."

The quaintness of his characterization, 'squabble,' made her feel desperately sorry for David Samuel, knowing what she did. She stared at the speckled pattern of the slick granite. It was like a body of water reflecting a dark sky full of stars. "You and your dad really don't get along, do you?" she said to the sky below her.

David Samuel scoffed, or possibly briefly choked. She wasn't sure which.

Ruzanna had no hope of an appetite with what she needed to say to him sitting like a cannon ball in her stomach, so now was the time, she decided, to launch into it. "Do you know that thing I wanted to tell you?" she said quietly, her eyes welling with tears, despite her intention to deliver this news with calm compassion. "I know about something that…happened to you. At Oswald Park." Here, she looked up at David Samuel to confirm his reaction. Briefly, he stopped chewing, his cheek a pocket of under-masticated corndog. Then, his jaw began again. He eyed her, chewing slowly, as if her words had caused him to reset and he needed time to build up to the gusto with which he'd previously enjoyed his food. "I didn't know about it until a couple days ago," she said, thinking how now that she'd revealed this dangerous information, such a clarification was necessary to lessen its potential to injure her as well.

"Mm-hmm," David Samuel intoned before swallowing, with a tip of his head that suggested she go on.

She cleared her throat. "The other day, Collin… my old… *Collin*…told me that he was…one of them… in the park that day. And the reason they were there… to do that to you…is because…they were paid to do it…by…your dad." Ruzanna couldn't look at David Samuel for what felt like a long time. When she did, raising her head from her plate, settling her eyes on him, she found him sobbing in silent, disturbing heaves. And, as if taking his tears as license, she also began to violently cry. "I'm so sorry David Samuel," she said. "I wasn't sure if I should tell you…but you've been so nice to me and I thought that if I didn't, I'd be a bad person, and I didn't know what else to do."

David Samuel abruptly rose from his stool in a manner that caused its wooden legs to groan, shockingly loud, against the floor tile. He rested his forehead on top of fists that were clenched on the counter, half in his plate, mashing the fried potatoes that were trapped beneath it and ejecting others onto the counter and the floor. The plate angled and lifted. A second corndog rolled and rested against his fingers.

"Do you want me to go?" Ruzanna wailed. "I'm sorry. I can go if you want me to."

"I can't believe it," David Samuel was saying, over and over, to his spoiled food. "I can't believe he would do that."

"I know. I know. It's awful." She had an urge to touch him on his broad back, but she kept her hands in her lap.

"I can't believe he would do that—for me."

"It's," she said, then nothing more.

"I can't believe I made him do that. I must have… yes, I must have really gotten to him. Sometimes, I wasn't sure, but—I must have." He was still crying, but his face had contorted into a manic smile, his eyes those of some dangerous clown. He raised from the counter, suddenly animated, and addressed her with excited gestures, the heel of one palm coated in ketchup. "I won," he said. "I beat him."

"But, I mean, aren't you, like…pissed?"

"Pissed? Ha!" he spoke this word of merriment rather than actually laughing. "When a boxer defeats his opponent, is he pissed? When a terrorist brings down a government, is he pissed?"

"But," Ruzanna began, trying to make sense of this reaction, "when I saw the video, it was so awful what they did."

"There's video? I knew it." This seemed to inspire particular delight. She perceived wheels turning behind his eyes. "I have an idea," he said. "I know what we should do." He licked his lips and, in so doing, extracted a crumb of breading that she'd noticed but not brought to his attention. "Let's go through all his private places: his office, his bathroom drawer, *his bed*. All of it. We'll make our own video. You, the outsider, invading his private spaces. I don't know how I'll use them, but I'll think of a way." He leaned in and whispered: "Let's make the old codger lose his mind."

And, before she could refuse, David Samuel had grasped her fingers and was leading her, the ketchup that was smeared on his hand a kind of blood oath, transferred to her own hand, making it impossible for her to refuse.

Chapter 38

"Elysian Fields Taxidermy. Bob speaking."

"Hi, Bob. My name is Lillian Ochs. How are you tonight?"

"What can I help you with, ma'am?"

Before her on the coffee table, Lillian had arranged Bernie's ears; a small tube of Super True super glue that had arrived that afternoon in a bubbled mailer; and the bald rabbit himself, his face turned away from her as if in shame. "Well, Bob," she said, "I was wondering if you could give me some advice. I'm repairing a rabbit and I was curious if you could advise on the appropriate amount of super glue to use. To make it stick, I mean, without flowing out of the seams and getting stuck in his fur."

"What's the nature of the repair, ma'am?"

"My son ripped his ears off."

Bob clucked then said, "I might can help you, ma'am. But you really ought to treat your taxidermy pieces the way you would any other artistic sculpture. Keep them away from young children and that."

"My son is twenty-three years old. But what I'm wondering is: do I brush it on the underside of the fur or just squeeze it straight onto his scalp? Which do you think?" She lifted the ears from the table in anticipation of specific questions about their physical properties that would lead Bob to an educated conclusion.

"You're a hobbyist?" Bob asked.

"No, Bob, I'm a lady."

"Well, ma'am—"

"*Lillian*," Lillian corrected.

Bob sighed. "Lillian, for a major repair like that, I'd advise you to find a professional. For one thing, I'd probably go with a latex caulk rather than a super glue. But, I can't say that for sure, since I can't see what you're dealing with. This isn't the kind of thing you want to get wrong, believe me. I've seen some DIY monstrosities. Did you ever see one of those TV shows about botched plastic surgery? Think that but with woodland critters."

"Oh, darn!" Lillian said, bringing the ears close to her face. "There's a rip right between his ears. I hadn't noticed."

"There again, ma'am. All the more reason to get it in front of someone that knows what they're doing."

"Can a rip like that be fixed?"

"No way for me to say. Even if not, though, you'd have options. You might consider going crypto, for example."

"Crypto?"

"Yes, ma'am, cryptozoological. Mythic, I mean. Take the salvageable parts and work them together with the parts of some other critter to make something new. I mean, you're working with a rabbit that's got no ears and a ripped scalp. Sounds to me like this thing's just crying out to be a jackalope."

Behind her, Lillian heard David Samuel and Ruzanna barrel through the living room and down the hall. Distractedly, she inquired, "Jackalope?"

"That's a jackrabbit with antelope antlers, ma'am. Real funny, Lillian, real funny. The bigger the antlers, the funnier I find them. You'd have some choices to make concerning the impact you're trying to achieve. Me, I'd cut its head off and put it on a wall mount and then give it great big gnarly horns. But, it's all in the eye of the beholder, of course. For a lady, maybe something more refined."

Lillian replaced the ears on the coffee table and rose from the sofa, curious to peek down the hall after David Samuel. "Bob," she said, "You've really given me something to think about. It sounds like I need to powwow with my son to figure this out."

"I agree, ma'am, don't go in blind. And, also, you should Google jackalopes. Real funny, you'll see."

"Okay. Thanks, Bob. Goodbye." She disengaged the phone and tossed it onto the sofa before heading toward the hallway. Just as the realization occurred to her that David Samuel had led Ruzanna into Phil's office, there was a knock at the door.

Bothered, Lillian changed her course and entered the foyer. "Yes?" she called through the door.

"Um, is this…are you…Ms. Ochs?" a male voice asked.

"Yes?"

The voice said nothing.

"Yes?" Lillian asked again, seeking identifying clues from what she could see of him through the door's small window.

"Would you, like, be able to talk to me for a minute please?"

Life's little impasses, she thought, looking over her shoulder toward the commotion in the hall. Lillian took the doorknob in her hand and pulled it open. Standing on her porch was a tall, thin young man with timid eyes. "Yes?" Lillian said to him. She began to step out onto the porch but froze when she saw what he was holding. "Where did you get that?" she asked with a strained calm in her voice.

"This, um, belongs to your son," the young man

said.

"Yes, I know. It's David Samuel's notebook. What I wonder is where you got it."

The young man raised the notebook and she hesitated before taking it, but once she had it, she clutched it at her chest protectively.

"There's, uh…I need to tell you something," he said. His head was low and, when he spoke, his eyes shifted far to the left, directed at her flower bed. "I… followed Ruzanna when she came here," he explained. "I have to tell you…" His voice sounded to Lillian as if he had recently cried or might soon begin to.

"David Samuel!" she called behind her.

"No," the boy quietly scolded. "Don't do that."

Behind her, there was a clatter followed by David Samuel's heavy footfalls. He appeared at the door beside his mother. "Oh," he said, startled to see the boy, "hello."

"God!" the boy wailed, beating his forehead with the edge of his fist. "God! God! God! I'm sorry, I shouldn't have come here." He took two backward steps on the porch, then turned to run away.

"Collin?" Ruzanna said. She'd come behind Lillian and David Samuel, just close enough to see him.

Collin stopped and turned back to her. "Hey, babe," he said then sniveled a deep and beaded intake of air.

"What are you doing here?"

He seemed more comfortable to ignore Lillian and David Samuel, willing them away: "I've been, like, trying to talk to you. Going where I think you'll be, you know? I saw you leave your house tonight. I wanted to give you that…" Here, he looked up and threw out a hand to indicate the notebook, but the motion was halted when he realized that to do so meant acknowledging the woman holding it. "I wanted you to give it back to…him." He said to his shoes.

"To David Samuel," Lillian said to the boy sternly.

"Yeah."

"You've been following me?" Ruzanna asked.

Collin took a step forward. "I had to, babe. You're, like, all I ever think about. You and this…trouble." He nodded toward David Samuel. "I need you, Ruz. I want to do what you want me to do here. Tell me what you want me to do." He was back on the porch now, towering over them on the other side of the door.

"I can't tell you that," Ruzanna said.

"Does anyone want to know what I think?" David Samuel said, staring Collin boldly in his eyes, "I think, Collin, here, should be invited in."

Lillian and Collin each shook their heads, but David Samuel persuaded his mother away from the doorway with an outstretched arm, then that same arm bade Collin's entry. The boy took a grudging step forward.

When the children were all in the living room— Collin and Ruzanna on the sofa, David Samuel in his father's recliner—Lillian appraised them all from the room's doorway. She held the notebook at her side.

"Dude," Collin began, staring past David Samuel, "I don't know how to say this. I was, like, really uncool to you."

"Uncool?" Ruzanna shouted beside him. "You beat him up, Collin. You and your little brother and that dickhead, AJ."

This confirmation of her guest's identity caused Lillian's heart to race. She'd known it, of course, but there was a comfortable margin between knowing it and hearing it confirmed as fact. She clenched her jaw.

Collin nervously rubbed his fists on his blue jeans, forward and back. "Mm-hmm," he nodded, a tear escaping his left eye and spotting the denim. "Mm-hmm. I'm really sorry, man. I'm really sorry, Ruz."

"What about his mother?" Ruzanna demanded.

"I'm really sorry, ma'am," Collin said, turning to her, fully blubbering now. "I'm really, really sorry." A violent sobbing overtook him, and he buried his face in his lap. He was just a boy, a baby. Lillian's own tears rested in her eyes, providing her a refracted distance from what was unfolding, a lens to watch it through.

"What I want to know," David Samuel began, sitting forward in Phil's recliner. "Are you listening, Collin?"

The boy raised his face, a pathetic face wet with the fluids of grief.

"Collin, what I want to know is: did you read my notebook?"

Collin nodded pathetically.

"I see. And secondly: did it inspire you?" His fingers bloomed in the air with a suggestion of magic.

Collin tucked his face into his armpit then wiped away its dampness along the length of his arm. "I mean…I don't know. I couldn't stop thinking about it. I even had dreams about it."

Lillian watched her son and saw that he appeared titillated by this revelation.

Ruzanna, in a tentative show of affection for the boy, placed a light hand on his knee. The conciliatory feeling of that moment caused Lillian, for the first time, to speak her mind. She stepped forward and said to Collin, "I think we need to call your parents. We need to figure out where we go from here. And I need to talk to Phil, to see what he thinks."

She wasn't sure what she'd said, but the room seemed suddenly to tense and stiffen. Ruzanna's eyes fell to the carpet. Collin looked first to Ruzanna and then to David Samuel and, finding no help from either, settled on their bald coffee table rabbit.

"David Samuel?" Lillian said, taking a step toward the recliner, intuiting that he was the authority on whatever it was that was happening here.

David Samuel sighed then rose as abruptly as his girth allowed. "Mother," he said, offering her the recliner, "you should sit."

She listened quietly as David Samuel explained the motivation for Collin's attack, those protective tears spilling from her eyes only once before welling again.

She promised that she would remain uninvolved in Phil and David Samuel's warring, in concerns of the restaurant and the campaign. But hearing David Samuel's account of the assault, the sick things he was telling her, she felt there was one thing more to do before washing her hands of all of it. So, when he was through, Lillian sat for a moment before rising and looking her son sternly in the face. "David Samuel," she said, "I want you to call Jim Trebek. And I want you to ask him for Gilda Cranston's phone number. I don't know what your father was thinking, but that's not my primary concern right now. Call and get the number, then I'll figure a way to put an end to all of this." And for once, David Samuel did as he was told without commentary or sass.

Chapter 39

The manager of the Columbia DMV was a short, solidly-built woman named Gussie Ford. She was younger than Eddie, he supposed, but she projected a world-worn confidence that suggested she'd seen a thing or two, and that she'd let not one person more take even the softest of steps over her. "I told you no, man," she said.

"Let me just tell you what I was thinking," Eddie said. They were standing on the sidewalk to the right of the DMV's big front window, Gussie Ford working on the last third of a Parliament Light, Eddie projecting his palms to her like a physical frame around his vision. "So, the future Senator walks in through that door," he continued, pointing. "The camera's behind him. He doesn't make a fuss, gets right into the line and waits. And, when it's his turn, you call him over and he tells you he's here to legally change his name— he already has all the paperwork filled out, so we'll take up as little of your time as possible. And then, when it's all over, I was thinking you could shake his hand, maybe, and say congratulations." Eddie raised his eyebrows as if the offer of a spoken line in their video may be just the carrot she'd been holding out for. "Have you ever met a Senator?"

"Man, I met everybody," Gussie Ford said. "Last week I reissued the license of the mayor's little drunk-ass daughter. And I told you: ain't no cameras allowed in the DMV." She finished her Parliament but used Eddie as an opportunity to light another.

"Why not?"

"It's the rules, man. All them people in there got business that ain't none of your business."

"We'll focus tight on the future Senator—and if we get any other faces on camera, we can blur them out."

Gussie Ford lifted her Parliament toward Eddie. "Do you see this?" She turned it back toward herself. "Do you see *me?* Let me ask you, where do you think I'm more comfortable: standing on this sidewalk like a goddamn hooker, or sitting behind my desk? I got a varicose vein running up my leg that looks like a slinky pulled out of a lawnmower blade and it aches me from coming out here, standing three, four times a day. I got a chair in there," she pointed, "with lumbar support. But, nope, here I am on this sidewalk—people driving by thinking we're out here negotiating the price of a goddamn blowjob—when I'm the manager of a government facility. And do you know why I'm out here? Cause there ain't no cigarettes allowed inside the DMV. It's the rules, man."

"Do you watch *Chat!?* They're going to air this video on *Chat!*"

"I got a job and a son, and the only thing we watch in the morning is *Teen Titan's, Go.* So, you get Robin and Cyborg to air your video, maybe I'll see what I can do. I'll even let you make me a bad guy: Vericosia Veins." She chuckled, then looked at Eddie decisively. "Otherwise, I think we're done."

"You'll be the first to learn the winning name."

Gussie Ford's frown was as belittling as if he'd just

asked to crash on her couch for a few nights.

"He's ahead in the polls," Eddie said weakly.

"And I'm *a-head* back inside," Gussie Ford responded, pleasing herself again. She flicked the Parliament into the parking lot then left Eddie alone on the sidewalk.

He'd been aware that there were no cameras allowed in any branch of the SC DMV, of course. But he'd figured it was worth a shot. And this wasn't the first he'd taken. The previous afternoon, he'd made a series of phone calls that culminated with an unanswered try for the governor himself.

Frustrated, Eddie walked back through the parking lot, and by the time he made it to the oversized news van, he had a passable idea and a smile to rally his troops. "It's a no-go," he told Doris, the local news producer who'd been loaned to him to oversee the video recording.

"For real?" Doris said, perturbed. She was chain-smoking the same brand of cigarettes as Gussie Ford. "New York expects a video intro."

"I know," Eddie said. "So, I was wondering: do you have any of those body cameras? The kind the police have to wear now?"

Doris laughed in his face. "So, you want the first national footage of your candidate to be of him breaking the law?"

Eddie's eyes found Phil across the parking lot. He was yelling something about Welfare Queens to a homeless man. "Well, I mean, he's kind of a renegade, right? And, you know, being an asshole isn't necessarily off-brand. So, yeah, maybe it could work. What would be the harm in trying?"

It wasn't that Phil appeared out of place in a ball cap—in fact, it suited the casual look invoked by his polyester tracksuits and ever-bright, spotless tennis shoes. There was simply a part of Eddie that delighted in forcing him to wear it against his will.

The camera was hidden in the second 'O' of the cap's South Carolina Stingrays logo, its tiny microphone similarly secreted in the cartoon mascot's left eye. An earpiece, visible but passable as a hearing aid on a man of Phil's age, would allow Eddie and their Local 5 producer to guide him from the station van.

"I look like a twit," Phil said, appraising himself in the side mirror of his Lexus.

"You look great," Eddie said. "Is Lillian coming out? David Samuel? It could be good to get a shot of you with the family."

Phil scratched his scalp under the brim of the cap and made a quiet, displeased sound. "She wasn't around this morning. Probably had some DAP what have you. And David Samuel—forget it. He'd burst, the little weasel, with the cameras and the crowd."

Yes, Eddie thought, *the crowd*: two people who were probably homeless, a three-person news crew, and eight or ten people stopped, probably only temporarily, by the site of the news van as they moved to or from the Dollar General that shared the DMV's parking lot. "That's a shame," Eddie said of Phil's absentee family. "Tell, you what, I'm going to talk to the camera man who'll get the long shot of you walking in and out to make sure he's clear on everything, then I'll go ahead and get seated in the van. Do you have everything? The forms I gave you?"

Phil presented him with a crumpled fold of papers from the muffler pocket of his track jacket.

"All right," Eddie said with a smile, "Goodbye forever, Phil Ochs."

Phil winced conspicuously at the sound of his name.

*   *   *

"Okay, Phil," Eddie said into a headset microphone, "can you hear me?" The image on the van's central monitor bobbed up and down in reply. "Cameras are rolling. Go ahead and go." The scene in the monitor bobbled forward.

Seeing the world from the perspective of Phil Ochs, even via a camera placed several inches above his sightline, was like seeing the world from the height of an average-sized middle schooler. More correctly, given the grunts and grumbles picked up by the camera's audio, it was like looking through the eyes of a rather tall bear, one released as some promotional spectacle for the Irmo Dollar General clientele.

"Hey there, buddy," a voice said from off-camera.

"Who's that," Eddie said. Stop and talk to him for a minute. It will look good in the long shot."

The speaker came into view. Eddie recognized him as one of the homeless men he'd identified earlier. He turned to the side monitor to see how the scene looked from the external camera. "Go ahead and shake his hand, Phil. It's gold."

"I'll pass," Phil said, the monitor image taking in a full-bodied appraisal of the man. He was holding a thin wooden sign.

"How's that, brother?" the man asked.

"Then just ask him about himself," Eddie said. "Keep it light and nod and then move on." He was resisting the impulse to swivel his chair around and watch the interaction from the van's back window, perhaps because not doing so would provide him greater distance from all that may go wrong with Phil's attempts at graciousness.

"What's that sign mean?" Phil asked. "Are you some kind of protestor?"

"This sign?" the man asked, apparently indicating it in some way that Phil's camera didn't pick up. "Now, what would I have to protest with this here sign? This is merely an advertisement of my services in the spiritual arts."

"You're some kind of lunatic, then? Is that it?"

"Keep it light, Phil. Ask him to hold up the sign. Spend a few seconds looking at it. You know, like you're interested in what he's all about."

The microphone captured the sound of Phil grinding his teeth. "So, what's the deal with the sign, then?" he said. The monitor image lowered and fixed on its painted words: Two-Headed Root Doctor.

"Never mind that now, buddy," Eddie heard the voice say. "You look familiar to me, you know that?"

"Tell him you're running for state legislature."

"I'm a community leader," Phil said. "A well-known political actor."

"You don't say," the man said, his face now squarely in the camera's frame. "Ain't that good for you? But—no, I don't think that's it, come to think of it. No, sir. I believe you was the subject of a dream I had two nights back."

"This guy's a crackpot," Phil said.

"Yup," Eddie agreed. "Move on."

The monitor again began to shakily advance toward the DMV.

"Hold on a minute," the voice yelled from a distance. The pace of Phil's movement increased. The man's face flashed close in the monitor and caused Eddie to jump back in alarm. "Don't you want to know what you was doing in my dream? You was on a roof, and you opened up your hand, dramatic-like." There was a manic jumble on the screen and a persistent crackling in the microphone that caused Eddie to rise and look out the van's back window to confirm his fear: Phil had begun running toward the building's entrance. "And in your hand, you showed me you had a bird. Then you smiled at me and started plucking out its feathers, one by one." His voice was beaded with the percussion of heavy footfalls. From the van window, Eddie saw that Phil had arrived at the DMV entrance. The man slid in front of him and blocked him from going in. "And I tried to stop you," the man said, "and do you know what you did? You pushed me."

"Don't push him," Eddie instructed. He watched through the window as Phil pushed him.

"You pushed me right off the roof," the man continued, undeterred.

"Don't push him," Eddie said again and watched as Phil pushed the man to the ground.

Phil pulled the door open and in the tinkling of welcome bells, Eddie heard the man yell, "Wait, brother. As I fell, I looked up and I saw what happened to you. Your fate, brother. It wasn't the bird that done it, it wasn't the bird that—"

And then, the door closed the man out. Eddie turned back to the monitor and saw its image heave with the labor of Phil's breathing. All eyes of the DMV's long line of waiting customers stared back at Eddie.

The camera image turned with choppy motion as Phil looked over his shoulder through the DMV's big glass window to the homeless man on his knees shouting something indecipherable to Phil.

"Creeping Jesus," Eddie heard Phil say.

He watched a parting of the crowd on the monitor. From its center bounded Gussie Ford. She grew larger and larger in the frame like a slow-motion fist with the aim to cold-cock him in the jaw. In the van Eddie sounded a frightened, "Eep."

"What the hell kind of ruckus are you making up here?" she asked the monitor.

"Oh, shit. Here we go," said Doris to the producer, both smiling in delight.

"And who is that out there, banging on my glass? *Hey, you, knock that off.*" Then to the monitor, she said, "You got business with the DMV, man?"

"I came for a legal name change," Eddie heard Phil say, his voice wispy and short of breath.

"Name change?" Gussie Ford said. For a moment, she appeared to search the air as if for why such a need struck her as familiar. Suddenly, her face was closer, her eyes directed at the monitor's lower edge. "You that politician-guy?"

"I'm running for state Senate," Phil huffed. He sounded so uncharacteristically weak that Eddie quietly wished he could see his face.

Gussie Ford's eyes rose to stare directly into the camera. "What's the deal with that hat?" she asked, cocking her head slightly as she looked at it. Her closeness to the camera created a fishbowl lens affect, rounding and broadening the center of her face with cartoonish distortion.

"It's a hat," Phil said.

"Mm-hmm," Gussie Ford said. "What's it say on it?"

"What?"

"I said, what's it say on that bullshit hat?" She barely gave him time to reply before saying, "That's what I thought. You trying to pull something on me, man?"

"No," Eddie heard Phil croak before a deafening crackle filled his headset as Gussie Ford wrenched the hat off his head. "Oh…hell…no," he heard her say, the words broken and distorted, before the image on the monitor became a succession of still images of the ceiling, of the floor, of faces in the crowd, of a wincing Phil as Gussie Ford repeatedly struck him with the hat. All the while, snatches of audio picked up pieces of her angry ranting: "fool me," "told you fools," "camera in the DMV," and, repeatedly, the phrase, "the rules."

After nearly a minute, Doris reached forward and switched off the monitor. "I don't think we'll be able to use any of this," she said.

Eddie swallowed.

"And you know that if she breaks that camera, the station's going to charge it to your campaign, right?"

"Do you think we should rescue him?" Eddie said to her.

Doris laughed, pinching a Parliament from her pack and tossing her headset onto the keyboard before her. "You go right ahead," she said. "I'll be leaning on the van here if you need any back up." She pushed open the backdoor of the van and stepped down to the pavement. "Just, you know, flash me a signal or something."

Chapter 40

Ninety seconds of usable footage. In fifteen minutes of taping that morning, that's what their two cameras had captured. 'Usable,' was a distinction made by the Local 5 remote video editor to mean any footage that didn't include Phil running from or assaulting a member of South Carolina's homeless population; cowering from or being assaulted by the manager of the Irmo DMV; any miscellaneous footage made useless by Phil's audible grunts, groans and burps; and moments lost to curious crowd members waving hands, middle fingers, or similarly lewd gestures as if hypnotized into states of involuntary clownishness by the camera's small red light. As the edited seconds of salvageable footage was played in the van for them, Eddie realized that 'usable' did not mean gripping. Most of those seconds were of an old man in a stupid baseball cap, shot from behind as he walked through a parking lot. *Riveting,* he imagined the hosts of *Chat!* saying. *Let's roll that again.*

"Fuck my life," Doris said. "There is no chance I'm feeding that to New York." She glowered at Phil, who sat in the van with a blanket draped over his shoulders like a rescued hostage in a terrorist film. Her eyes were accusatory.

"So, what do we do?" Eddie said.

The eyes she turned on him were no softer. "Well, I guess I get to call New York and tell them I let your man screw the pooch. See what they want us to do—" here, she checked the time on her phone before adding gravely, "with twenty-five minutes to air." She shoved her fingers so hungrily into the cigarette box that Eddie was surprised when they didn't reemerge scissoring multiples of them. She stepped down into the parking lot, the phone to her ear, a single Parliament in her lips.

With quiet delight, the video editor cued the cut footage. Rapt, he chuckled, "Man, for what it's worth, this is, like, the most amazing thing ever."

"How are you doing, Phil?" Eddie called.

"What's our position on the homeless?" Phil said to the carpeted floor. "We don't like them, right?"

"Some of us have been accused that way."

"Good."

Eddie moved away from him and sat on the closed lid of a steel storage box near the van's open rear doors. The chemical-smelling smoke of Doris's cigarette blew into the van in a greedy breeze. He could hear her on the phone with New York. "Just a weasel little dipshit," she was saying. Of himself or of Phil or of the homeless man, he wasn't sure.

After a moment of eavesdropping, Eddie became aware of a change in the language of Doris's body. The manic, animated gesturing of one intent on shifting blame suddenly quieted and became reflective. She peered over her shoulder, first, briefly at Eddie, and then for a long time, at Phil. "For real?" she finally said into the phone. And, from this point, her half of the conversation became relieved and grateful, lighthearted and compliant. Eventually, she pocketed the phone and joined them.

"What up?" the video editor said, the line invoking all the ironic charmless-ness of a balding, bespectacled white man who makes his living at a van's computer deck.

"What did they say?" Eddie inquired.

Even Phil turned his head in anticipation of her answer.

Doris smiled in a way that seemed involuntary, as if it were impossible for the muscles in her face not to smile. "They said to have him ready for air in fifteen minutes."

"Sweet," the video editor said, "They're not pissed about the intro?"

"No," Doris said. "They said they'd already decided to go in a different direction."

"What different direction?" Eddie asked.

"Hmm?" she questioned, as if he were out of range of her hearing. "Oh, they just said they have an alternate video intro. Something they'd rather show instead."

*   *   *

A solid green screen had been lowered on one wall of the van, one that was notably like the projector screens Eddie remembered from his school days: the same finger hold that doubled as a hook for the floor mount, the same unsatisfying sound of makeshift entertainment when it was lowered. Phil had been arranged on a stool in front of it, the blanket removed from his shoulders, a comically-lowered camera trained on his face. Something would appear behind him in replacement of the green screen. A flag, Eddie hoped, Phil's state's or his country's—even something shlock-y like a generic image of voting booths, or the Fry Buddy logo would be fine—though no one could tell him.

"Should we have audio?" he asked Doris.

"Shouldn't there be something in these cans?" He tapped his headset. It was sixty-seconds to air.

Doris shushed him with an erect finger and studied the New York feed.

A male impotency commercial ended and then the ear pieces in the oversized South Carolina news van burst to life.

"Welcome, welcome, welcome back," said a voice that was graveled and aged, the cigarette-weathered voice of an actress who was a favorite of Eddie's twenty years earlier, before her infamous starring role opposite an anamorphic canine private detective relegated her to the tabloids and then the television. "Boy, do we have an interesting story now for y'all."

"It's a political story," said another recognizable voice, this one of the pretty daughter of a former American president, the one panelist for whom this talk show didn't represent a last act in a career, but, rather, what was likely to be the accomplishment that most identified her as a public commodity separate from her famous father. "Hey, did I hear some of you groan? Politics is important, you guys," she pouted.

The voice of the celebrity attorney bolstered this sentiment, whipping the crowd to applause.

"Although, this particular story may be one y'all won't be so proud to have clapped for," the former-actress interjected with a punctuation of self-righteous laughter. "Let's show them the video so we all can chat about it."

"What video is this?" Eddie asked, his heart racing. He leaned over Doris's shoulder. He, Doris, and the video editor crowded the small monitor playing the New York feed. The video was choppy. Grass and sky. Close-up legs and feet. Voices yelling and laughing, some of their words censored with harsh-sounding beeps. And then, Eddie saw him: David Samuel. "Phil?" he whispered, taking a step back from the board.

Phil's head was turned toward the monitor too, though it was unlikely he could see the video from where he sat. Nevertheless, his eyes were wide.

When it ended, the audience gasped and intoned sounds of condemnation. "Okay," the attorney-host said, "let me explain: that exclusive video was sent to our producers just this morning, and since then they've been working to verify its sourcing and the context of the savage assault you just saw. And, while it was provided by the source with a strict understanding of anonymity, we can validate their connection to our next guest, and we can tell you that the poor man in that video," she said, pausing for emphasis before concluding, "is our guest's son."

The audience sounded a collective shock.

The former-president's daughter continued: "Let's bring him on. Our guest for The Interview is running for a special election Senate seat in the South Carolina legislature."

"This is it," Doris called. In the monitor that was soon to go live, Phil looked straight ahead. He seemed reduced in size by the slight downward tilt of the stationary camera. Behind him, the green screen was replaced by a still, close-up image of David Samuel's face pinned to the ground by a hand with splayed fingers.

"He achieved national attention when he agreed to let voters legally change his name," the host continued, with a tone that suggested a verbal roll of her eyes. "Please welcome, remote from South Carolina, the soon-to-be-renamed Phil Ochs."

The audience cheered. It was that long, uplifting cheer that daytime talk audiences reserved for heroic victims. Eddie was confused by what was happening, but had the sudden and brief realization that, whatever this video was, it might be great for them.

"Mr. Ochs, welcome," the former actress said.

Eddie raised his eyebrows and nodded at Phil to encourage a response.

"Yeah," Phil said.

"Look, I want to get right down to it. You saw the shocking video we just aired."

"I didn't see any video," Phil said.

"You didn't see it?"

"I'm in a van right now," Phil explained. "If it was about the boy getting jumped, though, I don't know anything about that."

"It was, indeed, footage taken by one of your son's attackers when he was jumped in a local park. You can't tell us anything about that incident?"

Phil was quiet for what felt to Eddie like an uncomfortable period of seconds. Finally, he said, "Well, he wears these vests, you know. Out in public even. And he's got this long hair. It was only a matter of time before someone clobbered him. But, it's a private matter. I'm here to talk about this name-change business."

A brief twitter arose from the audience.

"But, Mr. Ochs," the former attorney said, "the source of this video has told our network—and our producers have confirmed with secondary sourcing—that you, in fact, paid those men to arrange the assault we saw in that video."

The audience's collective intake of air, heard in Eddie's headset, may as well have been the elemental force that drained the color from his face. "Phil?" he said into his headset microphone.

"Yeah?" Phil said, turning to look at Eddie.

There were mob sounds from the crowd.

"Did you just admit to paying for this crime?" the former president's daughter asked.

"I didn't admit to anything," Phil said. "I was talking to this moron who's talking into my earpiece. The boy got whipped, I made him a store manager. Now he's leaving me. It's a private matter. Move on."

"Wait," the actress said, "are you saying you can justify arranging an assault on your son because you made him a manager at one of your Fry Buddy fast food restaurants?"

The audience hooted, smelling blood.

"I didn't say that. I didn't say anything. I'm not saying anything about this." Phil stood, not to escape the interview, but out of what appeared to be an involuntary reaction to the stress of the questioning. The top of his head grazed the van's ceiling. He paced back and forth as if unaware that the camera wasn't moving with him. For the remainder of the interview, the audience of *Chat!* was treated to shifting perspectives of Phil Ochs's abdomen.

"Sir, please sit," the attorney said, but continued when he didn't do so. "Sir, our sources tell us—"

"Your sources are slanderous punks," Phil barked. The audience, by now, sounded less like that of a talk show than of a prizefight. "Was it those kids? You're going to listen to kids who'd beat up a guy for money over the word of a community leader? What kind of program is this?" He appeared to direct this last question at Eddie, who only stared blankly as if watching Phil tug the red carpet of his political future out from under him.

"Mr. Ochs, the source of this video has asked to remain anonymous, but I can assure you it's someone intimately connected to you."

"David Samuel?" Phil said, "That creepy little geek. This is exactly the kind of thing—"

"David Samuel, that's your son, correct?"

"That's what his mother tells me. He does this. This is what he does. I wake up with poems he's written laying on my chest. And filthy bird's nests in my underwear drawer. And then, after I give him everything, he abandons me. Did your source tell you that? That he abandoned his own family? I don't know how he set this up, but this is exactly the kind of thing he does."

"Is that why you paid to have him assaulted, sir?"

"If I did, I ought to ask for my money back, clearly." To Eddie, he said, "Did you help him set this up? God knows he's not bright enough to have pulled it off himself."

Eddie had pulled off his headset. He held it at his side.

"Well?" Phil demanded.

"I don't know anything about this," Eddie said to the man directly.

"About what? Embarrassing me on national television? Because it seems to me you know a good deal about that. Setting up these hens with this 'gotcha' video and all? Tell me I'm wrong."

Eddie shook his head, his eyes fixed on the monitor beyond Phil's body. "You're a monster, Phil," he said.

"And you're as much a traitor as that kid of mine."

Light flooded into the van when Eddie pushed open its backdoor, frying the camera's video until he slammed it shut again from the parking lot.

It wasn't Eddie's departure that stopped Phil's pacing. It was a sudden shock of meaning he saw in Lillian's absence that morning, the woman whom he'd counted on for twenty-five years to have his back, unexplainably missing on his most important day. And from this realization, he correctly guessed, "Lillian?" Once aware and sadly certain of her betrayal, he found he couldn't separate it from the assault he was being subjected to in this interview, three on one, ambushed with no protection, trapped inside this stinking box, his assaulters like invisible ghosts yelling at him through intimate whispers in his ear. Lillian, who up until now had always been predictably at his flank, was nowhere in sight, and so, he had no one to take his side. He felt vulnerable and alone. "Creeping Jesus," he moaned, pulling his earpiece and tossing it to the floor like it was something unholy, a devil doll or cursed monkey's paw. He fled the van quickly, leaving its backdoors open behind him, frying the video again, running for safety, needing to call home for the very comfort of having a home to call. A safe space where no ghosts malevolently whispered and where someone was always there to trust his word and to believe he was a winner.

"Okay, we don't know what's happening there, South Carolina," the former actress said. "Mr. Ochs, you're not on camera…okay, I'm being told we're going to take a break. We'll discuss whatever it was we just saw on the other side. We'll be right back."

In an earpiece, idle on the van's floor, a satisfied audience applauded.

Chapter 41

"Thank you for calling Miracle Products. This is Raj. Who am I speaking with, please?"

"Raj?" Lillian said.

Raj swallowed audibly. "Lillian Ochs?"

"Yes. Hello, Raj."

"How is the stuffed pet?"

"Battle-scarred, I'd say," she sighed. "Last I saw him, anyway. But, that's not why I'm calling."

"There was something I could help you with today?"

"There is something in my craw, if you want to know," Lillian said. "Raj, can I ask you: are you married?"

Raj was silent for a moment before saying, "Miracle Products forbids all telecommunications specialists from calling, meeting, or otherwise seeking involvement with their callers. With romantic interests or not."

Lillian blushed. "Oh, no, Raj. That's not what I was implying."

"It's policy."

"I'm sure. But, what I meant was—and I know

this is forward of me, but you've been so helpful to me, a blessing really, and I could use your advice right now. But, what I was asking is: have you ever been betrayed? In matters of the heart, I mean."

There was another long pause before Raj said, "Love renders the senses mad and blind."

"Yes," Lillian said, "exactly. The blindness, I mean. Dumbness too, don't you think? So that when you find your loved one has betrayed the very thing that's dearest to you—you waffle. On what to do, I mean."

"A waffle iron burns hot like the passions of the heart. Miracle Products' Two-in-One Waffle Griddle has five browning settings to let you choose the perfect temperature for your family's waffle pleasure."

"That's fascinating. But you're right. About passions, I mean. So, what do you do? Do you burn everything down? Or risk betraying yourself by sticking with the person who's left such a terrible stain on things?"

With an air of confidence, Raj said, "Stains can be stubborn to remove. But they can be lifted to make a surface like new. This only requires a miracle product."

Lillian was silent while she considered this.

"Lillian Ochs?"

"Sorry, Raj. Yes, I'm here... So, what you're saying is that, no matter how bad the stain seems, there's always a way to repair it? The stained surface, I mean?"

"Yes. With the correct miracle product."

"But you can't buy a magic fix for something like this, so...the miracle is the product of your own actions. You rebuild things in a way that's true to yourself and to what you hold most dear, and that will allow you to maintain the relationship with the source of the stain. Is that right?"

"Yes. I think that's right."

Lillian shook her head demonstrably, as if he could see her show of awed wonder through the phone. "My goodness, Raj," she said eventually. "Do you know what I think? I think you might be my miracle. I feel two tons lighter. I swear, Raj, I could hug you."

"Miracle Products forbids physical affection from customers," Raj reminded her.

"Can I tell you? I've been staying at a hotel for two days."

"You are on holiday, Lillian Ochs?"

"I've been avoiding a stain. Or the man who made it, anyway. But now, I mean, you've made me want to roll up my sleeves on this thing and scrub it out. I feel like I can do it now."

"Miracle Products encourages you to do it yourself."

"That's marvelous. Listen, Raj, I'm going to go. But I want you to do something for me: if you *are* married, I want you to tell your lovely wife to give you a giant hug for being a wonderful man. And tell her it's on behalf of Lillian Ochs. Never mind the policy. Will you do that?"

Raj was silent.

"Raj, will you?"

"I will do that," he said. "Never mind the policy."

Chapter 42

In his parting act as campaign manager, Eddie got Phil on the national news one last time. He bribed the Local 5 remote video editor for the raw footage of Gussie Ford beating the shit out of Phil with his camera hat, then he emailed it to three of the network's producers. Within hours, the video caught fire. It was the feel-good segment on three of the network's primetime programs and a source of bad-faith discussion about partisan violence on two others. The women of *Chat!* picked it up the next day, as did the other two political cable news networks. By the end of the week, PUG Ochs was a joke on the lips of Americans nationwide. Memes of the video, and of his *Chat!* meltdown, flooded Eddie's inbox. Gussie Ford was interviewed on at least four of the major midafternoon talk shows, each of which welcomed her as a hero: the underpaid single-mother government worker who'd given come-uppance to the wealthy political villain who'd paid to have his own child assaulted. She was the long arm of justice for the nation's outrage, and in a manner of thinking, Eddie had given this to her. If nothing else, he would always have that.

"You did the right thing," Cindy said. "I'm really proud of you, Eddie."

They were sitting at the big, rustic dining table in Gail's kitchen, a kitchen to which Eddie had never previously been invited, and to which he would not have previously come. But he was now a man without friends or a job or direction, so there was nothing for him to do but to take a two-handed grip on his family, such as it was, and not let go.

Penny was seated to his right, coloring on the paper tablecloth that Eddie had to grudgingly concede to be a touching effort by the woman who'd stolen his daughter away from him. Gail, herself, was on the back porch, tending to the grill. Half of the women's six dogs—those who'd found a more appealing source of interest than lapping dripping hamburger fat from the tile beneath the grill—were taking turns filing under the table to nose and occasionally bite at Eddie's crotch. It was currently the pug who was head-butting him in the balls, an irony that wasn't lost on him.

"What are you going to do now?" Cindy said.

Eddie lifted the pug's chin away from his chair. "Oh, find a freight brokerage, I guess. I paid myself pretty well during this thing, so I can afford to take my time with that. I don't know, maybe I'll take a road trip first." A fleeting look of jealousy played across Cindy's face, prompting in Eddie a small wave of satisfaction. "What are *you* going to do now?" he asked.

Cindy's eyes moved to Penny, whose head was hung low over her coloring. "You mean, long-term?" she said, her words chosen carefully. "I don't know for sure. There's still, you know, the buyer's remorse."

"Well," Eddie said, "I'm sure you'll figure that out."

The storm door slapped loudly, stealing all their attentions. Gail came toward them with a metal tray of burgers, seemingly carried by a platoon of enthusiastic miniature dogs. "Hope you're hungry, sperm donor," she said, touching Eddie on the back and setting the tray on the table near him.

Gail's playful sparring had taken him by surprise when he'd arrived, but he figured it was at least a way to avoid the awkward silence he'd expected from this meal, so maybe she was onto something. "You better believe it, home-wrecker. I plan to keep you on your feet serving me the entire time I'm here."

"Trying to steal my woman?" she said with a good-natured wink.

"No. If that was the plan, I'd keep you around so you could give me tips on how that's done."

Gail laughed a big, bellowing laugh, and Eddie did too. Penny looked up and stared from one to the other, then silently queried her mother for direction. Cindy had reddened and fixed her face with a fraudulent smile. Noticing this, Eddie nodded to her and, as if to coach her, offered her that same look, only warm and genuine.

Gail pulled out a chair opposite Penny, taking care not to endanger a stray paw or tail that seemed always to circle her feet.

When she was seated, Eddie said, "Gail, thank you very much for inviting me. It was really thoughtful of you."

"Edward," she said, taking his hand and leaning into him with a smile, "have you been into my booze? That sounded awfully earnest."

It occurred to Eddie that he might have gotten away with an offended reaction to this comment, but he was tired of the politics of the weird turn his family had taken. Still, he hoped Cindy was offended, that there might be a fight later between these women, an epic blowout after he left, but now he only squeezed the hand that held his and said, "No ma'am, I'm just really happy to be here." And all of them, even Eddie himself, understood that it was true.

Chapter 43

PUG Ochs stared down at the name that was stenciled on the parking space that belonged to him. He exhaled audibly and flattened his lips. "All right," he said, "get rid of it."

The man who was with him set down a white gallon bucket, took a knee, and began to extract its contents. He unscrewed a can of stripping gel and set about covering the painted letters in a single viscus band, right to left, as if erasing its existence backward in time.

"It's only going to take about five minutes with this shit for me to be able to power wash off them letters," the man said.

PUG nodded and said nothing. He stared through the window of the Columbia Fry Buddy, watching the movements of a dining room packed with customers. They rose and sat, roared back in laughter or leaned together for privacy. It was just now dinner rush and the dining room had been busy for nearly an hour. Recent days would suggest that it would be well after seven o'clock before the crowd would start to thin.

For the first week after the *Chat!* interview, the crowds at PUG's franchises barely ebbed at all. Each morning, lines would be waiting as his managers unlocked the doors, then the lobbies would fill and stay full until the end of business. Customers came and went and then more came, bussing crumbs and spills left by previous occupants at tables they didn't want to wait on to be cleaned. For days, at each of his stores, it was like this: the crowds coming in hopes of seeing PUG, telling him to his face that he was despicable, then convincing him to take a photo with them. And PUG welcomed them, stood calmly while they berated him or asked what one of those *Chat!* women was like behind the scenes. He took and took their money and heard more than once from someone who claimed to have written in his name when they voted for state Senate, despite his having removed himself from the race. Several told him they were the submitter of his winning name.

"I think that ought to do it," the man said, tossing a cigarette into the parking lot, then lowering himself to his knees. PUG watched the smoking butt roll and stop in the lot and made a mental note to send out a kid to collect it.

The man took a fist-sized metal scraper in one hand, a plastic shopping bag in the other and set about scooping the ruined gel from the blacktop into the bag. "Well, hell," he said, "it comes off real neat. Look at that. It almost never wants to come up that easy. Won't take anything to blast the rest away."

From the jacket pocket of his tracksuit, PUG's phone began to vibrate. "Yeah?" he said after accepting the call.

"PUG? It's Lillian," Lillian said.

"Yeah?"

"Do you have a moment?"

"Mm-hmm."

The man was through connecting the power

washer to the store's outdoor faucet and electrical out-let. He was now working to start its engine with a pull string. PUG walked away as it roared to life.

"Listen, PUG," Lillian said, "I have something important to ask you: how much do you like corn on the cob?"

"Corn on the cob?"

"Yes, the vegetable."

PUG closed his eyes and lifted his face toward the sky. The winter sun turned the darkness of his eyelids red. "I like it fine," he said.

"I know you like it, but that wasn't my question. What I want to know is how much do you like it?"

"Fine," PUG repeated. "I like it fine. What's this about?"

"Well, all last week, I was craving a really good breaded fish sandwich. And then, this morning, I tex-ted David Samuel to ask what he wanted for dinner tonight, and guess what he said? A breaded fish sand-wich. Isn't that wild?"

PUG wasn't sure where this was going, but he was certain it would involve a major financial expenditure. In the two weeks since he'd ended his campaign, Lil-lian's spending had spiked. Many of her purchases had been safety-themed—a telescopic police-style baton to be kept in the driver's door of the used Corolla she'd purchased to "keep David Samuel off of that scum-my city bus"; said Corolla; life vests for storage in that same car's trunk, as if David Samuel were in danger of tripping while writing at Lake Murray then falling and overcoming all physical laws of friction, sending him rolling with unencumbered acceleration into—and straight to the bottom of—that lake's peaceful waters.

When PUG didn't respond, Lillian said, "Anyway, it got me thinking about why I had never made myself a really good breaded fish sandwich last week when I was craving one. It was the same thing that's stop-ping me now: the right buns. I mean, call me old-fashioned, but a breaded fish sandwich just isn't a breaded fish sandwich with a bun that's grilled or toasted, you know? It needs to be steamed. And that's the kicker: I don't have anywhere to steam my buns.

"Did you ever think of just going through a drive-thru and buying a fish sandwich?"

"Of course not," Lillian said flatly. She'd lately taken on an air of authority when dealing with him. "But, I did begin to look around at industrial steamers."

PUG leaned against his Lexus for support. He'd parked in a far corner of the lot under a dogwood tree.

"Anyway, the one that I think would look best in the kitchen is full-sized. A six-pan convection steamer. There's another one too, a smaller one, but it's a tabletop model and I really don't want to give up the counter space, you know? And, like I said, I think that first one would look best in the kitchen."

"So, why does it matter if I like corn on the cob?"

"Well, I was just thinking of other things we could do with a full-sized steamer. It would be too much for just steamed buns, wouldn't it? And no one in the house eats vegetables, except maybe corn on the cob. I was even thinking that we could reserve a few of the trays for socks and underwear to heat them up on cold mornings? If we only used the same trays every time, what would it matter? Our clothes are clean."

"Lillian," PUG said, "I have to go now. But my answer is that I love corn on the cob. And you should get whichever one you think would look best in the kitchen. Will that make you happy?"

There was a momentary silence before his wife clarified, "It was never in question that I would buy the one that made me happy, PUG. I just wanted to extend the courtesy of letting you give your input."

"And now you have it."

"And now I do. Be home early tonight. Bye, PUG." The phone disconnected.

PUG placed the phone back into his tracksuit

jacket. As he returned to the man with the power washer, he saw a large object filling the majority of one dining room window. It was the broad back of David Samuel, posing for a photo with two female customers.

At first, David Samuel had been less of an attraction than PUG. PUG was the face of evil, after all, a villain from the television. David Samuel had been more of a concept: the symbol of every child who'd ever been abused by his father. All it took, though, was one look at him for people to know that David Samuel Ochs wasn't a symbol of everybody's anything. He was a singular hiccup in the genetic pool, one who didn't offer himself easily to simile. And when they got him talking about the park and Collin and Phil Ochs, with all that showmanship and drama he excelled at, people got hooked. He entranced them with his oddness and that flourish he had with words. In the last week, as it started to seem less worthwhile to people to get in a car and drive from Fry Buddy to Fry Buddy to tell off some villain from the television, PUG found he could walk around his restaurants again basically anonymous. David Samuel, though, seemed to have become the stuff of weirdo cult legend, like the world's biggest ball of twine or Georgia's Jimmy Carter peanut statue. He was South Carolina's most dramatic little twit. But they kept coming to Columbia to see him. And they kept buying meals. By now, it was so many thousands of dollars-worth of meals.

With all this attention, David Samuel had decided to stick with Fry Buddy, and in his first act as long-term manager, he'd replaced Ruzanna with Collin Radaszewski, who'd been quietly removed from the Mt. Early athletics program for 'bad social citizenship.' His parents had thought it a fitting restitution to work under David Samuel, provided PUG wouldn't be around to influence him. And PUG had little time to hang around anyway while he negotiated the purchase of his two new stores. At home, David Samuel said that Ruzanna still stopped in from time to time to see him and Collin, whenever she was able to sneak away from the house arrest her parents had imposed on her. The whole thing made PUG feel good, thinking of his son socially chatting with the girl, imposing himself on Radaszewski, the better man submitting and doing what he was told. It satisfied him to think of it. Truly, in a way he hadn't felt for years.

"How's it looking?" he asked over the growl of the power washer.

The man kicked off the engine and said, "You tell me."

Where it had once said, 'Phil Ochs,' the soaking wet parking space now said nothing.

PUG pulled forty dollars from his wallet to pay for the work. "Tell you what," he said. "Once that dries, go ahead and stencil, 'David Samuel Ochs: Manager.'"

"You're the boss," the man said.

PUG turned and walked back to the Lexus. He figured he could live with giving away his Columbia parking spot. After all, he had other franchises, and each would have a spot that read *Restricted: PUG Ochs*. And besides, as many customers as David Samuel was bringing in, a personalized parking space seemed a reasonable concession to keep the little shit happy.

Made in the USA
Middletown, DE
04 June 2022